KIDNAP

Also by L.R. Wright

Acts of Murder
Strangers Among Us
Mother Love
A Touch of Panic
Prized Possessions
Fall From Grace
A Chill Rain in January
Love in the Temperate Zone
Sleep While I Sing
The Suspect
Among Friends
The Favorite
Neighbors

KIDNAP

An Edwina Henderson Mystery

L.R. Wright

Seal Books

Seal Books and colophon are trademarks of
Random House of Canada Limited.

KIDNAP
Seal Books/published by arrangement with Doubleday Canada
Doubleday Canada hardcover edition published 2000
Seal Books edition published April 2001

ISBN 0-7704-2796-0

Cover photographs by Linda Gustafson (background)
and Tom Hussey/The Image Bank (inset)

Seal Books are published by
Random House of Canada Limited.
"Seal Books" and the portrayal of a seal, are the property
of Random House of Canada Limited.

Visit Random House of Canada Limited's website:
www.randomhouse.ca

PRINTED AND BOUND IN CANADA

UNI 10 9 8 7 6 5 4 3 2 1

ACKNOWLEDGMENTS

The author wishes to acknowledge the information and assistance provided by Susan Ackland, MD; Elaine Ferbey; Maggie Nevin; Staff Sergeant Lenton Robinson, RCMP; Sergeant Sharon Woodburn, RCMP; and — again — by John Wright. Any inaccuracies are her own.

Let's make us medicine of our great revenge,
To cure this deadly grief.

Macbeth

AUTHOR'S NOTE

There is a Sunshine Coast, and its towns and villages are called by the names used in this book. But all the rest is fiction. The events and the characters are products of the author's imagination, and geographical and other liberties have been taken in the depiction of the town of Sechelt and the Royal Canadian Mounted Police detachment there.

PART ONE

THE PRESENT

ONE

They saw the row of poplars when they came around a long, slow curve in the road, and almost immediately the real estate agent in the VW Bug ahead of them slowed and began signaling a left turn. They followed her in Arthur's Jeep Wagoneer up the long, tree-lined driveway. On this April day the poplar leaves were the fluorescent spring green that usually caused Susie Wilson's heart to stutter with awe, or longing, or an abstruse nostalgia. Today, however, she merely noted that the trees established a landmark, tracing the course of the driveway from the country road up to the house.

They bumped along through rainwater puddles, following the Volkswagen, a brand-new sleek and yellow thing that looked to Susie the same from the front as from the back. For a moment she fantasized that the real estate agent had reversed direction and was speeding down the driveway toward the Wagoneer instead of toward the house. There would be a huge collision and she would be killed, and then she wouldn't have to worry any longer because her project would die with her and nobody would be the wiser. Susie shook her head, wanting to detach it from her shoulders and grip it in her hands and shake it up and down like the can full of pennies she had used to try to train Mutt not to gnaw on the furniture. Oh dear, oh dear, she thought, wiping her damp palms on her long, flower-scattered skirt.

Arthur must have seen this, for he placed a big heavy hand on her thigh and squeezed. "I've got a feeling, Suze," he said. "I've just got a damn good feeling about this place."

The agent's vehicle was parked now, its sides splattered with streaks of mud. There were many things to be said about Arthur Bentley, Susie thought as they pulled up next to the yellow Bug, and most of them were not good, but she readily admitted that he was an excellent driver. He had propelled the Wagoneer slowly up to the house, following the ruts, and had created hardly any splashing at all. The real estate agent was out of her car, standing next to it and waving for some inexplicable reason, even though Arthur's vehicle wasn't more than four feet from her. She had a clipboard tucked under her arm and was wearing an expression of such relentless affability that Susie felt like fleeing. Instead, she slid out of the Jeep, marched up to the agent and briefly touched her arm.

"We'd like to wander around on our own this time," she said, fixing a smile on her face. "Why don't you wait here, and when we've had a good look, we'll ask you whatever questions we have."

Arthur was already at the front door. "Key, please," he said.

Joanna Leery's robust exuberance crumpled somewhat as she stepped in her high-heeled shoes up the not entirely sturdy steps and unlocked the door. But Susie thought she sensed relief. This was the third day the woman had traipsed up and down the Sunshine Coast looking at rental properties with Susie and Arthur. She had to be sick of the sight of them by now.

She would never admit this, though — especially since they had hinted that if the property suited them, after two or three months they might want to consider buying.

"You two are picky, yes, but I respect that," she had said at lunch, her perfect eyebrows raised, her brown eyes wide.

They were looking for a three-bedroom house in the country. "No neighbors," Arthur had told the agent. "We don't want any damn neighbors."

"It has to be just right," said Joanna. "Of course. You don't want to be even the slightest bit dissatisfied," she went on, measuring a tiny chunk of air between her thumb and index finger. "Oh yes. I know."

"Nothing showy," Susie had insisted. "Nothing pretentious. Just a plain ordinary house in the country. Furnished. With the basics."

Joanna laughed. "I don't mind how many places I have to show you, Mrs. Williamson," she said merrily. "We're going to find exactly what you want." She leaned across the table. "I tend to be a perfectionist myself." She was an extremely well groomed woman in her late fifties, slightly younger than Susie. She had light brown hair, cut short, that flowed away from her face in buoyant waves. Susie felt considerable sympathy for her, since in her real life Susie herself worked in a real estate office, although not as a salesperson.

Her real life, Susie thought, following Arthur through the door, seemed not only miles away but shockingly distant in time as well. She wondered if she would ever find it again. But I've made my decision, she thought, breathless, feeling suddenly weak, leaning heavily against the kitchen wall. This is what I want to do. She dragged her hand from the wall and forced herself to catch up with Arthur, who was springing from one room to another as if in pursuit of someone.

There was one large bedroom on the ground floor, and up the creaking stairs they found two more. Susie decided in favor of the house the moment she entered the smaller bedroom, which overlooked the driveway.

It's perfect, she thought, slowly turning around. It contained a cot, a washstand, a night table, and a small bureau. As if it had been furnished to her specifications. There was a pleasant view of the poplars from the window, which was divided into several small panes: paint was peeling from the sash bars, but this didn't bother Susie. She tried to open the window, but it was firmly sealed by many coats of paint, inexpertly applied. Good. The door had a glass knob and in its keyhole was a long old-fashioned key. Susie removed it and closed the door. She had to push gently and turn the key firmly to get it to work.

She rested her forehead against the locked door for a moment. She felt like saying a prayer of thanks. This would have been inappropriate, however. Susie didn't believe in God and if she had believed in Him she knew He would not have approved of what she was going to do. And so she didn't pray. But she felt for the moment unburdened, as if the room, the house, had awarded her license. She unlocked the door and slid the key into the pocket of her skirt before joining Arthur in the hall.

"So what do you think?" Arthur said, folding his arms and leaning against the wall. His black eyes were bright with — well, Susie wasn't entirely sure with what: antic-ipation, maybe; glee, perhaps. It made her uneasy, what-ever it was.

"I think you're right," she said. "I think it will do. But let's take another look downstairs, and then outside, before we tell Joanna."

"There isn't much furniture, that's for damn sure," said Arthur, clattering down the stairs after her, "but we aren't gonna be here long, after all."

Susie turned quickly. "Shhh!"

"Sorry," said Arthur in a hoarse whisper. "We'll have to rent a TV," he grumbled as they entered the living room. "I'm not gonna do without a TV."

"And I need to get some linens," said Susie, peeking into the bathroom. "Sheets and towels. This will be your room, Arthur," she said severely, indicating the bedroom at the back of the house, "and I don't want to hear any argument."

"Fine." He came up behind her suddenly and swiftly, wrapping his big arms around her. "But I'll visit you upstairs." He was whispering again, his breath husky in her ear. "And you can visit me down here."

"I'm going to have only one thing in mind while we're here, Arthur," said Susie, moving away from him. "And you know it." She felt shaky again and straightened her thin body, lifting her head high, hoping she had enough strength left to finish what she had begun more than two months earlier.

Outside, the late-afternoon sun bored through the trees. Susie could feel it on her back. She also felt the anxious gaze of Joanna Leery, who was sitting behind the wheel of her car, the door open.

Susie studied the house, a brown-shingled, two-story structure that was located several miles southeast of the village of Sechelt. It sat on the eastern edge of two acres of land that was mostly woods and brush. Horses grazed in the field next door; the house in which the horse-owners lived was out of sight behind a steep rise.

"This junk, here," said Arthur, waving toward the piles of broken-down furniture and rusted machinery that stood between the house and the large barn behind it.

"It'll be gone, Mr. Williamson," said Joanna quickly, clambering out of her car. "Before you move in. If you should decide you want the house. Gone. I guarantee it."

"In that case, I think it will do," said Arthur, nodding. He looked over at Susie. "Agreed, hon?" He had never called her hon before. It sounded ridiculous.

Susie was standing in the driveway, looking up at the window of the second-floor bedroom, fingering the old-fashioned key in her pocket.

"Yes," she said.

She imagined that she could see a small figure behind the glass.

"Yes," she said again.

A child's face materialized in the window, disfigured by dark stripes because of the sash bars. Unmoving. Gazing expressionless down upon Susie.

Susie turned to the real estate agent. "Yes," she said. Her heart was beating alarmingly fast and hard. She placed her hand on her chest, summoning calm. "It will do," she said quietly.

Just north of Vancouver, there is a blue crack in the continent called Howe Sound, ten miles wide. Across it, the province of British Columbia juts abruptly west and then extends northward for almost a thousand miles. Its intricate coastline is fissured by innumerable inlets and channels, cluttered by countless small islands, and is at first sheltered from the open Pacific by Vancouver Island, 285 miles long.

Highway 1, the Trans-Canada, comes to a halt on the shores of Howe Sound, at Horseshoe Bay. Ferries leaving from here provide the only access from the mainland to the Sechelt Peninsula, otherwise known as the Sunshine Coast. This is the southernmost forty-five miles of that long, long coastline. Along its seaside are towns and villages called Langdale, Granthams Landing, Gibsons, Roberts Creek, Wilson Creek, Selma Park, Sechelt, Halfmoon Bay, Secret Cove, Madeira Park, Garden Bay, Irvines Landing, Earls Cove, Powell River.

Gibsons, at the southern end, has a population of 3,800 and was named for the first white settler there. About 7,400 people live in the village of Sechelt, which is a native Indian word that some people say means "a place of shelter from the sea." The center of Sechelt is less than a mile wide, with Georgia Strait on one side and Sechelt Inlet — the "Inland Sea" — on the other.

This part of British Columbia gets more hours of sunshine every year than most places in Canada — five hundred more hours, on the average, than Vancouver. Because its winters are also very mild, things grow here that will not grow anywhere else in the country — apricot and fig trees, even palm trees, it is said.

There is only one major road, a mostly two-lane highway that follows the coastline for eighty miles and then ends, in the northern reaches of the Strait of Georgia.

In the summer the area is clogged with tourists, even though it is not a quickly accessible place. Getting there depends upon ferry schedules, and once you've arrived, traversing the coastline takes time, because the narrow highway is winding and hilly.

The tempo of life on the Sunshine Coast is markedly slower than that of Vancouver, and its people, for the most part strung out along the shoreline, have a more direct and personal interest in the sea.

The coastal forests are tall and thick with undergrowth, but they come gently down to the water and are sometimes met there by wide, curving beaches. The land cleared for gardens is fertile, and the things growing there tempt wild creatures from the woods. In the sea there are salmon, and oysters, and clams, and crabs; there are also otters, and thousands of gulls, and cormorants. There are Indian legends, and tales of smugglers, and the stories of the pioneers.

The resident police force is the Royal Canadian Mounted Police, with detachments in Gibsons, Sechelt, and Powell River. They have their fair share of crime to deal with, but in comparison with most urban areas the Sunshine Coast is a gratifyingly law-abiding part of the world.

Murders are infrequent, for example.

And there is very seldom a kidnapping.

TWO

Sechelt might not on the surface seem a premium post-ing for an ambitious young policewoman, thought Sgt. Edwina Henderson on a sunny day in early May, pulling in to the fenced parking lot behind the detachment. Nothing particularly exciting had happened here in almost two years.

Except that she was in charge. She was the boss. It was her detachment.

Well — temporarily hers. She was filling in until the RCMP brass found a suitable staff sergeant to succeed Karl Alberg, who had left a little more than a year ago. Their first candidate, instead of putting his house in Port Coquitlam up for sale in preparation for a move to the Sunshine Coast, had abruptly quit the Force, and so far they hadn't come up with a second. Sometimes Eddie allowed herself to imagine that they'd forgotten all about Sechelt.

She swung herself out of the car and entered the detachment through the back door, striding along the hall to the reception area, where Isabella Harbud shoved a handful of pink message slips at her.

"Didn't get a chance to write it down yet," she said to Eddie, "but your fishing buddy called. He wants to know if you're going out with him tomorrow."

This was her neighbor, Alvin McKechnie, a retired ferry captain. He was enthralled to have a lady cop living next door and had taken it upon himself to acquaint her with various aspects of seafaring.

"Yeah, okay. I'll call him." Eddie rifled through the messages. "Anything else I should know about?"

"No, ma'am," said Isabella, sing-songing it.

Eddie gave her a sharp look but Isabella apparently hadn't intended sarcasm.

Isabella had slung over her shoulders a black and white cardigan that displayed a Canada goose in full flight on the front and another on the back. She owned a collection of extraordinary sweaters that she wore without apparent reference to the rest of the day's wardrobe. Today she had on a red skirt and a sleeveless blouse in a muted shade of orange.

Eddie went back down the hall to her office, taking off her jacket as she went, and once in there draped it on an object she had picked up at a yard sale a few months earlier. It looked like a set of antlers on a pole.

Eddie loved yard sales. She spent her days off, when she wasn't on the water with Alvin, going from one to another. She put on jeans or shorts and a sweatshirt, and her Saskatchewan Roughriders cap and a bum bag and if the weather was good a pair of big round sunglasses, hopped into her old green Mercedes and prowled the peninsula in search of bargains. It was fun, and it was also a good way to get to know a place and the people who lived there. She had spotted the coat rack in the sprawling backyard of a couple recently arrived from Nova Scotia. She had turned in to their driveway because of a handlettered sign that advertised free range eggs and homemade bread for sale and found that they were setting up a yard sale for the following day. Eddie had left an hour later with two dozen eggs, three loaves of bread (sourdough, raisin, and cheddar cheese), and the coat rack.

She had also acquired since her arrival in Sechelt an ancient rusty wheelbarrow, which she had scraped, oiled, and repaired and which Max, who mowed her

lawn, had filled with pots of flowers. Then there was
the old wringer washing machine that now occupied
a corner of her garage. Several lanterns that would
come in handy, she had been told, when the power
went off during winter storms. A scrubbing board like
one she remembered seeing in her grandmother's
basement. Et cetera, et cetera, et cetera.

Eddie sat at her desk, that which had once been
Alberg's, hauled paperwork from her in-basket, and set
to work. She was halfway through the pile when Isabella
phoned her.

"There's this guy on the line," she said, "maybe you
know him? Buzz Diffley?"

"Diffley?" said Eddie. "What kind of a name is
Diffley?"

"Canadian," said Isabella irritably. "It's a Canadian
name. How should I know what kind of a name it is?"

"What does he want?"

"He's got a corner store in that new subdivision up
the hill. He knew Karl. So now he wants you."

"For what?" said Eddie, drumming the end of her pen
on the desk blotter.

"He says he's got somebody in custody. For stealing.
Or trying to steal, I guess."

"Oh shit," said Eddie.

"Cornie Friesen's out here," said Isabella, "with nothing to do and no place to go."

"Yeah, okay. Tell him to meet me at my car."

Five minutes later Eddie was barreling the patrol car
down the hill. She didn't bother trying to make conversation, aware that Cornie Friesen didn't like her much.
When they had been introduced he had shaken her
hand and said hi, like everybody else, but his face had
been expressionless; no welcoming smile from Cornie
Friesen. Among all the Members, Eddie felt that he was
most critical of her appointment, and most resentful of
her seniority.

She slowed down as she turned off the highway, and made her way along streets that hadn't existed when she had moved to Sechelt two years before. She turned a corner, then another, and then a third.

"Good god. Look at this place," she said, parking in front of Buzz Diffley's store, which obviously predated the subdivision. Two antiquated, nonfunctioning gas pumps stood in front of the building, which was situated smack in the middle of a large corner lot.

"The developer must love this guy," said Cornie Friesen dryly as he got out of the patrol car.

Willow trees swept the sky along one side of the property, rhododendron bushes offered a riot of blooms at the back, an untended laurel hedge presented a disorderly countenance to the side street.

A tall, angular man appeared in the doorway to the store and waved at them to hurry.

"Mr. Diffley?" Eddie said. "I'm Sergeant Henderson. What's this all about?"

Diffley looked at her blankly. "Who's this, then?" he said, nodding at Cornie.

"Constable Friesen, sir," said Cornie. He had an amiable manner, Eddie had to admit, that went over well with civilians.

"And you're the boss?" said Diffley to Eddie.

"What can we do for you?" she said briskly, hands on her hips. She drew her shoulders back, making herself taller — slightly taller, in fact, than Cornie Friesen.

"It's more what I've done for you," said Buzz Diffley. His green eyes reminded Eddie for the briefest of seconds of Alan. His black hair had been carefully arranged across the top of his head, kept in place with liberal quantities of gel. He was wearing a longsleeved undershirt beneath a pair of overalls, and worn running shoes. "Come on," he said.

The store window gleamed, Eddie noticed as they went through the door, and inside, the creaky wooden floor had been swept clean and the shelves, crammed with merchandise, seemed to be dust free.

"He's over here," said Diffley, leading them around behind the counter. "There," he said, pointing.

On the floor a teenage boy lay on his side, hands and feet secured with rope, his mouth covered by a knotted red bandanna. His eyes were open. Eddie couldn't determine whether he was scared or angry.

"Untie him, Constable," she said.

Under the counter were shelves with neat stacks of torn newspaper for wrapping purchases, and used plastic bags hanging from a spindle. Eddie saw no weapon there.

"You want to tell me what's going on?" she said, watching Cornie, who had removed the bandanna and was now working on the knots in the rope. The boy remained limp.

"He tried to rob me," said Diffley. "Came in, I was behind the counter here, he says, 'Gimme some money.' I says, 'Forget it, kid.' He leans over and waves his fists in my face. 'Gimme some money,' he says again. And I tell him, 'Go away, kid, or I'm gonna call the cops.' He leans over closer." Diffley thrust out his chin, lifted his own fist, and brushed it lightly, then harder, against his jaw. "And he goes like this, bump, bump, bump."

Cornie Friesen untied the last knot and got to his feet. "Okay, kid." He offered his hand. "Stand up."

The kid drew his feet under him and got wearily onto his hands and knees. "What a bunch of bullshit," he said, shaking his head.

Eddie repressed a grin. "What's your name?"

"Ryan," said Diffley.

Eddie glanced at him, then back at the boy, who remained on his hands and knees on the floor, and as she studied him, she was pretty sure she knew who he was.

The bell over the door jangled. "Yo, Buzz," said a tall young man wearing jeans and a T-shirt. "Been working on my car." He spread his hands, displaying grease stains. "Time for a break." He started for the refrigerator in the corner, then noticed the cops. "Uh-oh. What's going on, Buzz? You got some kind of trouble here?"

Behind the counter, the boy Ryan pushed himself to his feet.

"Same old trouble," said Buzz, almost proudly. "But he's gonna learn his lesson this time. Yessir."

The boy was younger than Eddie had thought at first — about fourteen, she figured.

Ryan looked up at her, his face flushed, eyes dark. "He's my dad," he said. "He's my goddamn father. I only wanted my goddamn allowance."

Buzz Diffley's arm lifted so fast Eddie almost didn't see it move. The boy flinched, and Cornie Friesen took an involuntary step closer. Diffley's arm remained upright.

"Watch your language," he said. "You just watch it, you damn kid, you."

Eddie looked from one of them to the other. "Okay. I want you to close up shop, Mr. Diffley." She moved to the door and flipped the sign. "Outside, please," she said loudly, above his protests, "and into the car, the both of you."

"Uh, Sarge — " Cornie Friesen began.

"What the hell're you doing?" said Diffley. "I'm not going anywhere with you guys. No damn way."

"You called us for help, sir," said Eddie, ushering him firmly outside. "You wanted us to deal with this problem, and we're going to deal with it. Come on, Ryan, get a move on."

"Sarge?" said Cornie.

"What is it, Constable?" Eddie snapped.

Cornie shrugged an it's-your-funeral shrug.

Right, thought Eddie. That it is. "Get them into the car," she said.

"Hey," said the customer, faintly, standing in the dust between the gas pumps and the storefront. "What about me?"

"Come back in a couple of hours, sir," said Eddie.

"In the back seat, Ryan," said Cornie. "You, too, Mr. Diffley."

"I might have to get me a lawyer," said Diffley, climbing inside.

"That's very interesting," said Eddie, getting behind the wheel. "We can talk about it at the detachment."

An hour later Eddie left the Diffleys glaring at one another across the table in the interview room and went to the washroom. She wet a paper towel, wrung it out as best she could, and wiped her face, her throat, the back of her neck, then patted herself dry with a fresh towel. She leaned on a sink and studied herself in the mirror.

It occurred to her that she hadn't had sex in months and months. More than a year, in fact. As always, when she thought about sex, she thought about Alan, whom she'd met when she'd worked in Burnaby.

She had seen him for the first time in the gym.

"Is he married?" she had asked Marjorie.

"Who?"

"That guy on the StairMaster. With the red hair. Reddish."

"Alan McCurdy. Nope. Divorced. But I don't recommend him."

Eddie didn't hear this, though. Or already knew that she didn't want to hear it.

She was experiencing an amazing rush of exhilaration. Not married. Divorced. Eddie laughed out loud, with relief.

"Jesus," said Marjorie, hands on her hips. She told Eddie later, and Eddie believed her, that in that moment she saw the whole thing, the whole torrid appalling ignoble affair beginning, continuing, slamming finally to a halt. "Jesus," she said quietly, shaking her head.

Eddie lay in bed that night bright-eyed and sleepless, the skin of her body aching.

It wasn't her first infatuation but it was the most intense, and it was the only one that rendered her totally defenseless. Later she was to acknowledge it as something virulent, almost lethal.

In the gym she had seen him first from the back, and remained indifferent despite admiring his butt, the strong calf muscles, the powerful thighs: maybe she even imagined running her hands down that smooth back, from the base of his thick neck along the spinal cord down to the exquisite dip that happened just before the flaring of the buttocks. Maybe she was even smiling to herself, full of confidence, as she imagined this.

Just as Eddie was about to move her head to gaze appreciatively upon some other captivating male body, he turned. And even then she might have been safe, except that he happened to look right into her eyes.

Eddie forgot how to breathe. A tumult grew, she was plunged into confusion, she had a horrifying over-whelming urge to touch herself.

Thank god, she thought, thank god I'm hanging on to my gym bag. His eyes were intensely green. That's all she was aware of.

"Come on, for god's sake," said Marjorie, and Eddie allowed herself to be hauled around the corner and into the women's locker room, where she sat down on a bench. Her skin was hot, and her muscles were weak. By the time they had changed and returned to the gym, Alan was gone.

"I'll be your mentor," he said to her two days later, his lips against her temple. He was standing behind her in the cafeteria lineup.

"I don't need a mentor thank you very much I'm well past the mentoring stage I'm a goddamn veteran is what I am," said Eddie, babbling, trying to concentrate on the sound of her voice, the tray in her hand, the food in front of her.

She had to go to bed with him. She knew this. Otherwise she'd never get her mind back on the Job, on

the rest of her life. She couldn't go around like this —
jumpy, shivery, all her nerve ends exposed and quivering.

"Let's go out," he said, sitting across the table from her.

Eddie looked down at her plate. "Out where?"

"Does it matter?" said Alan.

She couldn't see anything in his face. Maybe there
was nothing showing in hers, either.

On that first date they kept their clothes on for
maybe six minutes, for the time it took him to drive
them from her apartment building to Central Park.

He parked the car, turned immediately, and reached
for her. Thank god, thank god, Eddie thought, and it
occurred to her that this was what being an addict must
be like.

The sounds she made astonished her.

When he tore open his jeans, and hers, kneeling
astride her, awkwardly, in the front seat of his car, when
he finally entered her, Eddie came, and came, and came.

Was that why for a while she worshipped him?

She wanted him again almost immediately.

For too long, this was all she knew about him.

There was a polite rap on the door of the washroom,
and Cornie Friesen called out, "Sarge? Can I send these
two on their way now?"

Eddie, still leaning on the sink, said sharply, "Not just
yet, Constable."

She looked into the mirror. She didn't want to be
addicted. Not to sex, not to booze. She straightened and
headed for the door. But oh boy. She sure did want her
fair safe share of each.

"He wants to go home, Sarge," said Cornie Friesen
wearily, leaning against the doorway of Eddie's office.
"They both want to go home. *I* want to go home. Don't
you want to go home?"

Eddie leaned back in her chair and stretched, and
couldn't help but laugh. "Yeah, I do. Okay." She tossed her

pen on the desk and stood up, shrugging on her jacket. The constable backed into the hall as she approached. "Let's go let them loose," said Eddie.

"Thank god," said Cornie Friesen.

"I wonder how come he changed his mind, never asked for a lawyer," she mused.

"We didn't charge him with anything," said Cornie at her heels.

"They should have just walked out," said Eddie. "I sure as hell would have."

"Yeah, well, most of the world ain't as — assertive as you are, Sarge."

Eddie stopped, turned, leveled her blue gaze at him. Cornie Friesen raised his eyebrows and shuffled his feet. Was he laughing at her? Being sarcastic? Trying to be friendly?

She continued along the hall and pushed open the door to the interview room. She glared at the Diffleys, *père et fils*. "I've had it with you two," she said with disgust.

"What the hell —?" said Buzz Diffley.

"You don't know diddly-squat about your son, sir," said Eddie, "and you, Ryan, know even less about your dad."

"Excuse me," said Diffley, "but who the hell do you think you're talking to? It's none of your damn business what I know about my kid. Which is more than plenty, by the way."

"If it's none of our business, sir, then why did you call us?" She pulled over a chair and sat down. "This is not the way to solve family disputes, Mr. Diffley. You call the cops when you get into serious trouble, not when your son wants his allowance and you don't think he's done anything to earn it."

"Tying me up and all," said Ryan. "What is that, anyway, that's some kind of assault, right?"

"I'll assault you, you little turd," said Buzz, turning swiftly in his chair and leaning across the table toward the boy.

"That's enough," said Eddie sharply. She looked from one to the other. "You two are on your own?"

Buzz Diffley turned impassive eyes upon her.

"The old lady walked out eighteen months ago," said Ryan. "Went off with some stupid bastard."

"I think you guys need some help," said Eddie.

Diffley snorted. "Yeah. Sure."

Eddie scribbled on the back of one of her cards and put it face down on the table. "I'm going to have this man call you. He's a counselor."

"Oh shit," said Diffley. "A goddamn counselor."

"Give him a chance," said Eddie calmly. She stood up. "Constable Friesen will take you home now."

Back in her office, she left a message for the counselor to return her call. Then she phoned Cindi Webster, and they arranged to meet in the bar an hour later.

She had a friendly relationship with Cindi but it was also circumspect. Cindi was, after all, a reporter. But tonight Eddie felt like talking about men. About sex. And even vicarious experiences were better than none. She hoped that Cindi had some stories to tell. Preferably of recent vintage.

THREE

Samantha caressed the grass with an open hand, sitting on her haunches with her chin on her bare knees. Her hands were dirty, but she didn't mind. She wasn't thinking about that as she stroked the lawn, trying to make the strokes even. She brought her fingers together — it didn't work so well with the thumb in there, too, so she let the thumb go its own way but kept the other fingers together as she stroked, doing it again and again, until her motions were rhythmic and even.

"What's she doing out there?" said Eleanor at the kitchen door. She had pushed the creaky screen door open a couple of inches to have a space to see through. She crinkled her eyes against the sun's glare. "What's she *doing?*" she said again, but not loudly enough for her mother to hear. Her mother was doing the breakfast dishes and humming to herself and what with the water running and her humming Eleanor hadn't really expected her to hear. Eleanor didn't know if she'd been talking to her mother or not, actually. Probably she was just talking to herself again.

Samantha was now sitting on the grass, reaching for one of the pansies growing in the flower garden that edged the lawn. She was pretty sure that if she touched its little face just so — not roughly, but hard enough to be felt — then the pansy would say something to her. Samantha didn't know what it would say but she imagined that its voice would be high and squeaky, like that of a cartoon character. And maybe when it spoke it would suddenly have big eyes with long flopping lashes like a cartoon character. But maybe she didn't want to find cartoon characters in this garden.

"Eleanor? Come here and dry these dishes, okay?"

Her mother sounded happy, which Eleanor found very hard to accept. Yet at the same time her mother's good mood lightened Eleanor's heart somewhat. It was always harder to have bad feelings when her mother was having good ones. She didn't want the whole world to know this, though, so she didn't reply but continued to look through the space between the screen door and the jamb, her face still screwed up against the sun, against the sight of Samantha out there looking at the flowers.

"Eleanor? Did you hear me?"

"Coming," she said, which would give her another few seconds. She stood on one leg and rubbed the inside of one knee against the other, trying to relieve an itch.

Samantha gave the pansy a poke right in the middle of its flowerface, which had dark purple petals and white ones: poke, poke. And the pansy ducked its head down, then lifted it again. Samantha thought it was definitely going to speak then, and maybe say something angry because of the way she had poked it. But then she realized that it was only moving because of the wind. There was a big gust of it all of a sudden and the air was filled with tiny pink petals. Samantha looked up and saw that they were falling from the flowers that crowded the branches of a big tree that grew next to the fence, sitting side by side on the branches like a flock of pink furry birds. And she laughed. This was because of the pink petals, and the blue sky behind the tree branches, and the sun making the top of her head warm.

"Eleanor! Get in here and dry these dishes!"

"What's she laughing at?" said Eleanor to herself, watching Samantha from behind the screen door. "What's she up to now?"

"It's like full summer out there," said Eleanor's mother, "it's so warm." She paused in her work to look out the window. Her hands were covered in soapsuds. Eleanor wished she would wear protective rubber gloves like sophisticated women did. Although she had to admit that her mother's hands looked pretty good even though she didn't protect them.

Eleanor couldn't see much through the window because she wasn't tall enough yet. Her mother insisted that Eleanor hadn't stopped growing — that nobody stopped growing when they were only ten, especially girls — but Eleanor worried about it anyway. She definitely didn't want to be a short person for the rest of her life.

Through the window she could see wisps of the vine that spread up the side of the house and sent out shoots that would have totally covered the window if not regularly pruned. And she could see some of the sky, of course. And part of one of the apple trees. And the very top of the swing set. Which she was too old for now, but which she used anyway, sometimes.

"So," said her mother. "What're you going to do today?" It was a teachers' professional day, and there wasn't any school.

Eleanor finished drying the plate and put it down on the counter. Now there were only the knives and forks left to do. She didn't understand why her mother hadn't bought a dishwasher. Everybody Eleanor knew had a dishwasher, except her mother.

"I don't know," she said, clutching a handful of silverware. She saw her mother notice this, and knew that her mother thought Eleanor had taken hold of too many knives and forks at once. She waited to see whether her mother would mention it. This time she didn't. She just glanced around the kitchen making sure she hadn't forgotten to wash something, then she let the soapy water drain out of the sink.

"What do you mean, you don't know? On such a lovely day? I'd have thought you'd have all kinds of plans."

Through the window Eleanor saw that one of the swings was moving. It was a motion too slow and regular to be caused by the wind. She stood on her tiptoes and saw the top of Samantha's head.

"Maybe I'll call up Karen," she said, quickly drying the silverware. "See if she wants to get some kids together and play ball."

"That sounds like a good idea," said her mother, wringing out the dishcloth, smiling at her.

Eleanor, in a hurry to finish, dropped some cutlery on the floor. This made a big clatter that for a moment threatened to shift her mother's mood. "Sorry," she mumbled, picking them up. She rinsed them, shook them over the sink, dried them, and put them away.

Her mother looked out the window and smiled again — she was smiling at Samantha this time, of course.

Eleanor slammed the cutlery drawer closed. "Is that all?"

Her mother looked at her calmly. "Have you made your bed?"

"Yeah."

"Then, yes, that's all."

Eleanor eased out of the kitchen.

"Let me know when you go out," her mother called after her.

"I will."

"And where you're going."

"I will."

Eleanor fled to the dining room, where there were glass doors that led out to the backyard. She hid behind the pulled-back curtain, inched up to the edge of the glass, and zeroed in on Samantha, swinging.

Samantha had had to stand on her tiptoes to do it but she'd gotten up onto the swing all by herself. The wooden seat, warmed by the sun, was smooth like flower petals. The chain ropes were warm, too, and very thick — almost too thick for her fists to grab tightly enough.

She looked hopefully at the back door — really it was the side door, since the kitchen was at the side of the house, not the back — but nobody was coming outside to give her a push. She pumped for a while but couldn't get herself very high, and was soon bored.

There was a slide in the backyard, too, but Samantha didn't like sliding unless she was wearing her jeans, and today because it was so warm they had put her in shorts.

She sat on the swing, dangling her feet, which wore the sneakers that closed with Velcro. She sang softly to herself, thinking. She had been promised a pet at the end of the summer, and had to decide if she wanted a kitten or a puppy. Kittens maybe weren't so friendly when they grew up to be cats. But puppies on the other hand got to be very, very big when they grew up to be dogs. Samantha was having a hard time making the choice.

She gripped the chain rope and let herself lean back as far as she could go. She felt the seat tilting backward. If her hair were still long it would be dragging in the dust underneath the swing by now.

"What are you doing?" Eleanor shouted. "What do you think you're doing?"

Samantha was so startled that she almost let go. She struggled to get herself upright and looked, amazed, across the grass at Eleanor, who was standing at the sliding glass door.

"Nothing," said Samantha. "I'm not doing anything."

Eleanor had made fists of her hands, and her head was scrunched down into her shoulders. Samantha let go of the swing and jumped down. The seat smacked her in the middle of her back, and the pain made tears squirt into her eyes.

"Nothing!" she said again, her voice shrill with apprehension.

Eleanor took a furious step toward her and Samantha bolted for the kitchen door, trying not to cry. Halfway there she looked back over her shoulder to see if Eleanor was chasing her and she stumbled and sprawled on the grass. She scrambled to her feet as fast as she could, before Eleanor could grab her.

But Eleanor wasn't chasing her.

Samantha looked cautiously around the yard, rubbing the scar on her knee, which hurt again because she'd fallen on it.

Eleanor had disappeared.

Just like a ghost, thought Samantha. Just like a mean old ghost.

FOUR

Susie Wilson was sitting in the sun, waiting. She and Arthur were about to go on another reconnaissance. She was getting more and more nervous every time they did one of these surveys. Wondering how much more information she needed to accumulate. Knowing that someone was going to notice them eventually.

She was no longer sure that they were going to be able to carry off Plan A. Yet she would abandon it with the greatest reluctance — it seemed to Susie less evil than to invade the child's home. She sighed and twisted the green ring on her right hand and smoothed her dress over her knees. It was dreadful, looked at in the abstract, this thing she was going to do.

Susie was tall and thin, a decidedly bony person, sharp-featured, definite. An unequivocal-looking person, with a long straight nose, a small pointed chin, and a long neck. She had dark silver-streaked hair that was cut straight across about two inches past the bottom of her ears, and she wore bangs, also cut straight across. Her hands were long and slender, with slender fingers that were almost never still.

She became aware that she was kneading her thighs and stopped, and again smoothed the long blue dress she wore, which had narrow white stripes that made her look even taller and thinner than she was.

Her hands were brown and strong. For a moment she

could believe that they were young hands again. The green ring glowed and she polished it with some spittle and the fabric of her skirt. On her feet she was wearing socks and sneakers.

She pressed her hands to her sides, where her waist had thickened despite her thinness. Her small breasts sagged, too. These things ought not to bother her any more, now that she was sixty. And they didn't, either. Not really.

She looked at her watch. No, it wasn't time yet, another half hour had to pass.

Susie stood up and walked to the row of rustling poplar trees and followed them down the driveway toward the road. It was a warm and quiet morning. She was soothed by the smell of cut grass, and manure, and the confessional whisperings of the poplars, and her feet padding in the packed-down dirt of the driveway, and a squeaking, banging door somewhere far away. She felt suddenly drowsy, listless, and stopped walking, stood still with her head bowed, wishing that her dress had pockets. Her hands hung at her sides like deadweights, large and awkward, dangling uselessly.

She looked back at the house, at the second-floor window. The room was completely ready now. The basin and matching chamber pot she had found among the clutter in the barn. She had bought a bar of Pears soap and placed it on a saucer, next to a brand-new towel.

The mail truck trundled into view, trailing a small cloud of dust, and stopped at the end of the driveway. The mailman reached across the passenger seat, thrust a handful of mail into the box, and raised the red flag. He gave Susie a wave before he drove away. It continued to startle her, the reflexive friendliness of people who lived in the country. She walked on to the box and collected the mail — which was entirely junk, of course, she certainly hadn't given the post office in Vancouver a forwarding address — lowered the flag, and headed back to the house.

As she shuffled absently through the supermarket flyers, the real estate notices, the political proclamations, she
thought about the letter she had written. Brief, to the
point, it sat in the drawer of the desk in the living room,
all ready to go. Oh, that had taken some thought, all
right. That had been a toughie, that letter.

Her palms were wet and her underarms felt sticky and
she had a headache coming on. Not one of the bad ones
that had begun to afflict her over the past several
months, just an ordinary headache, the kind that was
only mildly distracting. She squinted against the sunlight
that was less kind now that her head hurt.

But she couldn't wear sunglasses. Not when doing
surveillance. She would wear them when they took the
child, large dark sunglasses and a sun hat with a huge
brim: these would be her disguise. And a pair of jeans
and a plaid shirt. Arthur wouldn't need a disguise, the
child's eyes would be covered so quickly. Susie had
planned her project with considerable attention to
details such as these.

Arthur appeared in the living-room window. He bent
his arm and pointed in an exaggerated fashion at his
watch. Susie nodded impatiently and pointed in the
same way at hers. She knew what time it was. Whose
project was this, anyway?

The glass in the window was gimped in some way
and Arthur saw Susie through it as elongated and wav-
ery. She was pretty elongated in her natural state, but
looked at through this window he thought she resembled somebody in a hall of funny mirrors.

He stepped back and picked up his can of beer. She
was right. It was too soon to leave. The woman and the
kid came out of the house and went down the lane and
ended up at the library almost every day at almost the
exact same time. Somebody in that house read a hell of
a lot of books. Two mornings a week they went to the
grocery store — usually just the two of them, the

woman and the kid — every day, same damn time. Susie
had written in her notebook every coming and going
from that house over the last two weeks. So far the damn
kid had never been out of sight of the woman or the
other kid.

Arthur dropped into a chair and spread his legs in front
of him. He was just about out of patience. He wanted to
break into the damn house, get it over with. He didn't have
the agility or the stamina he'd had in his youth — and
there was his injury to consider, he reminded himself,
slipping his hand under his T-shirt to touch his scar. But
after all there were only two little kids and one woman in
the place. Shit, he thought. They probably left a key under
the damn mat.

Night would be best, he figured. They would sneak
inside, find the right bedroom, then Susie would slap a
hand over the kid's mouth while he tied her arms and
legs together. Piece of cake.

The front door opened. "Okay," Susie called. "Let's go."

"I've been thinking," Arthur began, getting to his feet.
He set the beer can down on an end table. "Why don't
we just forget all this reconnaissance shit and go into the
damn house and get the damn kid. In the middle of the
night. Tonight, maybe."

She leaned her head against the edge of the door. She
was an attractive woman, Susie, despite her age and the
lack of beef on her. She had a backbone of steel, and she
could be annoying as hell, but he liked her.

"I'd really rather not do that, Arthur," she said wearily, "unless we absolutely must." She gave him a smile, a
peculiar smile, with more sadness in it than pleasure.
"But if nothing occurs to me after today, I guess we're
going to have to."

FIVE

Eddie parked the patrol car, got out and locked up, and walked reluctantly into the beachside restaurant. She felt conspicuous in this place, with its huge windows and masses of indoor greenery. She would much rather have gone to the old Earl's.

Earl's Café and Catering had changed hands. It had once been small and self-effacing. It was conveniently located on Sechelt's main street, and in Earl's day cops had felt as comfortable there as had the town's bank tellers, mechanics, restless seniors, and gossipy adolescents. It had also been clean; the waitress was efficient, if not particularly friendly; and the food was good.

But no more, thought Eddie gloomily, tucking her cap under her arm as she waited to be seated. Earl's — the new owner had bought good will and the café's name as well as the property — had expanded to incorporate the neighboring space that had been vacated by the stationery store. Gaudy rainbows covered the walls inside and out. The windows were smeared, loud music played all the time, and the food — when it finally arrived — was in Eddie's opinion inedible. Black-haired, opinionated Naomi Hellyer still worked there as a waitress, and she still snapped at the patrons and vociferously (but ineffectually) complained to the chef, but Naomi wasn't enough of a draw to keep Eddie going there.

"You want a table by the window?" said the hostess, and Eddie said sure.

She ordered coffee and a chicken salad sandwich. While she waited for her lunch she pulled out her notebook and made some notes for her work diary. Eddie didn't consider herself to be particularly introspective, but she was occasionally contemplative and enduringly ambitious. From the start of her career she had been recording and studying not only the events in her work days but her reactions to them. She did this at home. In private.

She was halfway through her first cup of coffee when Cindi Webster slid into the chair opposite, deposited her enormous shoulder bag on her lap, and folded her hands on top of it.

"Hi," said Eddie.

Cindi gazed at her reproachfully.

"What's the matter with you?" said Eddie, closing her notebook.

"We're sitting there in the bar for how long? An hour? Two?" Cindi was slightly out of breath, and her plump face was flushed. Her hair was loose.

"Who, you and me?"

"You and me. Last night."

"Yeah," said Eddie. "I remember."

"And I'm confiding in you, right? All manner of private and personal things."

"We confided in each other, I think," said Eddie, grinning. "What's the matter — are you having regrets? I told you," she said, placing a hand on her heart, "your secrets are safe with me."

Cindi shoved her bag under her chair and waved away the waiter's offer of a menu. "Vegetable soup, white toast, and a glass of milk," she said. "You really are something else," she said to Eddie. "I thought we were friends."

"What the hell's your problem, Cindi?" Eddie shoved the notebook and pen back into her pocket.

"It never once occurred to you to tell me you had Buzz Diffley and his kid in the slammer?" Cindi was bright-eyed, relentlessly inquisitive, and surprisingly organized for one who spoke in a rush and always sounded slightly dismayed.

"We let them go."

"That's not the point."

Eddie leaned across the table. "You're right, Cindi," she said coldly. "It isn't. The point is that I'm a cop and you're a reporter and when we get together the thing we do not talk about is work."

Cindi let herself fall back in her chair. She shook her hair over her shoulders.

Eddie gazed out the window, beyond the walkway and the strip of grass and the wide rocky beach to the blue sea. Trail Bay. She imagined a ship — a big yacht — sailing slow and stately into the middle of the bay and anchoring there.

Cindi planted her elbows on the table. "Okay. Sorry."

"Okay," said Eddie, and she imagined herself piloting a little boat out there to meet this yacht — a motorboat, maybe even a rowboat.

"I guess they're not under arrest, then. If you let them go."

Eddie saw the side of the yacht looming higher and higher as her small boat approached. It was almost blindingly white. A rope ladder was being thrown over the side . . .

"Eddie?"

"Right," said Eddie, still gazing out at the water. "We didn't arrest them." What she couldn't tell was whether the yacht had come to collect her, to whisk her off to glamorous faraway places, or to deliver something to her. Or someone. She blinked, and turned away: the brightness of sunlight on blue water was hurting her eyes.

As they left the restaurant Eddie looked at her watch and decided she had time for a quick trip home.

She stood by the patrol car smiling after Cindi, who was bustling off with her long brown hair whipped by the wind in all directions, wrestling her gigantic bag into a more comfortable position on her shoulder. Suddenly, without turning her head, she lifted her hand in a wave. Eddie experienced a mild shock, realizing that Cindi knew Eddie was watching her. Sure enough, Cindi turned, then, to look back at Eddie.

Eddie waved, laughing.

All the way home she pictured the day's mail sprawled on her hall floor just inside her door, and winking up at her from the middle of the pile was a letter she'd been waiting for: perhaps it was from the owner of the imaginary yacht. I need some excitement in my life, she thought. This is getting ridiculous.

As she wheeled around the last corner and pulled up in front of her house, Eddie remembered the Charles Atlas stuff she had sent away for when she was nine or ten. She was still short, then, and thin, and woefully lacking in muscle power. She remembered the looks of amazement on the faces of her parents. "This came for you today, Edwina," they had said, meticulously courteous. But Eddie heard their curiosity, and maybe some amusement, as well. She ignored this, though. She took the big thick envelope from her mother's hand and ran into her bedroom to peruse its contents and plan the program that would transform her into an Amazon.

She got out of the car and hurried up the walk to her house. Her very own house, painted primrose yellow with deep blue trim, colors that even though they'd proven slightly more dynamic than she had expected, she liked very much. She would get some lilac bushes planted along here, she thought, on each side of the walk, so that eventually in the spring when she strolled from the front door to the sidewalk she would pass through the drenching fragrance of their blossoms and the droning of incipiently threatening bees. But it would

take a couple of years for the bushes to start blossoming,
she thought, unlocking the door, and maybe she wouldn't
be here that long.

She swept the mail from the floor and flipped
through it.

Then tossed it onto the hall table.

Eddie sank onto a fragile round-backed chair, its
needlepoint seatcover created years ago by her grandmother. Really. These fantasies were doing her no good,
no good at all.

She went into the bedroom, undid her thick yellow
braid, bent from the waist and brushed her hair, energetically, almost viciously, until it flew and crackled. Then
she stood up, face flushed, scalp throbbing, her hair tum-
bling on her shoulders, and made a new braid.

As she watched herself in the mirror she reminded
herself that although Charles Atlas hadn't come through
she had eventually been transformed. She actually felt
quite Amazonian, studying herself: tall and sturdy and
strong, and not bad looking, either, with her yellow hair
(Eddie refused to think of herself as a blonde) and blue
eyes. Good cheekbones, too.

In the kitchen she stood for a minute by the window
looking out into her backyard, which was tended every
week, now that spring had come, by Max, the skinny,
toothless handyman who had been recommended by
her neighbors. She drank a glass of water and had just
put the glass in the sink when the phone rang.

Eddie knew before she picked it up that it was Alan.
She felt a spasm occur along the vulnerable skin of her
back: how had he known she would be home in the
middle of the day? It was as if he could see her, from
Burnaby — all the way across Greater Vancouver, and
over the waters of Howe Sound, and halfway up the
Sunshine Coast highway.

He couldn't see her, of course. He hadn't known that
she'd be home. He called when he felt like it, that was

all, and if she was there he got to say something and if
she wasn't at least he got to hear her voice on the
answering machine. That's what he'd told her, anyway.

"Don't hang up," he said. But she did.

Eddie took her time, then, checking the windows and
the back door, making sure the heat was down and no
taps were dripping — habits laboriously acquired over
the two years she had been a homeowner. She took her
time because she knew he wouldn't call again. Not right
away.

At least she no longer shook when she got his damn
phone calls, she thought as she left the house.

Eddie turned the key in the door and jiggled the
knob to make sure it was locked.

She tried not to think about him as she jogged down
the sidewalk to the car, but she couldn't help thinking
about him, because he was calling her again, damn it, and
there was a sharpness in his voice, an impatience that
Eddie found disquieting.

He had called regularly and often when she first
moved to Sechelt. She hung up on him every time, but
still he called. Never left a message. Never sent her a letter, a note, a fax. He was too smart for that.

And finally: "Leave me alone, you goddamn psychopath," she had said to him, rage flaring, consuming
her fear. "Or I swear to God I'm gonna report you."

Eddie had decided that her outburst must have been
what he'd been after, because he had left her alone then.
For months. For more than a year. But three weeks ago
the calls had begun again.

Was it harassment? she thought, firing up the patrol
car, glancing in her rearview mirror.

Or could the fact that she had once had an affair with
the sonofabitch really mean that she was fair game?

SIX

After lunch on the following Saturday Eleanor's mother told her she had a headache and had to lie down for a while, and she told Eleanor to keep an eye on Samantha.

"But first come in here for a minute," she said, standing in the hall outside her bedroom. "I want to talk to you." So Eleanor followed her, reluctantly, and when they were both inside her mother closed the door. "What's the matter with you, anyway? Why are you so mean to your cousin?"

Eleanor scuffed her feet on the carpet, which was blue, with a pattern of big pink roses on it. Eleanor found these roses embarrassing. They made her think of women who had large breasts and wore kimono-like things that hung open in the front. "I am not mean to her."

"Look at me, Eleanor," said her mother sharply. So Eleanor did. "She's only five. Her mother's dead. Her father hasn't been . . ."

Eleanor saw her hunting around for the right words. "Around much," she offered.

Her mother frowned. Then her face softened. She sat down and patted the bed.

Eleanor sat down beside her.

"You're right," said her mother. "He hasn't been there much lately."

She sounded tired. Eleanor thought she could hear the headache throbbing in her voice.

"Don't you like her?" said her mother, putting an arm around Eleanor.

Eleanor shrugged. "She's okay."

"Then what is it?"

Eleanor thought she ought to be able to figure it out for herself. Samantha didn't have a mother. Well, Eleanor didn't have a father. Was a person supposed to get used to that? She hadn't got used to it. She didn't think she ever would.

"She gets treated like she's special," she said sullenly. "I don't think she's so special."

"You're right, she's not special," said her mother. "But she's your cousin. And she's our responsibility — yours and mine — until her father comes home."

"Huh." Eleanor, rubbing the toe of her sneaker against one of the roses, wondered whether she could rub hard enough to erase it.

"Okay?" said her mother, giving her a one-armed hug.

"Yeah. Okay," said Eleanor. She went to the door. "What time should I wake you up?"

"I won't really sleep. I just want to rest for a while." She looked pale, thought Eleanor. The little bit of tan had faded because of her headache.

Eleanor went out into the hall and closed the door. She paused there for a moment, looked down the stairs, then retreated into her room.

Samantha crept up to the kitchen doorway and peered around the edge of it. The big plant sitting on the floor by the window seemed to be okay. She was worried about it, though. She hadn't much enjoyed her lunch, and had managed while nobody was watching to sneak most of her soup into the dirt in the pot. It was aspara-gus soup, so Samantha had figured that the plant would probably like it.

Now she was having second thoughts. Maybe it was like if somebody gave her a hamburger made of people meat. She knew that she would throw up if she had to eat people meat, and maybe she would even die. And so she had several times crept back to peer anxiously at the plant, whom she had named Angus.

Now she ventured all the way into the kitchen. "How you doing, Angus?" she whispered, examining the soil. "How you doing, huh?" She saw bits of asparagus, and a large damp spot where the runny part of the soup had soaked in. "I'm going to give you first aid," said Samantha. She got a spoon from the drawer and scraped off the asparagus pieces and dumped them into the garbage container under the sink. "There." She petted the plant's long, wide, pointed leaves. Samantha liked plants very much.

"Can we go to the park today?" she had asked Patsy, swirling her spoon in her Cream of Wheat. That wasn't what she had wanted to say. She wanted to say something that was very important, something she had been trying to say for days and days but it just wouldn't come out.

"Depends on the weather, I think, sweetie," said Patsy. She was taking a loaf of bread from the breadbox. "Do you want some toast?"

"No toast," said Samantha. She sat back in her chair and folded her arms. "No porridge."

"What's the matter?" said Samantha's father. "How come you're not hungry?" He was leaning against the kitchen counter, drinking coffee from a big mug.

"Well, I'm having some," said Patsy, putting two slices of bread in the toaster. She wore blue jeans and sweaters, and tied her hair back in a ponytail, and drove to Samantha's house every day in a very old car. She said she was tired of school, she wasn't ready to go to university yet. She said she'd sooner have the job of looking after Samantha.

And all of a sudden Samantha, staring at Patsy, then at her father, knew she could say it. And so she did. "Who's going to look after Mommy's garden?" She folded her arms around herself and squeezed.

Her father sat down at the table next to her. "What do you mean, Samantha?"

Samantha pointed to the potted plants crowding the kitchen windowsill.

"What about them?" said her father.

Samantha glared at Patsy.

"Oh my god," said Patsy. "I'm sorry, Samantha." She turned to Samantha's father. "I'm sorry. I forgot to water them." She grabbed a pitcher from the cupboard and filled it with water.

"There's more upstairs, too," said Samantha. "And in the living room." She began to cry. And the more she cried the angrier she got. "And there's the roses in the backyard. And the — the — all that stuff in the front. What's going to happen to it all?"

Her father picked her up and put her on his knee and hugged her, and he and Patsy promised that they'd take care of the garden, and Patsy said maybe Samantha would help her remember the inside plants and maybe she could even water some of them herself . . .

It had become very quiet inside the house. Samantha knew where everybody was, but it was a big house and with one of them in one upstairs room and the other one in another upstairs room, downstairs was very quiet.

Humming under her breath, she sat at the kitchen table and started rubbing the smooth clean surface with the palms of her hands. Soon her hands felt hot, and squeaking sounds were slipping out from under them. The harder she rubbed, the hotter her palms became, and the louder the squeaking. She stopped when her hands began to hurt. Besides, she didn't want anyone upstairs to hear the squeaking and come down to investigate.

Almost every day Eleanor's mother took Samantha — and Eleanor, too, if it was a Saturday — to the library. Usually they went right after lunch. Today, they had to wait until later in the afternoon. Samantha didn't know why, or couldn't remember why, anyway.

Upstairs, Eleanor emerged barefoot from her room and started down the stairs, passing the closed door to the guest room silently, feeling stealthy, in her own house, and indignant about this.

Samantha got up from the table and wandered into the living room, dragging the toe of one sneaker along the floor with each step, making a thick, clumpy, stuttering sound that she thought was very interesting. But then she got to the big carpet that took up the whole middle of the floor and had to stop.

She climbed up on the piano stool and twirled around, pushing at the edge of the keyboard to launch herself. First she made the stool go higher and higher. Then she went the other way, all the way down, so that not only her toes but her entire foot could touch the floor.

Eleanor reached the bottom of the stairs and caught a glimpse of Samantha. Her heart pitched like a little boat struck by a big wave: she'd been certain that Samantha was in the guest room reading library books.

Samantha had been taking piano lessons for almost a whole year — since the very beginning of kindergarten, away back last September. She twirled the stool upward again, until the keyboard was in the right place. Samantha began to play, very softly, one of the pieces she had memorized. But the piano keys were sticky. She didn't like the way they felt under her fingertips — which she was trying to keep wide and flat, like little spatulas.

Eleanor thought about her grandmother's house, the grandmother who had been her father's mother, not her mother's mother, who had died a long time ago. In her grandmother's house, in a corner of the living room between two windows sat a low round table with a cloth on it that went all the way to the floor. If there'd been such a table here, in her own living room, Eleanor could have crawled under it and been invisible. She flattened herself against the wall in the hallway just outside the living room and listened to Samantha at the piano. It sounded awful. She must be making a lot of mistakes.

Samantha sighed, slid off the piano stool, and made her way into the dining room, over to the glass doors. She was supposed to stay inside the house. But Samantha was impatient. She was, after all, quite a big girl by now. She knew how to read; she could play the piano; she knew how to speak politely and directly to grownups but not to ever go anywhere with anybody she didn't know.

Samantha rolled the door open, stepped out into the backyard, and pulled the door closed behind her. She blinked, because the sun was so bright, even brighter and hotter than it had been in the morning. She closed her eyes and let her head fall back to feel the strength of it on her face. She opened her mouth wide, filling it with sunshine, then closed it and gulped, imagining a brilliant blizzard of sunlight shooting down her throat and spreading into all the parts of her insides. She imagined that she now had a see-through body, thanks to the sun.

Eleanor watched her set off around the house. She hurried to the front door and stood on her tiptoes and watched, through the small window in the top of the door, as Samantha went through the front gate and out onto the sidewalk. She watched Samantha dawdling along, swinging her fat little arms, looking at the dandelions that grew next to the neighbors' fence. Sometimes she hopped for a few steps. Sometimes she skipped. A couple of times she turned around and walked backwards, looking up the sidewalk toward the house she had just left.

Eleanor watched Samantha until she was out of sight. Then she hurried upstairs, very, very quietly, and went into her room and closed the door, soundlessly.

Eleanor lay on her bed, hands behind her head, looking up at the ceiling, waiting for her mother to emerge from her room, waiting for her mother to notice that Samantha was gone, waiting for her mother to call out to her in alarm.

SEVEN

Arthur had driven his Jeep out from behind the house, where it was parked next to Susie's station wagon. The wagon was fifteen years old and not entirely reliable, which was why they weren't using it.

Susie climbed in, adjusting the long silky scarf that she'd wound around her neck.

"Okay?" said Arthur as she settled herself in and fastened the seat belt. "Ready?"

"Ready." Her voice was firm and steady, not a wrinkle in it.

They set off down the driveway, bumping along the ruts, and Susie in her mind started going through the list of things they would have to take with them when the day came. It wouldn't matter if it was Plan A or Plan B, the list would be the same.

She had decided they could afford to wait one more week. If she hadn't figured out how to make Plan A work by then, they would have to do the break-in.

Arthur saw her glance into the backseat. "It's all in hand, Susie. Trust me. It'll be there when we need it." They bounced off the driveway onto the road. "A blindfold. Some rope — strong, but not that rough stuff that might hurt her. Something to use as a gag." He gave her an encouraging wink. "See?" He tapped his temple. "Nothing you tell me gets lost. It all gets stored away, right in here." She was looking out the window, acting like she hadn't heard him. He was filled with exuberance all of a sudden. He reached across and squeezed her thigh, and although she pulled away, just slightly, he knew she wasn't offended.

And she wasn't. She liked the firm touch of his hand on her leg, liked the way it warmed her, inside and out. Arthur straightened his arms, pushing himself back against the driver's seat, and he looked so expansive, so cheerful, that Susie almost expected him to burst into song.

He couldn't be called handsome. Not any more, anyway. Maybe he had been handsome in his youth. But although his hair had thinned and his waist had certainly enlarged, there was something about him that Susie had found attractive almost from the moment they met.

There was a lot of the rascal in him, too. Susie thought he had probably toned down since he was young but the recklessness she thought he'd been born with was still there, and the dissatisfaction, and a spring of anger, too. Oh, she had become well acquainted with his anger, though it had never been directed at her.

But she had to admit, it comforted her to know that Arthur was in this with her, all the way. She sometimes worried that her palpitations might return, and at exactly the wrong moment. Even though she'd been given a clean bill of health by the specialists, those people never knew as much as they pretended to know. And so it was good to have a partner, someone who could take over if necessary.

She fervently hoped it wouldn't be.

Arthur glanced at Susie as they turned from the road onto the main highway that led to town. "You've worked hard at this. All that snooping and following, it's gonna pay off."

"It was research," said Susie stiffly. "Not snooping."

They drove along in silence, and in her mind Susie began going through the contents of her kitchen: cupboards, refrigerator, deep freeze . . .

"How long do you figure it's gonna take?" said Arthur. "Once we've got her?"

"I don't know."

" 'Cause you know I've gotta get back to town by the end of the month."

"Good heavens, it isn't going to go on until the end of the month."

"Good," said Arthur.

They were driving past acreages, houses set back from the road, swing sets in some of the front yards, or tires tied to the thick branches of trees. Susie wished she knew the names of more trees. She knew the poplar, of course, and the Japanese maple whose leaves were that lovely burgundy, and she could identify a maple tree and an oak because she had learned way back in elementary school to recognize their distinctive leaves. But all the evergreens, for example. She couldn't tell a fir from a hemlock, and she'd lived here in the rain forest for her whole life.

"Relax," said Arthur. "Quit jiggling your foot. I told you, everything's gonna go smooth as glass." He reached over to squeeze her thigh again. "Teamwork," he said. "We got good teamwork going here. You'll see."

He's enjoying himself, thought Susie, amazed, studying his profile. He's actually enjoying this.

"Your kid would be proud of you," he said comfortably, resting his left arm on the open window. "If she knew what you were up to — and hey, who knows, maybe she does, eh? — she'd be damn proud of you, Susie."

Susie breathed in, quick and hard, and out again.

Arthur, when she had been silent for several moments, glanced at her. She was motionless. Rigid. Oh jesus, he thought. Bad move. Got to learn when to keep my trap shut. He looked out the windshield and drove on.

EIGHT

Eddie knew she should have let somebody else take this call. She wasn't delegating enough. She had taken too many calls herself when she was Alberg's second in command and she wasn't doing any better now that she was in charge.

But she and the Blakes had a history. They had arrived in Sechelt at about the same time Eddie had arrived, and she had responded to the first complaint about them. They were a pitiable couple in their sixties, permanently estranged yet unable, apparently, to live apart.

And this time it wasn't a neighbor who had called but Donald Blake himself, and he had specifically asked for Eddie. And this had gotten her attention.

She stood by the patrol car, waiting, and knew she ought to go on waiting for at least a bit longer, to make absolutely sure that Ralph Mondini had had time to get around to the back.

But she didn't.

Eddie proceeded up the sidewalk toward the front door of a familiar bungalow, which she noticed now was in need of painting. She was acutely aware of her body — of its strength and agility; of her size and substance. She felt almost weightless. She felt — despite the fear that thickened her tongue, sharpened her senses, and set her heart to thundering — indestructible.

The uniform was very hot. Eddie wanted to tear off her clothes, rid herself of the jacket, the shoes, the pants. As she approached the house — the door loomed larger and larger, like something out of *Alice in Wonderland* — she imagined herself in the middle of the Blakes' front yard wearing only socks and her underwear. Might be a good way to diffuse the situation, she thought. Get everybody laughing.

The uniform felt heavy, too, especially around the waist, where all the paraphernalia hung from her belt.

Eddie walked slowly, her hands swinging slightly, held out from her sides. She knew she looked somewhat threatening. And truthfully, she didn't mind that.

She was almost at the door now. Two concrete steps, cracked but not yet crumbling, led up to a small concrete porch. Hydrangea bushes flanked the porch. Someone had pruned them: they were nice and tidy, covered in new green shoots. Do you do that in the fall? Eddie wondered. Or in the early spring?

She was on the porch. She couldn't remember going up those steps and, recalling the childhood chant, wondered if she had trodden upon the cracks. It was too late to worry about that, though, because her mother was already dead.

Eddie rapped on the door. She heard a scurrying inside the house and rapped again, harder. "Hildy?" she called out.

The scurrying stopped.

"Hildy? Donald?"

All was quiet.

"Come on, you two. Answer the damn door. I'm sick of coming over here, you know. We're all sick of coming over here."

She heard something behind the door — breathing? A whimper?

"Just like the neighbors are sick of hearing you yell at each other." She waited, listening. Mondini must be

around back by now, she thought, and lifted her fist to
bang again on the door.

And then it was opened — at first, quickly. Then
whoever was on the other side changed his or her mind
and pulled on the door slowly, opening it slowly, carefully, which was a damn fine idea, Eddie thought, her
hand on her holster: she had unsnapped the leather flap.
The hand rested there casually and she shifted her
weight to her left leg, right knee bent, as the door
opened all the way.

"Hi," said Eddie, tilting her head at Donald Blake.

His face was blotched, his eyes were bloodshot. He
was barefoot but dressed, wearing jeans with dirty
knees and a faded plaid shirt that was only partially
buttoned, and half pulled out. No belt. An undershirt.
Eddie noticed that the shirt buttons weren't done up
properly.

"Hi," she said again.

Donald Blake just looked at her.

Eddie tried to see around him. He wasn't a large man
— in fact he wasn't as tall as Eddie — but he was looming awfully big just at the moment. One hand hung
empty by his side. The other clutched the edge of the
door.

"Where's Hildy?" said Eddie.

"Who wants to know?" said Donald, as if he'd never
laid eyes on her before.

"I want to know," said Eddie, putting an edge on it.

"It's none of your business," said Donald Blake, mum-
bling it to the door. He had shuffled behind it now, and
Eddie was afraid he was going to slam it shut so she
stepped forward, across the threshold — just that far, no
farther — and looked around.

"Of course it's my business, Donald. You called me,
remember? Told me I ought to get over here." She
relaxed somewhat then, seeing no discarded baseball bat,
no bloodied butcher knife, no disarray. The floor was

clean, the place looked orderly. The fight was over, apparently. "So here I am."

"You can't come in," Donald said sullenly.

Eddie smiled. "I'm already in. So where is she?"

"I told you, it's none of your business." Donald's shoulder twitched as he tossed frantic glances to the right and to the left. Even his balding head was covered with blotches and gleamed pasty white where it wasn't red.

"You need help, right?" said Eddie.

"Where'd you get that idea?" he said, astonished. "I don't need nobody's help. I can look after things just fine. I don't need your damn help, or any other sumbitch's, either." He glared at her, sullen. "I didn't phone you. I don't recall it."

"You just forgot," said Eddie. "Do you have some coffee going?"

His mouth moved as he stared at her, but nothing came out.

Eddie listened intently while she waited for him to speak, but heard nothing: the house was quiet. She was aware of other sounds, though, coming through the open front door. Someone was mowing a lawn. A bunch of birds were having an argument. Some kids cycled past the house, calling out to one another.

"I don't know," Donald said finally. "I don't recall that either."

"Why don't we go into the kitchen," said Eddie, "and find out."

She looked down the hall, which led right through the house, from the front door to the back, and saw Mondini's shadow on the other side of the window in the kitchen door. There was a curtain over it but it was thin, almost worn through in places, and Eddie made out Mondini's head — his cap — with no difficulty.

She said to Donald, loudly, "What do you say, huh? Coffee?" She stepped farther into the house and put a hand on Donald's shoulder, pushing him gently around until he was facing the kitchen. She took a furtive sniff as she came close to him, but smelled no booze.

Donald shuffled obediently down the hall, walking on the outside edges of his feet, the toes curled together and turned inward. "Shit," he muttered in dismay. "My feet're cold. Where the hell're my shoes?"

"Don't know, Donald," said Eddie. "Maybe you left them in the kitchen."

She saw the back door open.

Donald lifted his head just as Mondini slipped inside. "What the hell?" said Donald.

Mondini lifted a reassuring hand — but his attention was caught by something out of Eddie's range of vision. He froze. Eddie thought he looked ridiculous, one hand raised as if he were stopping traffic, his head unwisely averted from the cars and trucks barreling toward him.

"Who let you in?" said Donald, no longer shuffling, walking quickly down the hall, striding toward Mondini, his bare feet making faint sucking sounds against the tile floor.

Eddie hurried to keep up with him. When they reached the kitchen doorway Donald abruptly stopped. Eddie almost ran into him.

"She might be dead," said Donald.

Eddie stepped to his side and looked where he was looking, where Mondini was looking.

Hildy was sitting motionless at the kitchen table, face-down on the bare surface, hands hanging at her sides.

"Mondini," said Eddie, and she nodded toward Hildy.

Mondini checked for a pulse, and shook his head.

Eddie's flesh prickled, with heat, with sweat.

Donald had clasped his hands and was looking at his wife's body with an expression Eddie couldn't read. "Yeah. She might have died," he said.

"What makes you think she died, Donald?" said Eddie. It seemed a logical inquiry, the woman's obvious lifelessness notwithstanding.

Donald sighed and his breath caught in his throat. Eddie saw tears sparkling in his eyes. "I think she died of fright," he said. He looked at Eddie, blinking, nodding. "I think I might have scared her to death." He reached out with his bare toes and nudged a long slim belt that lay coiled at the dead woman's feet. "Poor Hildy," said Donald. "Poor her."

NINE

Eleanor looked again at the big round alarm clock that sat on the table next to her bed. Its hands didn't seem to have moved at all, either of them. She picked up the clock and held it close to her ear: it was ticking, all right. She shook it, uselessly, and put it back.

She was fed up with lying there, waiting for her mother's nap to be over. She was getting more and more restless.

Finally, she couldn't stay still any longer. She got off the bed and moved around her room, picking things up, putting them down. She gazed for a while out the window, into the side yard, looking at the grass and the flower bed and the big tree with the pink flowers — they were exactly even with her now that she was upstairs looking at them.

Eleanor peeked out into the hall. A long, narrow carpet on the floor led from the top of the stairs right across the width of the house.

She slipped out of her room, closed the door behind her, and followed the carpet to the little window at the end of the hall. She looked outside at the slide, and the swing set, then walked quietly back down the centre of the carpet to the door to the guest room, which was now Samantha's room. She didn't know how long it would be Samantha's room. Every time she asked, her mother got mad. At first she had said it depended on

Uncle Blair. Now she just told Eleanor to shut up about it.

It occurred to her that Samantha might have come back. Snuck into the house and up the stairs without making any noise. Maybe she was in there reading library books. Or even sleeping — she was only a little kid, after all.

Eleanor opened the door, very quietly, turning the knob carefully, pushing the door just far enough so she could look in. But Samantha wasn't there.

Eleanor stayed where she was for a minute, thinking.

Then she pushed the door all the way open and went inside, straight to the big window that looked out onto the front yard and the sidewalk and the street, which was deserted, now, on this hot, slumberous afternoon. The window was open, but only a couple of inches. Eleanor's mother had been afraid that Samantha might topple right out if it was open too far, being too young and stupid to know any better, and so she had wedged the top of it so it could be opened only a little way.

Eleanor turned from the window. The bed wasn't made, and there was a pile of clothes on the floor, and the closet door was half open. Library books and books that belonged to Samantha littered the top of the desk. In the middle of the unmade bed lay a teddy bear — only it was a donkey, very soiled and worn, named after Eeyore.

She squatted next to a box of toys and poked through it. There was a painted drum with no drumstick, a doll that was missing one arm, a dog-eared coloring book, and a half-empty box of crayons. Eleanor was shocked at such carelessness. She didn't know if all five-year-old kids were like this or if it was only Samantha.

"It isn't so long since you were that age yourself," her mother told her whenever Eleanor complained about Samantha. But it was a long time, it was years since Eleanor had been five, so long ago that she couldn't remember the faintest thing about it.

She pulled open the folding door to the closet and examined the contents. The higher rod didn't have much on it, only two or three dresses Eleanor figured must be for good, and a coat Samantha for sure wouldn't need since it was so hot outside. On the lower rod were a lot of little shirts and little pairs of jeans. Eleanor thought of Samantha as being bigger than these little clothes, and wondered if this might be stuff she'd grown out of.

There was a dresser in the closet, too, because the room was small, only meant to be a guest room after all, just a place for people like Eleanor's grandmother to stay for one or two days while she was visiting, and visitors didn't need a lot of room. The dresser drawers were filled now with little kid clothes, underwear and shorts and socks mostly. Eleanor slammed the drawers closed in sudden disgust.

Then she stood very still, half crouched, listening — but heard nothing. Her mother was still asleep, then.

She swiped her gaze around the room one more time but couldn't see anything interesting — by which she meant revealing.

But then she asked herself, impatiently, what had she expected to find in the room of a five-year-old kid?

At the door, she took a last look around. A little table stood next to the bed, with a lamp on it, and there was a drawer in the table. She pulled the drawer open. Inside was a photograph in a silver frame, not a large photograph, about the same size as a paperback book. It was a picture of Samantha's mother. She picked it up and studied it. Her aunt Donna had been a very pretty woman, in her blue jeans and V-necked sweater.

Eleanor sat on the edge of Samantha's messy bed with the photograph in her lap. She didn't have a picture of her father, not one that was only hers, not one in a silver frame that she could keep next to her bed. She wiped her hand across her cheeks, first the right, then the left, getting rid of her tears.

After a while she put the photograph back in the drawer, face down, and left the room, closing the door quietly behind her.

Eleanor was downstairs, looking in the fridge for something to eat, when her mother finally woke up. She heard the door to her room open, and then her mother hurried down the stairs, saying, "Dear me, why didn't you wake me?"

Eleanor didn't answer, just rolled her eyes.

"What are you doing in there, Eleanor? Please don't eat anything, you'll spoil your dinner."

Eleanor slammed the fridge door shut and collapsed on a kitchen chair.

Her mother washed her hands, then opened the fridge and got out a chicken in a plastic bag. "It's so warm today, we could have had a cookout," she said, "but I haven't cleaned the barbecue since we used it last fall. Where's Samantha?" she said with a casual glance out the kitchen window.

Eleanor shrugged. "Don't know."

Her mother looked at her sharply. "What do you mean, you don't know?"

"I mean I don't know where she is, that's what I mean."

Her mother intensified her scrutiny of Eleanor, just like turning up the flame in the gas stove. "Go and find her," she said, and each word had its own sharp edges.

Eleanor pushed herself out of the chair.

She started upstairs, looking into every room, calling. Then she did the same downstairs, feeling her mother's piercing eyes upon her even when walls separated them.

Finally Eleanor stood in front of her mother, looking at her sandals. "She's not here," she said.

Her mother had put on a sundress and her legs were bare. Her sandals were made of leather. Eleanor looked up into her mother's face, which was every bit as pretty as Aunt Donna's, even when she was angry, like now, and worried, like now.

"When did you see her last?"

"She was playing the piano," said Eleanor. It wasn't a lie. Only a kind of a sidestep. "I went into my room." She put the flat of her hand on her stomach. "I wasn't feeling good." She saw this information register, and saw her mother decide to ignore it. "So I lay down," Eleanor concluded, "and I guess I fell asleep." She scratched the inside of her knee, which was itchy again. Was it too early for mosquitoes? she wondered.

"Please look for her outside," said her mother coldly.

Eleanor, her head bent, went through the swinging screen door from the kitchen into the yard. Maybe Samantha was hiding in the cherry tree, she thought. Hiding behind the pink flowers in the cherry tree. She would look there first.

TEN

"She'd be damn proud of you, Susie, your kid would."

It echoed in Susie's head, making her slightly dizzy. She gave herself a little shake, and then another, to clear her brain. Arthur's Jeep shuddered across a rough spot in the road and she grabbed at the dashboard to steady herself.

"Oops. Sorry," said Arthur.

She couldn't think about Leigh-Anne. She had moved her daughter from her head for the duration, like she would transfer something rare and breakable from a shelf to a safer place if an earthquake threatened: she would take it down, wrap it in something soft, and stow it safely in a drawer until the danger had passed.

A figurine, for example. She owned only one, a Hummel figure that Buddy had given her when they got married. It had been an odd choice for him to make and Susie had always thought that somebody had suggested it to him, probably a salesperson at the Bay. She had loved it, though, and still did. It was a small boy wearing a green hat and a blue jacket and brown shorts, climbing a fence to escape a goose. The boy's suspenders showed under the jacket, which had ridden up on his shoulders as he bent over the fence, and the goose appeared to be laughing at him. Leigh-Anne had loved the figurine, too. Susie never told her it had been a gift from her father. "Oh, somebody gave it to me," she had said carelessly, when Leigh-Anne had asked. "It was a long time ago. I can't even remember his name now."

Susie had once been chased by a goose, at the Fraser Valley farm of one of her mother's relatives. She wasn't going to school yet or even kindergarten so she must have been very young. In her memory the goose was as tall as she and uttered piercing squawks as it pursued her. She didn't know what she had done to make it angry. The adults had stood at the back door laughing, which had humiliated her. This piece of personal history was probably why she had such affection for the Hummel figure, and why she would hurry to protect it.

And that's what she had done with Leigh-Anne. Wrapped her up tenderly and closed her safely away in a drawer. But the drawer had now been opened a crack. By Arthur. Who ought to have known better.

"Whatcha thinking about?" he said.

"I was thinking about when you and I met," Susie lied.

Arthur chuckled.

They were still several miles from the village, but the houses were closer together now, on smaller lots, maybe an acre or so. In many front yards spring flowers were blooming. Susie wasn't a gardener, although she had tried. Vegetables she planted invariably became bug-infested, which caused her to shiver and uproot them. And she had never been particularly fond of flowers.

It took her utterly by surprise, then, as they drove along, to be swept away by a bed of brilliant red tulips in front of a two-story white house with fake green shutters, the kind of shutters that didn't close, their only purpose being to create a decorative frame around the windows.

There were hundreds of tulips. They filled half the space between the house and the street, arranged in rows that formed an immense triangle. An army of tulips, in strict formation. But they seemed to Susie to be laughing as they bent in the breeze, and shook their bell-shaped heads, and lifted wide green leaves like feminine hands raised to flutter at a passerby. She turned in her seat to gape at the sight: a sea of crimson, softly billowing.

"That was a while ago now," said Arthur comfortably. "When we met."

Susie watched the tulips, craning her neck until the Jeep rounded a bend in the road and they disappeared from sight. She looked out the windshield but continued to see in her mind a battalion of scarlet blooms, mirthful and content. She was astonished by her reaction, and embarrassed, too, because she didn't consider herself to be an anthropomorphic type of person. Quite the reverse, in fact. She knew very well where things belonged, and she kept them there.

"I wonder where we'd be now, what we'd be doing today," said Arthur, "if we hadn't run into each other in that park that day."

She didn't reply. She knew he believed that their project would never have been launched had it not been for him.

But Susie believed otherwise. She was convinced that if she had never met Arthur she would still have been here now, driving down this road, making final preparations to commit a grievous crime.

Arthur thought there was far too much tension in the Wagoneer. The open driver's window didn't even help. The sounds and smells coming in were having no effect whatsoever upon Susie: she was wound up as tight as one of those kids' toys — a yo-yo, that was it. He reached across to pat her leg again. "We'll be ready, Suze," he said before he remembered that she hated being called Suze. "When the day comes, when the moment comes, we'll be ready. I guarantee it."

She gave him a look that was so cold, so bleak that his own spirits plummeted, and he had to concentrate hard on his secret — on the rewards that he was convinced lay in store for him — in order to get them to rise again.

ELEVEN

Samantha walked down the narrow, dusty lane singing softly to herself. Big tall trees grew on both sides — they had new leaves on them; it looked like a great big green-gold cloud had gotten caught in their branches. She was holding a dandelion, pulling at the yellow part and strewing it behind her. The stem had leaked sticky goo all over her hand. She had tried to get it off by rubbing her hand on her shorts and now there was dirt too, as well, stuck to the dandelion sap or blood or whatever it was.

The lane was very, very long. Samantha couldn't see the end of it yet, but she knew where it came out. First the trees started getting farther and farther apart, with weeds and ferns growing in clumps among them, and then Samantha would be able to see across to the main street of the town on one side and to a street of houses on the other, and then the lane would end, next to a gas station. Samantha was a long way from the gas station. The trees were still tall and close together. She stopped walking, tossed the dandelion away, and looked into the woods, wondering if any wildflowers were growing there.

She glanced up the lane toward the town, and back in the other direction. And she thought she saw something moving. Maybe a wild animal: a skunk, or a raccoon. She started skipping back the way she'd come, to have a look.

But then she stopped. She'd never get to the library if she didn't keep going.

"You're a dawdler, Samantha, an honest-to-god dawdler," she heard her father say with a laugh, and this memory made her happy and sad at the same time. She felt nice and warm and loved, but also she wanted to sit down in the dust and cry. He hadn't said it for a long time now. Not once since her mother died. And he hardly ever laughed any more.

She started walking again, swinging her arms, lifting her knees high in the air like she was marching, imagining that she could hear marching music.

Behind her, Eleanor had ducked behind a tree, swearing at herself because she'd feel pretty stupid if Samantha saw her. She counted to thirty, then peeked around the trunk.

Samantha was walking away again, a little faster now. And Eleanor continued to follow her, slipping from tree to tree, feeling graceful, like a ballet dancer, leaping silently from tree to tree, touching the rough and scaly bark lightly with the tips of her fingers. Her feet in their hightop sneakers disappeared into the undergrowth with each bound.

When she couldn't find her in the yard, Eleanor had known exactly where to look. She knew all the places Samantha liked to go. She knew that Samantha was on her way to the library, and Eleanor had decided to follow her almost to the door, then she would grab her by the arm and haul her home, telling her the whole way how angry her mother was that she'd gone off on her own.

Bound — leap — jump — hurdle . . . there were a lot of different words for what she was doing, thought Eleanor, still pretending she was a dancer.

Suddenly she stumbled over a big fallen branch and had to scrabble at a tree trunk with both hands so as not to fall down. When she had recovered, she looked cautiously down the lane again. But Samantha was nowhere in sight.

Samantha had gotten bored with marching and had decided to run. One of the things she had discovered in kindergarten was that she was a fast runner. So she had suddenly bolted along the lane, pumping her arms. The trees whipped along at the edge of her vision — she could almost hear their whoops of encouragement and she ran faster and faster until she thought she could hear cars on the town's main street. She slowed down then, and was proud to notice that she was hardly out of breath.

Eleanor, meanwhile, had given up the idea of a stealthy pursuit and was stomping angrily down the middle of the lane, her sneakers creating puffs of dust. She walked rapidly, looking into the woods on either side and calling out, "Samantha! Samantha!" But she got no response.

Suddenly she heard a scuffling among the weeds and fallen leaves. Eleanor stopped and looked hard. She imagined that she had super-sight and could see through and around things. It didn't work, though — she couldn't spot Samantha in there. So she pushed through the brush for a better look.

"Samantha? Samantha!" she called.

She stood still, listening intently, with her whole body. She heard birds, and some rustling that was probably caused by a breeze, and a sighing noise that she couldn't identify, and car sounds from the street she knew was now close by.

But nothing more.

And she looked hard, too, into the woods that surrounded her and saw trees, and ferns, and weeds, and mossy fallen-down branches, and the leaves and the ferns sometimes shivered slightly.

And nothing more.

"Samantha! I'm getting damn mad at you," she said.

What was she *up* to, anyway?

Hiding, probably, to make Eleanor mad.

And so Eleanor pressed on, quietly, quietly, into the woods.

An hour later Eleanor's mother heard the kitchen screen door squeak open and slam shut. She hurried downstairs, calling, "Eleanor? Did you find her?"

Eleanor stood by the door. Her knee was skinned and bits of leaves and moss clung to her clothes and her hair.

"Eleanor?" Her mother took her by the shoulders.

"I didn't find her."

Her mother sat down on one of the kitchen chairs. "Oh god. Oh god."

"I don't know where she is," said Eleanor.

"Oh god," said her mother. "Oh god."

TWELVE

Susie collapsed into a kitchen chair and tried to lean against its back, but she was shaking too much. So she sat bolt upright, both feet on the floor, her hands twisting in her lap. Her eyes focused on the tabletop but she wasn't seeing it. She was seeing the child coming toward them, along the narrow dusty track that led through the greening trees. She had been partly running and partly skipping, her hands lifting with every second step or so, and creating the illusion that, pale hair bouncing, she was about to take flight. Behind her, the path had stretched, then curved. Empty.

"You didn't have a choice," said Arthur, slumped against the counter. "I know that. You had to do it. But Jesus H. Christ, Susie," he said, slapping the countertop with the flat of his hand. He looked at her helplessly. "What a mess. What a fucking screw-up. She's seen our *faces,* for chrissake! She's seen us!"

"We have to make the best of it," said Susie, striving for confidence, or at least for the sound of confidence.

"Yeah, right, well you just tell me how we're gonna do that." He jerked open the fridge and hauled out a can of beer. "And did you even look *around?* Do you even know if anybody *saw* you with her?" He shook his head. "Somebody saw you. Jesus. I know it. I just know it."

"I have to think." Susie placed her hands on the table, smoothing the grain of the wood. "I just need a little bit of time to think." She looked sharply at Arthur. "Give me some credit. I've gotten us this far, haven't I?"

"Yeah," said Arthur grimly, slamming the fridge door shut. "Right."

Samantha was sitting on the floor, trying not to be scared. She was hugging her knees and wishing that her aunt Harriet had told her to put on her jeans today, because this floor didn't look very clean. It was made of strips of wood that were a lot wider than the wood in the floor of her aunt's house, and not at all shiny like the floors there.

Samantha kept looking at the window. But she didn't get up. She stayed where she was, on the floor, with her back pressed against the wall. Here she would be hidden for a minute if somebody opened the door. She knew they'd look behind the door almost right away, but for a minute maybe she'd be able to see them and they wouldn't be able to see her.

She wanted badly to look out the window. Maybe she could jump out of it. But she was trying not to be too scared, and she thought that if she stood up and scurried over to the window, that would definitely make her more scared than she was now.

What if she took her shoes off and tiptoed over there? No — she'd still be scared.

What if she backed toward the window, watching the door all the time?

No — that would *still* be too scary.

Samantha felt a trembling in the place where you go to the bathroom: what if she wet her pants?

She pressed her back against the wall, hugged her knees tightly, and scrunched her eyes closed, concentrating on whatever was yelling at her from the middle of her head.

And when the door opened, she almost *did* wet her pants. It was like she had been making so much noise

inside her head that she hadn't been able to hear anything that was happening *outside* her head. Samantha
thought this might be an important thing to remember.

She watched the door slowly open. The lady poked
her head around it, and they saw each other at the same
moment.

Samantha looked straight into the lady's eyes. The
lady looked straight back, and Samantha saw coldness
inside of her. Yes. The lady had a big chunk of ice in her.
Probably in her chest.

The lady came all the way into the room and closed
the door. She lifted the edges of her mouth, as if she
meant to smile.

"I'd like to go home, please," Samantha said to her,
trying to be polite. "Or else to Eleanor's house."

But the lady was shaking her head.

Samantha hugged her knees more tightly and rocked
back and forth on her bum, looking across the room at
the window. They had walked up a whole entire flight of
stairs getting to this room so she knew it would be too
far down for her to jump. But there could be a great big
old tree growing out there, stretching its branches this
way and that.

"What do you want for your supper?" said the lady.
Her voice sounded almost ordinary, except for a little bit
of sharpness.

Samantha heard somebody coming slowly up the
stairs. It would be the other one, the man.

The lady paid no attention. "Did you hear me?" she
said. "What do you feel like eating?"

The slow footsteps came closer. Samantha's throat
suddenly felt swollen and dry. Maybe it wasn't that man
at all. Maybe those footsteps were made by a ghost;
maybe the lady wasn't ignoring the footsteps — maybe
she didn't even hear them, maybe it was a ghost out
there that only Samantha could hear. She listened intently: the footsteps went right past the room she was in, and

then she heard a door open and close. Samantha swallowed, which was very hard.

"I want to go home," she said. She was very tired — not sleepy tired but heavy-feeling tired. "I want to go home." She heard a quaver in her voice. "I want to go home," she said again. But the quaver was still there. Her eyes filled up with tears. "I want to go home!" she said, louder, clutching her knees.

The lady came close to her and knelt down. She was near enough to touch Samantha's shoulder, but she didn't. "After a while," she said firmly. "But not yet."

"Before it gets dark," said Samantha. She looked at the lady, who was old, with gray in her hair and a stiffness in the way she moved. But she wore a beautiful ring, with a big green jewel in it. "Please?" said Samantha. "Before it gets dark?"

THIRTEEN

"I got nobody to call," said Donald Blake. He was sitting on a metal chair in the interview room. His hands were clasped between his knees and he was staring at the floor. "Who would I call?"

"What about a lawyer?" said Eddie, who was sitting opposite him, while Mondini stood by the door. "You want to call a lawyer, Donald?"

"Ah, shit," said Blake, sitting back. His eyes glittered, and he wiped at them with his fingers. "It tires me out to think about it."

"You don't have a lawyer, right?"

He slid a glance at her, and shook his head.

"That's what we thought. So we're getting one for you," said Eddie.

"He's on the way," said Mondini. "The Crown, too, Sarge," he added.

"So," said Eddie. "Do you want to wait till your *pro bono* lawyer gets here, Donald? Or do you want to go ahead and tell me what happened?"

Donald lifted his hands and placed them on the table-top. He did this slowly and with considerable effort, as if they were extremely heavy. He studied them for a while before raising his eyes to Eddie. They were small eyes, bloodshot, trembling in a face that was pinched with pain. "She died on me."

Eddie nodded. "And how did this happen?"

Donald plucked his hands from the table and wiped them on his pant legs. He rested them in his lap, palms up, and bent his head to examine them closely — as if he were listening, Eddie thought, listening for his hands to tell him what they had done.

"Donald? What happened to Hildy?"

Donald lowered his face and lifted his hands and his hands covered his face entirely except for the tears that squeezed out from between his fingers.

Eddie sat back in her chair. "Okay, Donald. I'm going to have Constable Mondini take you to a cell now. You can wait there until your lawyer shows up."

Mondini took him by the elbow and pulled him gently to his feet. "Come on, Mr. Blake. Upsy-daisy. There we go."

"I need to go to the bathroom," said Donald, shuffling obediently toward the door.

"No problem," said Mondini. "We got all the perks here."

Eddie watched them make their way to the cells, then went to her office to finish the paperwork on Donald Blake's arrest in preparation for the arrival of the Crown prosecutor.

She was almost done when the duty officer buzzed her.

"What is it?" said Eddie.

"There's a kid gone missing, Sarge."

FOURTEEN

There wasn't any big tree growing outside the window. There were several trees — a whole row of them, in fact — at the edge of the yard, but they were very far away.

Between the house and the trees were several piles of junk. There was no grass for Samantha to look at out the window, no flowers, only heaps of junk. Dead machines, with rust all over them. Samantha saw an old stove lying on its side, its oven door open, and she imagined that when the wind blew the door would make a clattering sound, hitting itself against whatever was underneath it. And there was an old car; well, parts of it — the doors were gone and most of the glass in the windows, too. And she saw an overturned metal tub, and a whole pile of what looked like phone books. It was a real mess, that yard.

From her little window Samantha could also see the driveway, and the road that passed, a long way away, in front of the house, and the front part of a building at the bottom of the yard. She thought it must be a barn, because it had a rounded roof and a huge door like the barn in one of the storybooks she'd had since she was very young. The windows on each side of the door were cracked and clouded, so that even if the sun were to shine directly onto them Samantha didn't think a person would be able to see inside.

Samantha stayed mostly by the window all afternoon, looking out at the barn and the junk-filled yard and the road. Sometimes a car drove by, but not often, and they never stopped.

It was comforting, that road. If she could just get out of here, all she had to do was go down to the road and start walking. It wouldn't even matter which way she walked, the road would take her somewhere. She knew her phone number, of course. She couldn't remember Aunt Harriet's phone number but she knew her own, in West Vancouver. She wondered if there was a phone in this house. There had to be — everybody had a phone.

She wasn't allowed out of this room, even to go to the bathroom. The door was kept locked with a great big old key that didn't look like any key she'd ever seen before. It felt to Samantha like she'd been hurled back in time to the olden days, the really, really olden days, because of this key, which was long and skinny. In the round part at the top there was a hole shaped like the figure eight. Samantha would hear the lady approach the door and unlock it with the key and when the lady came into the room the key would be in her hand.

Also like the olden days was the big shallow bowl and the big pitcher of water that sat on a wobbly white table in front of the window. There was a piece of soap on a saucer, too, and a small folded-up towel. And when she had to go to the bathroom she was supposed to use a china pot with a handle that was kept on the floor under the bed. Samantha almost cried when the lady showed her this. She thought, what if she had to have a b.m.? But then she told herself that she wasn't going to be here long enough to have a b.m.

Samantha left the window and used the stepstool to climb up onto the bed, which was high and narrow with a metal frame. She sat on the edge and swung her feet. It was still a nice day outside but the light was changing the way it did when evening was near. And every time Samantha thought about the coming of darkness a frantic feeling started fluttering inside her, reminding her of the small bird that had flown into their living room by mistake one day, through the open sliding door, and then couldn't find its way out. But Samantha's father had held up a sheet and slowly moved toward the bird, who would rest for a moment on a windowsill, or the fireplace mantel, and then suddenly rise into the air again, flapping its poor little wings so frantically Samantha was afraid they'd come off. She had imagined its tiny heart pounding in its chest, so hard that she thought it might pound its way right out of that bird. Slowly, gradually, her father herded it back to the open door.

And now Samantha felt just like that bird must have felt, every time she thought about night coming and finding her here, in this strange place, with these awful people.

For the old lady must be an awful person. Because she had taken Samantha, stolen her, like she was a watch, or five dollars.

Samantha knew the man who had helped her was in the house, too, because of the footsteps, which she had really known all along weren't from a ghost. She didn't believe in ghosts. But she'd been scared by the slowness of those footsteps, and besides the old woman hadn't looked like she was hearing them. But Samantha had heard the murmuring of people talking, too, so she knew he was there. And the man was just as awful as the lady, because he'd helped her bring Samantha here, and was letting her keep her locked up, like she was in jail.

And then Samantha had a thought.

Maybe they weren't the only people in the house — it was a big house, after all — and maybe the others didn't know that the old lady and the old man had a little girl locked up in this room.

This was a new and powerful thought, and Samantha acted upon it instantly.

She slid off the bed and started jumping up and down on the bedroom floor as hard as she could, all the while screaming "Help! Help!" at the top of her lungs. The more she jumped and screamed, the harder the jumps became, and the louder the screams. Her screams were so piercing that Samantha thought she might be deafening herself — but she didn't care. She was jumping so hard that she was making herself dizzy — but she didn't care. She was gripped and shaken by her screaming. She felt the impact of each jump in her hips and in the soles of her feet. Her hands were clenched, her face was covered with tears, when the door burst open.

"What the fuck are you doing?"

Samantha stopped jumping, stopped screaming. Her whole body was shaking. The old man filled the doorway. He was leaning forward, slightly stooped, and if it hadn't been for the anger in his face she might have thought he was waiting to start running in a race. He hadn't shaved today, or combed his hair, either. Samantha noticed these things automatically. She gulped a big breath of air, but didn't speak.

The man continued to stare at her. He waved the key. "You'll keep quiet," he said, "if you know what's good for you." He backed out of the room, pulling the door closed, and Samantha heard him turn the key in the lock.

She crumpled to the floor. Her throat was sore, and the bottoms of her feet hurt. She lifted her arm and wiped the shoulder of her T-shirt across half of her face, then did the same with the other arm.

She looked up at the window. The soft rich buttery light of evening flowed right through the glass.

FIFTEEN

It would be a momentary thing, Eddie was sure. A child not lost but ranging beyond authorized boundaries. Exploring, as children do. She would quickly be found, perhaps had been found already. Eddie was confident of this.

Yet when she turned onto Harriet Murchison's street she was struck by what an ordinary street it was, as if some part of her had already decided that this call wasn't an ordinary call.

Most of the places where crime happened, where dreadful things happened, most were ordinary places, even pretty places. And often even when they weren't pretty, there was something . . .

Her mind skittered to a rundown, smelly apartment building in Burnaby, to an almost empty room with a window that wouldn't close all the way. There was cracked glass in the panes and cold air whistled through the space between the bottom of the window and the sill.

A rumpled bed stood against one wall. An easy chair, ripped and stained, sat next to a small wooden table, its top scarred and blotched. Yellowed newspapers had washed up in the corners of the room like flotsam.

The body lay in the middle of the filthy linoleum floor.

The girl wore black boots halfway up her calves, a short black leather skirt, and a black leather jacket, both so shiny that looking at them stung Eddie's eyes. Her hair was magenta, cut short and spiked. She had rings in her ears, rings in her nose, rings in her bottom lip. She lay on her side and looked quite comfortable, as if she had arranged herself to sleep. But her throat had been cut and there was a pool of blood beneath her so large that Eddie was at first convinced that it could not possibly all have come from the slim, slight body of this fifteen-year-old prostitute and drug addict.

Eddie remembered all of this, all the details. She remembered the girl's parents, remembered the trial — this time they had caught the sonofabitch — but most of all she remembered the violet on the windowsill. An African violet crowned with dainty white blooms, growing in a green plastic pot.

And the tentative stop-and-start whistling of the wind through the crack between window and sill.

She locked the car door and headed up the walk.

It was a white house, two stories, with a veranda along the front, and it sat off-center on its large lot. There was lawn and there were flower beds and trees: a big ornamental cherry tree on the left was languidly tossing pink petals onto the evening breeze.

The door opened while Eddie was mounting the steps.

The woman wore a sundress, sunflowers on a white background, a white cardigan, and sandals.

"Is there just one of you?" she said to Eddie. She looked dismayed.

"We're organizing searchers. They'll be along in a few minutes." Eddie smiled. "I'm Sergeant Henderson. And you're Mrs. Murchison, I guess."

"Yes. We have to find her before it gets dark."

"I need to get information from you, ma'am, that'll help us do that."

"Yes, sure, of course," said Harriet, still in the doorway.

"You want to talk out here?" said Eddie. "Or inside?"

"Maybe out here." Harriet pushed the screen door open and stepped onto the veranda.

Eddie saw a woman wound so tight that a single touch could set her spinning like a top, spinning out of control down the steps, along the walk, and down the street, spinning and spinning until she dissolved. Eddie saw this in the clenched fists, and the rapidly blinking eyes, and the stiffness of her posture. Harriet's eyes ranged up and down the street, hungrily, desperately.

"Have you got a picture of her?" said Eddie.

Harriet looked at her with an expression so incongruous that Eddie at first didn't recognize it: it was relief. "A picture. Of course! A picture." She rushed back to the door and called through the screen, "Eleanor? Eleanor! We need a picture! Bring me a picture of Samantha!" She turned back to Eddie, who was flipping through her notebook, looking for the first empty page.

"The child's name?" said Eddie.

"Samantha."

"Samantha Murchison?"

"No, Decker." Harriet clasped her hands and brought them up to her chest. "She's my brother's child. She's visiting us. From West Van."

"And how old is Samantha?"

"Five. She's five."

"How long has she been missing?"

Harriet Murchison was hanging on to herself for dear life, almost panting with the effort not to weep, or scream. "Since about two o'clock. I've been up and down the street," she said, talking quickly, her words running into each other. She couldn't articulate fast enough to get them out one by one — they seemed to emerge from her mouth in jumbled-up clusters. "I talked to all the neighbors, I called the library, I drove there — people saw her walking along, walking that way, toward town, toward the library, I take her there after lunch but today, today I told her that we'd go like usual — but *later*," she cried out. "Not then! I had a headache." She wiped her palms on her dress. "And so I went upstairs to lie down. I told her, when I get up we'll go to the library."

Harriet was clinging to one of the posts supporting the roof of the veranda. A single light burned inside the house, in the front hallway. The golden light of evening suffused the yard in a glow that to Eddie seemed false, garish, like a badly lit stage set.

She sensed movement, then saw a silhouette. The screen door opened and a child came out holding a photograph. She handed it to Harriet, watched Harriet study it, stroke it, and begin to sob, then turned to look at Eddie. As she did so, she moved into the light from the hallway. She looked familiar to Eddie, but she couldn't think where she might have seen her before.

The child's head almost reached her mother's shoulder. She was wearing shorts and a T-shirt and hightops. Her hair was light brown, swept back from a high forehead into a ponytail. Her eyes were blue. There was a cleft in her chin, and her right knee had been recently grazed. Her teeth were still too big for her face and she moved awkwardly, self-consciously. Eddie knew from personal experience that this would get worse before it got better — she figured the kid was ten or eleven.

Harriet thrust the photograph at Eddie. "Hurry," she said. "Hurry. It's almost dark."

"They'll be here any minute, Mrs. Murchison."

"Will there be dogs, too?" said the child.

"This is Eleanor," said Harriet. "My daughter, Eleanor."

"How do you do, Eleanor. My name is Edwina, but everybody calls me Eddie." She offered her hand and Eleanor hesitated, then took it in a surprisingly firm grip.

Eleanor wished that her mother would turn on the porch light. She could hardly see this policewoman's face. She felt dizzy. Sick to her stomach. But excited, too. She couldn't concentrate on anything.

She knew she'd have to say something. Eventually. But meanwhile she hugged her secret to herself.

All she wanted to do now was sleep. But she couldn't sleep. Neither of them would ever sleep again, not Eleanor and not her mother, until Samantha was found.

She looked at the policewoman and even in the gathering dark saw her mouth. Eleanor knew before she uttered a word what she was going to say, this big tall woman with the man's name.

"When did you last see your cousin, Eleanor?"

"I saw her out on the lawn this morning, poking at a pansy. I saw her on the swing. I saw her pour her soup into the corn plant. I saw her playing the piano." And then Eleanor's mouth closed itself. The policewoman waited. "I went upstairs," said Eleanor. She shrugged her shoulders.

Eddie watched her, waiting. She was sure the child would go on. But she didn't.

"Does anybody else live here?" she asked Harriet.

"No, there's just Eleanor and me. My husband died three years ago."

"Have you been in touch with Samantha's parents?"

"No, it's . . . Her mother was killed in a car accident. My brother — he's out of the country. He — I don't want to try to reach him. Not until . . ."

Suddenly noise flourished in the street, in the dying of the day's light, as cars materialized and parked at the curbside up and down the block, wherever room could be found.

"Here they are," said Eddie quietly to Harriet Murchison. She touched her arm. "Now we'll go look for her."

Eleanor stepped back against the house, into deep shadow, and thought about the green glint from the lady's ring, glinting cold and green in the hot sun.

The policewoman had started down the steps toward the sidewalk where men and boys were piling almost silently out of their cars. Where are the women? thought Eleanor. And where are the girls, to go looking for Samantha?

Eleanor's mother opened the screen door, reached inside, and turned on the porch light. This, or something else, made the policewoman stop and turn around. She looked directly at Eleanor then, and Eleanor felt strong, terrible things. She knew the light was shining right on her and thought, maybe she can see these things in my face.

"I don't know where she is," said Eleanor.

The policewoman cocked her head, as if she hadn't quite heard her.

"I don't know where she is," said Eleanor again.

And this much was true.

SIXTEEN

Slowly, Harriet let herself slump into the clasp of the rocking chair, releasing molecule by molecule the tension in her limbs, torso, and neck, collapsing against the cushion, her head lolling, eyes closed. Eddie started to get up, certain for a moment that the woman had fainted; then she saw tears tracking down her cheeks in two shallow streams.

"I want him to know," she said. "It's been hours, now. He has to know. But I'm afraid to tell him."

"I'll speak to him when he returns your call," said Eddie. "If you like."

Harriet didn't respond. Eddie watched her, letting her rest, hoping she was resting.

The doorbell rang again. It was the side door, which chimed a single tone. The front buzzer had two. Eddie wondered what made some people decide to rap softly while others preferred the formality of the bell. The door was opened, Norah Gibbons murmured, the door closed. Harriet hadn't moved. Not even a twitch.

Norah returned to the kitchen and leaned against the counter. Eddie saw this through the archway, saw her fold her arms, heard the squeak of leather as her holster rubbed against the edge of the counter.

She looked around the living room, where pools of light were arranged artfully upon a wingback chair, an end table, an enormous spreading fern on a rattan stand behind which sat the child named Eleanor, leaning against the wall, hugging her knees. Half of one foot was in the light that spilled from the lamp above. As Eddie observed this, and the child's stillness, the foot slowly withdrew entirely into shadow.

"No," said Harriet. "Thank you, but I'll do it. I'll talk to him." She opened her eyes and sat up straight in the rocking chair, pushing heavily on the arms. "If she's been kidnapped, they'll be calling soon, won't they? Asking for money."

"I think you're jumping to conclusions, Mrs. Murchison. We've got no reason to believe Samantha's been kidnapped."

"I don't have any money," said Harriet. "Well, not much. Blair's got some. They must know that." She bent toward Eddie, clutching the arms of her chair. "*How* do they know it?" she whispered. "How did they even know she was here?"

"Mrs. Murchison," said Eddie firmly. "I'm quite sure that your niece is just lost. And that we'll find her, very soon. You know how many people we've got out looking for her. It's only a matter of time."

"We picked her up, Eleanor and I," said Harriet, "from Blair's house in West Van." She glanced across the room at her daughter, still and silent, secluded in near darkness.

Lurking, thought Eddie, behind that damn fern.

"When?" she said, taking her notebook and pen from her pocket. "What day, what time?"

"It was a Sunday. A week ago last Sunday. We got to his house before noon, and we all went out for lunch. Blair doesn't cook," she said with a touch of disapproval. "I think on the weekends they mostly eat out." She touched her forehead with her fingertips, delicately, as if feeling for a wound. "There was practically nothing in the fridge. Of course he was just about to go away." She looked at Eddie, who nodded obligingly.

"When you arrived," said Eddie, "while you were there, do you remember seeing anyone on the street? Near your brother's house?"

Harriet frowned, concentrating. "His house is in a cul-de-sac. I don't remember seeing anybody." Her eyes widened. "Do you think — somebody was watching them?"

Eddie was aware of the silence in the kitchen. The unringing telephone. The child's father wasn't calling. The child's kidnapper — if there was one — wasn't calling, either.

"I don't know," said Eddie wearily. "Probably not. I'm just doing the obvious here."

An hour later, the telephone did ring.

In the kitchen, Norah Gibbons picked it up. "Murchison residence." She looked at Harriet and nodded. "She's right here, sir. One moment, please."

Harriet grabbed the receiver. "Oh, Blair," she said, hunched over the phone, one hand pressing down hard on the counter. "Oh, Blair. I'm sorry. I'm so sorry."

PART TWO

THE PAST

SEVENTEEN

Later, Susie would see the whole dreadful thing as beginning on a glistening day in May almost exactly two years before its horrible end. It would encompass four deaths, this span of events, not to mention Susie's terrible crime. And it began, in Susie's memory, on a Saturday afternoon in springtime when she took her dog, Mutt — a yappy, self-confident creature who had taken possession of Susie's heart — to the park that occupied a square block not far from Susie's house. . . .

As she scampered inelegantly across the sidewalk and onto the grass, hanging on to the leash that Mutt, racing, kept stretched to breaking, Susie observed a man lying on a bench under one of the ornamental cherry trees. His face was covered with a newspaper, and the newspaper had a soft pink layer of petals on it. So thick and motionless was the layer of petals that for a terrible flesh-crawling moment she thought the man beneath the newspaper was dead.

She walked a bit closer to him and encouraged Mutt to bark, in the hope that the body might bestir itself at the sound. But Mutt, a small gray dog resembling a mop, was more interested in the corpse of a robin she had found at the foot of the tree. Susie yanked at the leash, and Mutt responded by growling at her. Susie promptly picked Mutt up and shook her, something she had read in one of the dog books that were now crowding out the fiction on the shelves in her living room. Mutt yelped piteously, and the man on the bench shifted and sat up, scattering pink petals in all directions as the newspaper slid to the ground.

"Sorry," Susie muttered.

Now Mutt began barking, as if embarrassed that she hadn't recognized the lengthy lump on the park bench as a human, and Susie backed away from the man and headed diagonally across the park, dragging the dog behind her. Mutt eventually lost interest in barking at something that was receding into the distance and began zigzagging through the grass, nose to the ground.

Susie heard footsteps and turned to see the man from the bench loping toward her, holding his rolled-up paper in one hand, waving it at her. Oh dear, oh dear, she thought, grasping Mutt's leash tightly, wondering if the dog would have any interest whatsoever in attempting to protect Susie from assault, and deciding it more likely that she would stand back and watch, her tousled head tilted, her small black eyes bright with interest.

"Hey, wait up," the man called.

But Susie kept on going, heading for the sidewalk that would take her home.

"I just want to ask you something." He sounded out of breath. When he caught up with her he stayed a respectful distance away. "Nice dog," he said.

Susie shot him a nervous but frosty glance.

"What kind is he?"

"She's mostly terrier."

"How come you've got him on a leash?" he said, slapping the newspaper against his thigh as he walked. "Can't you just let him run around on his own?"

Susie snorted. "If I did that, she'd run away."

This had occurred several times, causing Susie great distress as she searched the neighborhood, often catching glimpses of Mutt but never managing to catch her, eventually going home to wait, certain that this time there would be no scratching at the door, no mud-smeared, self-satisfied mongrel peering up at her from the porch, her tail wagging tentatively as she psyched out Susie, no, this time the dog would have been struck by a car — smashed to death — left bleeding in the street. After the fourth time Mutt ran away, Susie had vowed never to let her off the leash again.

"He's a runaway, huh?" said the man from the bench, keeping up with Susie easily even though she was hurrying now. "Maybe you ought to take him to dog school."

She had taken Mutt to obedience classes, of course she had. The instructor had told her that it was Susie's fault the dog wouldn't behave. "She'll get away with exactly what you let her get away with, Mrs. Wilson," the woman had wearily pronounced. Well, Susie had gotten into a huff then and refused to take Mutt back to class. Eventually they had reached a détente of sorts. Mutt had agreed not to urinate or defecate in the house, and in exchange, Susie let her do pretty much whatever else she liked.

Susie's job was that of office manager for a group of realtors, and she frequently worked overtime. Mutt had at first amused herself in her owner's absence by chewing on whatever was handy — shoes, purses, belts that Susie had left lying around. A can of pennies, shaken hard, discouraged Mutt from this behavior, but only when Susie was around to shake it. When Susie started putting her things away, the dog had turned gleefully to curtains, bedspreads, and the arms of chairs and sofas. So Susie had installed a baby fence to keep her corralled in the kitchen. And that put an end to that.

"I was wondering," said the man, "is there a coffee shop anywhere around?" They were out of the park now, crossing the side street that was only a block and a half from Susie's house. "I just got off the bus from

Prince Rupert," he went on. "Gonna be staying with a friend. He's not home yet, so I'm putting in time. And I'd sure love to have a coffee while I'm waiting."

Susie began giving him directions to a nearby Starbucks. But somehow she ended up taking Mutt home and accompanying him there: she couldn't have explained why.

His name, he told her, was Arthur Bentley.

He had the coffee of the day and Susie had a blackberry tea. She was off caffeine, because of that scare about her heart. Six months earlier it had begun to have alarming fits of stuttering, painless but frightening. She had worried and worried about it and had finally taken herself off to her GP, who could find nothing wrong but who sent her to a specialist just in case. The specialist had required Susie to wear a device that monitored and recorded her heartbeat: every time she thought about it during that interminable weekend she felt her damn heart leap and stumble. She returned to the specialist in dread. How much time off work would she need, she wondered, to get a bypass done? And would Leigh-Anne look after Mutt for her while she was in the hospital? But the specialist hadn't been able to find anything wrong, either. Susie continued to worry, certain that she would soon die of a massive heart attack. Gradually, however, she stopped worrying. And then noticed that her heart wasn't stuttering very often any more. But by then she had given up caffeine and had begun drinking various flavors of herbal teas. Arthur, when she got to know him better, had plenty to say about the kinds of people who drank herbal tea but that day he kept his mouth shut.

They fit in just fine, sitting there, she and Arthur. They looked like any other couple of people sharing a small round table, drinking their tea and coffee, making small talk.

He said, "I admire your house."

"Thank you," said Susie. "I like it too." Her house was small and brown, with the window frames painted white.

"Do you own," he said, "or rent?"

"I own," said Susie stiffly. Although she still had another five years of mortgage payments to make.

"You're not married, I guess."

Susie tucked in her tummy and lifted her chin, gazing at him dispassionately.

"I mean, you aren't wearing a ring," said Arthur.

Well, Susie wasn't about to tell this drifter her life story. She ignored the question and asked one of her own. "What kind of work do you do?" Dirt was ingrained under his fingernails and his hands were scarred — brutal hands they were, tough looking, powerful.

He told her that he had worked first in the woods, then on the fishboats, "until I got hurt." He lifted his T-shirt to reveal an irregular scar that slashed across his chest and midriff and disappeared under his waistband. He did this so abruptly that Susie hadn't enough time to turn away, and she stared helplessly at his damaged front for several seconds before he dropped the T-shirt.

He tore open another envelope of sugar, his third, and dumped it into his coffee. "That's why I'm down here. This friend I mentioned, the one I'll be staying with for a time, he thinks he can point me to a job that'll do me." He patted himself. "This tore me up inside. I gotta be careful, can't do anything too strenuous. What about you?"

"What about me?"

"Do you work?"

"Of course I work. I've got a job in a realty office."

"Oh yeah? Do you like it?"

"It's okay. The people are very nice." Susie sipped her herbal tea, feeling prim.

"Having a job's good," said Arthur, nodding.

"I hope it works out for you," said Susie. "What your friend has in mind." She stood, and he immediately pushed back his chair. Susie put a hand on his shoulder, which surprised her, but it was just to stop him from standing up. "No, you stay and finish your coffee," she said. "I've got some errands to do so I have to go now, but you stay."

"Maybe I'll run into you again," said Arthur, smiling up at her.

His eyes were very dark blue, almost black. Though he was unshaven, even unkempt (but after all, she rationalized, he'd just gotten off the bus), she found his easy manner attractive.

He had a fluid way of moving that she found sexy. He was apparently unaware of this, although he certainly knew that there was something about him that women responded to. At their first meeting Susie mistook his litheness for self-confidence that extended beyond the physical. But she liked his white teeth, too, and the strong chest she had glimpsed when he'd shown her his scar.

She patted his shoulder in what might have been a sisterly fashion. "If you're in the neighborhood for any length of time," she said, "I'm sure you will."

That evening she called Leigh-Anne, just to chat, and told her, casually, about meeting Arthur.

"My god, Mother, a complete stranger, sleeping in the park? How could you? The man's probably a psychopath."

"I'm sure I do not understand," said Susie, "why you assume that I wouldn't recognize a psychopath if I met one."

Leigh-Anne managed to laugh and sound exasperated at the same time, as if Susie in her late fifties had suddenly become senile and in need of a watchful eye.

(When Susie introduced the two of them several months later she didn't tell Leigh-Anne that he was the man from the park. Arthur took Leigh-Anne's hand in his and actually bowed over it, causing Susie to think of

Errol Flynn, and Leigh-Anne to present him with a
wintry smile.)

"If I come over after school on Friday," said Leigh-
Anne, on the phone, "would you give me a free meal?"

Susie smiled. "I think I can manage to whip something up."

Leigh-Anne was a big girl who always had to watch her
weight, or thought she did. She jogged, and visited a
gym regularly, aiming for three times a week. She had
described in great detail the machines and the exercis-
es, but Susie felt more pity than approval for Leigh-
Anne's exertions. Whenever Leigh-Anne launched into
an enthusiastic narrative about her exercise program,
she would smooth a long skirt over a bony knee and
wait patiently for her to finish. Susie was never rude
about it, though. She would raise an inquisitive eye-
brow, purse an admiring lip, make the occasional "tsk
tsk" sound to signify attention that was if not rapt, at
least undivided. If running and lifting weights kept
Leigh-Anne content with her physical self that was fine
with Susie.

But as her daughter sloughed off her coat in Susie's
kitchen Friday evening, Susie noticed that she was not as
big as she used to be.

"How long has it been since you came over?" she said.

"I don't know, Mom. A month, maybe? But good
grief, we talk on the phone almost every day."

"I think it's more than a month."

"Could be," said Leigh-Anne. She was wearing her
dark hair loose today and it fell across her face as she
leaned over to remove her sandals and place them carefully on a rubber shoe mat inside the back door. "The
time goes so damn fast." She smiled up at Susie, a sweet,
fond, familiar smile. "I don't know where that rain came
from all of a sudden." She looked absentmindedly into
the corner of the ceiling, sweeping her hair back behind

her head, and the sudden elation on her face, private and extraneous, squeezed at Susie's heart.

She knew, instantly, what was going on, although it would be several weeks before Leigh-Anne confirmed it. Susie was shocked and bewildered by her reaction. Her brain slowed to a crawl. She looked at her hands, flat on her knees, and at the kitchen's linoleum floor, and heard the wall clock ticking. "Well. Anyway. It's good to see you, like always." She got up and went to Leigh-Anne, and enveloped her in a hug. "You've lost weight, haven't you?"

"A little," said Leigh-Anne casually, hugging her back. Then she held her mother at arm's length, smiling at her. "What're we going to do for dinner, order in a pizza? Chinese?" She was teasing, knowing that although cooking wasn't one of Susie's greatest pleasures she always prepared homemade dinners when Leigh-Anne came to call.

They were eye to eye. Susie thought her daughter looked like a painting, suffused with light and color like only a work of art can be. For an instant she marveled: she had had a hand in the creation of this suddenly transcendental being. But only in her potentiality for transfiguration, she realized — something else had made it actually happen.

"Don't be silly," she said, dislodging Leigh-Anne's hands from her shoulders. "I've got a pot roast in the oven. I'm sure you smelled it as soon as you walked in the door."

Leigh-Anne, in her bare feet, wandered into the living room. "Mind if I watch TV?"

"Go ahead," said Susie, opening the oven door to check on the roast. She uncorked a bottle of inexpensive red wine to let it breathe while she set the kitchen table, two places, just like in the old days, when Leigh-Anne still lived at home.

That was the old days, indeed. It had been more than

seven years now since she moved out, a university graduate, a newly employed teacher, to a one-bedroom basement apartment.

"You're not leaving a single piece of yourself behind!" Susie blurted that day, watching her daughter and her friends carry box after box out to the pickup truck, and Leigh-Anne had ended up leaving her report cards with Susie, and all the dolls and teddy bears except one.

Susie decided to use a tablecloth instead of placemats, and cloth napkins instead of paper ones. She carved the roast and arranged the vegetables alongside.

In the living room, Leigh-Anne turned off the TV. She appeared in the kitchen just as Susie was sliding the platter back into the oven to keep warm, and watched while Susie fed Mutt, scraping out the roasting pan into her dish.

"A little bit of this stuff is good for you," Susie told Mutt, "but too much is not."

"You spoil that dog, Mom. Really. That dog rules the roost around here."

"She's a good companion," said Susie, setting Mutt's dish down next to her water, on another shoe tray. "And a good watchdog, too, I might add."

"I'll bet."

"You can pour the wine if you like."

"Wine. My goodness."

"I know you enjoy a nice glass of wine," said Susie, hauling the platter from the oven. "So do I, from time to time."

"Mom, that's an enormous roast."

"Plenty of leftovers. You can take some home with you."

Leigh-Anne smiled at her mother across the table and tilted her head to shake her hair back behind her shoulders.

They talked for a while about inconsequential things, although nothing is really inconsequential, Susie reflected, listening to Leigh-Anne, whose junior high school

English classes she found tough going except for the
one or two students for whom literature might eventually become important; whose relationships with her
colleagues were mostly but not entirely pleasant and
congenial; who was no longer happy in her basement
apartment and had begun looking for something bigger.

"And sunnier," she said grimly. "I need more light.
Well, you've been there, Mom. You can imagine how
dull and depressing it is most of the time."

"I've often wondered how long you were going to
stick it out there, as a matter of fact," said Susie. The pot
roast was tender and delicious. She decided that she really must cook more often.

"When was the last time you heard from Dad?"

Susie had to run that back through her head a second
time, it was so unexpected. She speared a piece of carrot
with her fork and dragged it through the gravy pooled
on her plate, put it in her mouth and chewed and swallowed. "Pardon?"

"When did you hear from Dad last?"

"My goodness, Leigh-Anne. It was years ago. Years."
She poured some HP Sauce on the thick slice of pot
roast she had selected for herself, thinking now that it
was altogether too thick, she would never be able to eat
a piece of meat that large.

"Do you know where he is?"

Susie stared down at her plate. "I think he went home
to Saskatchewan," she said finally. "I don't know. I really
don't know." She looked up at her daughter. "Why are
you asking me this?"

"I think about him, of course I do," said Leigh-Anne,
"now and then."

Susie pictured Buddy holding an infant Leigh-Anne
high in the air, both of them laughing: she could hear it
now, Buddy's chuckle and the baby's delighted squeals.
And then Buddy turned to look at her, at Susie, with a
wide grin, and he winked at her.

Leigh-Anne's tone was casual. She didn't sound upset or intense. Susie just hoped to god she hadn't gotten it into her head to go off and try to find the wretched man.

As if she had read her mother's mind, Leigh-Anne reached across the table and touched the back of Susie's hand. "My interest in him is purely theoretical, Mom."

"I don't know what that means," said Susie, studying the patterns the HP Sauce had drawn in the gravy and on the slice of pot roast she really did want to eat, but how to get it down her throat now?

"It means, I'd like to know if he's alive or dead, and if he got married again, and had more kids, and who his parents are, my grandparents."

"Were," said Susie. "They had him when they were old. They'll be dead now."

"And he didn't have any brothers or sisters, did he?"

"No."

"Like you."

"Like me." She looked up again, almost hostile, into Leigh-Anne's large limpid eyes, a warm golden brown, like her father's. "It was one of the few things we had in common. Why do you want to know? Why now, I mean?" She began cutting her meat, wielding the knife and fork like weapons, feeling like a besieged creature. "You already know the important things. You've known them since you were old enough to understand them."

"Yeah, I know, Mom."

"He left us," said Susie, whose slice of pot roast was now in several pieces. "He took off on us. He abandoned us, for god's sake," she said, throwing down her knife and fork, folding her arms. She looked across at Leigh-Anne. "I did what I thought was right. The best I could. And I kept on doing it. I do it now. The best I can."

EIGHTEEN

There was silence in the kitchen then, except for an occasional sigh from Mutt, who had arranged herself in her basket and was drifting into sleep.

Susie was staring at a spider plant in a green plastic pot that hung in a corner between the two windows. The ends of its fronds were brown and stringy because Susie regarded plants strictly as decoration, watering them the way she dusted knickknacks. She didn't think of them as live things, really, like Mutt was a live thing, and when they ceased being attractive she threw them out and bought new ones.

Buddy hadn't left them. At least, not in the way Leigh-Anne believed he had.

Her gaze wandered to the countertop, the sink — to the pan the roast had cooked in, a big stirring spoon, the spoon rest from the top of the stove. Maybe I'll leave the dishes until morning, she thought.

She had long ago stopped feeling guilty about the lies she had told her daughter. There were some things it was better Leigh-Anne didn't know. Susie had thought so at the time. She still thought so.

The working part of the kitchen was U-shaped, separated by a row of countertops with cupboards above from the rest of the room, which contained the round table with four chairs where she and Leigh-Anne were sitting, and a china cabinet in which Susie kept her good dishes: the silverware for special occasions stayed in the wide, shallow drawer, settings for four given to her and Buddy as a wedding gift by Susie's mother.

On the kitchen wall was a piece of fishing net, tacked up carefully so that it looked like it had been sent sailing through the air by an ocean breeze and come to a gliding halt on Susie's wall, artfully arranged by nature. In its folds seashells nestled, and seaweed, and small pieces of driftwood. It was a mural created as a birthday gift, Leigh-Anne's present to Susie when she became forty. Susie had been convinced for months afterward that Leigh-Anne had the makings of a real artist, perhaps a sculptor.

After a long time Leigh-Anne said, "I know you did the best you could, Mom. I know you tried."

"So what's changed?" Susie demanded. "What's going on with you, Leigh-Anne? I know something is." Her appetite was gone, the smell of the good pot roast turning her stomach now.

Leigh-Anne was playing with her food like she used to when she was a child, moving it around on her plate but never spearing anything, never carrying a forkful to her mouth. She was rearranging her food like someone rearranging furniture, trying to make a room look less crowded without getting rid of anything in it.

"I'm taking this course," she said.

Susie waited. "Okay. So? What kind of a course?"

"A writing course. A creative writing course."

Leigh-Anne had always been a scribbler. Susie saw this as yet more evidence of her daughter's artistic nature. She had even written a couple of poems in high school that had been printed in the year book.

"Well that's good," she said cautiously. "So — you want to write about your dad? Is that it?"

"Maybe," said Leigh-Anne. "I don't remember much about him."

"I'm not surprised," said Susie. "You were only five years old."

Leigh-Anne put down her fork and sat back. "I remember helping him shine his shoes. And wash the car. And I remember the sound of his laugh, I think. But I'm not sure about that. Was there something special about the way he laughed?"

"I don't really want to have this conversation," said Susie.

"Did he laugh a lot?"

"Not particularly."

"You told me stories about him," said Leigh-Anne. "When I was little. Remember? Nice stories. Funny stories."

"Of course I remember."

"But you never told me about when he left."

"Certainly I did. I certainly did tell you."

Leigh-Anne leaned forward and put her hand on Susie's. "No, I mean the details. On the day he left — what did he say? What did *you* say? What time of day was it? And where was I?"

Susie knew her face was flushed. She stood abruptly. She placed her hands flat on the tabletop and looked down at Leigh-Anne. "This is not fair," she said. "You're not being fair, Leigh-Anne."

"I've wanted to ask you for years," said Leigh-Anne steadily, with an expression both mutinous and pleading. She started to say something else but Susie lifted a hand.

"I don't want to talk about this," she said. She felt something brush against her ankle — Mutt had left her basket and was staring up at her uneasily. Susie scooped the dog into her arms and looked at her daughter. "I can't," she said more quietly. "You've taken me by surprise. I'm sorry."

The following afternoon, wielding a feather duster around the living room, Susie was still disturbed about their conversation. But the more she considered it the more she blamed the creative writing class. You get a person doing creative writing, they're supposed to delve into their past, Susie told herself. They're supposed to tunnel into their own psyche, looking for stories, for inspiration. What if Leigh-Anne continued to ask Susie about her father? What if in her innocence she were to write what she believed to be truth about him? Susie knew there wasn't such a thing. There were only elliptical glances — equivocal contemplations — ambiguous conclusions, inexpertly drawn. And in Leigh-Anne's case things were even more complicated. Whatever she wrote was bound to be pure fiction.

And who's to blame for that, Susie thought bitterly, but me.

Bits and pieces, everything's in bits and pieces, she reflected, and each of us gets to see a few of the bits and one or two of the pieces. Now if everybody looking at the same thing were to pool their observations . . . But no, she decided, dusting the photo of Leigh-Anne that sat on the mantelpiece in a silver frame, Leigh-Anne with her chin resting on folded arms, her glorious hair pinned on top of her head, looking straight out at her mother but not giving away a thing, no, Susie told herself, as she scrutinized Leigh-Anne's bland countenance with a mother's whetted gaze, that wouldn't work. We none of us can be trusted to translate what's seen, she thought. For it changes, doesn't it? As soon as you put words to what you see, or think, or believe you know, it changes. But you're committed then, and not about to admit to change. You'd have to start all over again. And who's got time for that?

She felt like a rainbow had arrowed through her head, splintering her brain.

"You've got to talk to me about it sometime," said Leigh-Anne on the phone the following week. "You owe me more than 'He left us,' Mom, you know you do."

"Why now?" said Susie, appalled. "Why didn't you ask these questions years ago?"

"I wanted to. I didn't want things to change between us. I was afraid you'd get angry."

"Well, I did get angry."

"I know. But that doesn't matter to me so much any more."

Susie thought about this, wondering if it was a good thing or a bad thing.

"Will you let me read something you've written?" she said finally.

"Will you tell me about Dad leaving?"

"Eventually," said Susie cautiously.

Leigh-Anne sighed. "Then maybe eventually I'll let you read something, Mom. But not until I get it right."

"What do you mean, get it right? How will you know if you've got it right?"

"Well, it'll be right when it works, you know?"

"Works?"

"Oh, Mom, when I've made something believable, okay? When I find just the right words to make some-body believe what I'm telling them, okay?"

So it's finding the right words that does that, thought Susie. Really. And although she felt whipped and exhausted, she smiled to herself, knowing better.

"Are you writing poetry, or what?" asked Susie tenta-tively, a couple of weeks later.

"I'm not writing anything," said Leigh-Anne. There had been a short silence before she answered. It was the silence that convinced Susie that she meant it. "I've quit the class."

Susie's immediate reaction was one of relief: perhaps now the questions about Buddy would stop. Still, she opened her mouth to protest, or sympathize, to do what-ever motherly thing was appropriate. But stopped her-self, because her daughter's tone lacked misery, was not despondent — she didn't even sound disappointed.

"How come?" she asked finally.

"Oh, I just wasn't getting anywhere. I'm not a writer, Mom," she said with a laugh.

"You filled up diaries year after year when you were going to school," said Susie. "And remember the pen pals you wrote to? The essay contest you won? Who says you aren't a writer? Maybe your teacher is no teacher, did you ever think of that?"

"Oh yes, he is," said Leigh-Anne quickly. "He's a wonderful teacher. It wasn't his idea that I quit the class — it was mine."

Susie carried the phone with its extra-long cord over to the kitchen table and sat down. "So that's it," she said, looking at the fishing net on the wall.

There was another silence.

"What are you talking about?" said Leigh-Anne.

"I'm not stupid," said Susie. "And you and I, we've known each other for a long time. You give yourself away to me, Leigh-Anne. And what's more, you don't even try not to, most of the time."

She heard a sigh, and a bit of a laugh, and another sigh. "He's truly wonderful, Mom. Honestly."

"Honestly," said Susie. "I wonder. Since you haven't said a word about this up to now, is he also married, by any chance?"

NINETEEN

Eddie Henderson was standing on a somewhat wobbly ladder, painting the outside of her house. She was transforming it from seagull gray to primrose yellow. She had rented the necessary equipment the previous week — power washer, sander, extension ladder — and done the preparation, including minor repairs and application of an undercoat, over the weekend. Now, three days later, wearing paint-spattered overalls and a sleeveless white T-shirt, her hair held back as usual in a thick braid, she was painting the fourth and last wall, balancing a paint tray on top of the ladder and wielding a roller with flourishes — like a conductor, she thought, wielding her baton.

She found physical work extremely satisfying, but it did leave much of the mind unengaged, free to wander about and get itself into trouble. Eddie, anticipating a visit to her father in Vancouver, was starting to get the shakes. She knew there was no chance she would run into Alan. He didn't work in Vancouver, he didn't live in Vancouver. But she thought about it anyway.

Hell, she thought about running into him here, in Sechelt, which was even less likely. But she had managed to get a handle on this. Going to the mainland, though, stepping onto turf near his, this always got her going.

Which was humiliating, of course.

She tried to get absorbed in the moment, concentrating on the sticky thwack of the roller against the wooden wall, the powerful smell of the paint, the prickling of perspiration on her forehead, the heat of the sun on the top of her head. It was warmer than she had expected. Maybe she ought to put on a hat. I'll do it when I quit for lunch, she told herself. And I'll quit for lunch when I've emptied the paint tray three more times.

"Hi up there."

Eddie looked down to see her neighbor, the retired seaman, standing in the yard next door.

Alvin McKechnie gave her a wave. "It's looking good."

"Thanks," said Eddie, dipping the roller in the paint.

"What color you gonna do the trim?"

"Blue," said Eddie. "Dark blue."

"Navy?"

She considered this. "No. Not that dark. Sea blue," she said, smiling down at him, a medium-sized roundish man of about seventy with thinning gray hair.

"Looking good," he said again.

Eddie swept the roller against the house, enlarging the spread of primrose.

"You've got yellow paint all over your deck shoes," Alvin observed. "Which by the way reminds me, are you gonna spend your whole holiday painting that house, or are you gonna find time for a few hours out on the water?" He was leaning on the fence and peering up at her, disapprovingly, she thought.

Eddie dug around in the tray with the roller and applied the last of the paint to the wall. She started down the ladder. "Well, I don't know, Alvin. What do you think, how much longer will it take me to finish?" She set the tray and the roller down next to several cans of paint sitting on a piece of tarp she had spread on the lawn. "Look at this, paint all over me," she muttered.

"This the last wall?"

"Yup." She squatted on the tarp and reached for a rag and a can of turpentine.

"Okay," said Alvin, nodding, "you finish this wall today, do the trim tomorrow, you'll still have three days left, right?"

"Right," said Eddie, scrubbing paint from her hands. "One of them I've got to spend in Vancouver."

"Yeah, shopping, I bet."

"I wish," said Eddie. She walked over to the fence, still scrubbing. "But if that was an invitation, Alvin," she said with a grin, "sure, when I come back from Vancouver, I'd love to go out on your boat for half a day or so." She flicked the turpentine rag at him across the fence.

"You watch it," said Alvin, ducking. "Or Bev's gonna come out here and see you flirting with me and I'll tell you, young lady, your goose is gonna be cooked."

The traffic from the ferry terminal at Horseshoe Bay into Vancouver had been horrendous, and when she finally got to the hotel Eddie had to drive around the block several times before a parking space revealed itself, so she was late meeting her father for lunch. He had chosen the Sylvia Hotel, in the West End. It was a great location, Eddie admitted, striding up the walk to the restaurant entrance. Only one street, a strip of grass and a beach separated the Sylvia from the Pacific Ocean. It was also within walking distance of her father's apartment building.

He half rose when he saw her, clutching a napkin in one hand and waving to her with the other. She kissed his cheek before sitting down opposite him. Their table looked out on a small courtyard that contained bushes Eddie didn't recognize and a groundcover composed mostly of blue-flowering periwinkle. "What are you having?" she asked him as the waitress approached to refill his coffee cup. "Me too," Eddie said to her with a smile.

"The clubhouse," said her father, looking at his watch. "I'll have the same."

"That was easy," said the waitress, collecting their menus.

"Sorry I'm late," said Eddie when the waitress had departed.

"These things happen. Especially when you have to use the ferry service." He smiled at her. "It's good to see you, Edwina. We don't get together often enough."

"I know, Dad."

She didn't particularly enjoy her father's company. To compensate, her attitude when in his presence or even talking to him on the phone was occasionally over-hearty: whenever she heard herself being an immoderately warm and friendly daughter she became momentarily depressed, and furious with herself. She had resolved to try hard not to let any of this happen today.

"I've got the whole afternoon," she said. "Do you want to do something?"

"Like what?"

"I don't know. What's at the art gallery?"

"What a strange suggestion. I have no notion. You know my interest in art is negligible."

"How about a movie?"

He shook his head. "Why don't we go back to my apartment and talk? There isn't enough conversation in the world these days. Making conversation — good conversation — is a forgotten art, in my opinion."

"I feel challenged to disagree," said Eddie. "But I don't possess an argument."

Her father regarded her warily, suspecting that he'd been mocked.

"Or we could walk the sea wall," she said as the waitress set down plates in front of them.

"Enjoy," said the waitress.

"We could do that," said Eddie's father. He lifted the top piece of toast and looked suspiciously inside. "I have to make sure there's no core in the tomato slice," he said.

He replaced the toast and picked up a sandwich. "Yes, we could do that. If the weather holds."

Eddie, munching on a french fry, glanced outside. There was high cloud and the day was pleasantly warm, with no hint of rain.

"How's your job?" he said politely. "Are you getting along better with — I've forgotten his name. Your staff sergeant?"

"Karl Alberg," Eddie said. "And we get along fine, Dad. We work well together. I'm happy."

He looked at her skeptically. "And what have you been doing on your vacation days, besides painting your house?" He bit into the sandwich and sat back. He chewed slowly. His wrists rested against the edge of the table, his fingers holding the sandwich above the plate.

"Painting my house was a pretty big job, Dad. I didn't finish until yesterday. It was damn near midnight by the time I got everything cleaned up and put away."

"You need a rest, then. Maybe you'd like to stay over for a day or two. I could put you up on my sofa."

Eddie, working on her sandwich, shook her head. When she'd finished her mouthful she said, "Thanks, but I've got to get back. I'm going sailing tomorrow."

"Oh? With whom?"

Eddie laughed. "His name's Alvin. He's my next-door neighbor. He's also married, and in his seventies. Give it up, Dad."

"Give what up?" he said indignantly.

"I'm perfectly contented, at the moment, to have nobody in my life. No man, I mean. No romantic interest." She sprinkled salt and pepper on her fries, and drank some coffee, then attacked her sandwich with zeal.

Her father wiped his fingertips with his napkin and leaned toward her. "Why don't you give him a call while you're in town," he said quietly. "Try to patch things up."

Eddie looked at him in astonishment. She put down the sandwich. "How can you say that to me? I've told you about his phone calls. How can you think that I might want to patch things up?" She lowered her voice. "The man is deranged, Dad. Possibly psychotic."

"Don't be ridiculous, Edwina. He's a police officer."

She stared at him, then shook her head. "Don't pretend you're that naive because I will not believe it."

"All right, all right," he said with a wave of his hand. He sat back in his chair. "I've lost my appetite." He looked at her, and sighed. "I love you, that's all. I don't want you to be alone. Like me. And you and Alan were such a good match. At least," he added quickly, "I thought you were. Maybe I was wrong."

"You were definitely wrong," said Eddie grimly. "But then, so was I."

"And this behavior you described," her father continued. "I told myself, it might not be as bad as Eddie thinks."

A vulnerable piece of her heart softened then, hearing him call her Eddie.

"He's just desperate not to lose her, I thought," her father continued. "And he may well be under some kind of unimaginable stress connected to his work."

Eddie pushed her plate away.

"I thought you might want to find out, before evicting him from your life forever, the reasons for his behavior."

"No, Dad," said Eddie. "I don't care what his reasons are." Her hands were cold and she rubbed them together, hard.

He had come out of nowhere, out of the shadows she hadn't known inhabited the lobby of her apartment building, and she thought she saw the flash of a knife, but it wasn't a knife, it was handcuffs.

"I don't care why," she said loudly.

She had fought back, grateful for her strength, but she had almost lost the battle as a result of her incredulity: this wasn't a perp, this was a friend, a fellow officer. Her former lover.

"Keep your voice down," said her father.

That was the only time his hounding had become violent. But the phone calls were still happening.

"I hate it that it you gave him my number, Dad," she said suddenly. "I just hate that."

He looked away. "He could have found it without me."

"But he didn't. He got it from you." She looked at their plates, crowded with limp fries and half-eaten sandwiches. "I guess neither of us gets to have dessert." It had been a rule when she was a child. No dessert unless you cleaned your plate.

"I'm sorry, Edwina," said her father stiffly. "I thought at the time it was the right thing to do."

She watched him smooth his silver hair, still thick and wavy. He was a good-looking man for his age. "I'm afraid of him, Dad. Literally. Afraid that he'll come after me, and try to do me harm."

Her father glanced quickly around, embarrassed. "Don't be silly, Edwina. Now you're sounding as crazy as you tell me Alan is."

She had never told him about what had happened in her lobby. She thought about doing so now. But he would say she had misinterpreted the incident. Or mis-remembered it.

"Do you ever see him?" It was a thought that hadn't occurred to her before. She sounded hoarse and severe even to her own ears, and her father flinched.

"Please. Don't sound like a police officer."

"Do you?"

He dabbed at the corners of his mouth with his napkin. "We talk, occasionally."

Eddie stood up quickly, her chair scraping against the floor. "I've got to go, Dad."

"Eddie, don't be silly. Why shouldn't I keep in touch with him? We became friends, he and I, why shouldn't — ?"

"Thanks for lunch," Eddie said loudly, and she strode for the door, her heart racing.

She drove straight to Burnaby. This took almost an hour, because of the rush-hour traffic, and by the time she arrived at the RCMP parking lot she had changed her mind about confronting Alan. Was this wisdom? she wondered. Or cowardice?

She drove past the detachment slowly, all her senses on full alert. She saw a couple of Members she knew and thought about pulling over — but what would she say to them? "Oh, by the way, how's that bastard McCurdy?"

Everyone knew how the affair had ended. She wondered if any of them knew he was still stalking her.

That's what it was, all right. She was being a stalked. She was a *cop*, and she was permitting herself to be stalked.

Eddie drove away, oblivious to the splendor of spring, to the bright sky, the flowering dogwood, the blooming rhododendrons, the magnolia trees. She took Canada Way to Willingdon, turned right, crossed the overpass and entered the freeway, which took her over the Second Narrows Bridge and along the Upper Levels Highway above North and West Vancouver to Horseshoe Bay.

She arrived at the terminal just as the Langdale ferry was being loaded, and had to wait for the next sailing.

Eddie sat in her old green Mercedes with the window open, thinking, while people from the other cars in the lineup wandered away to get soft drinks, or throw a ball back and forth, or take their dogs for a walk.

Thinking.

TWENTY

It was early summer when Susie and Arthur met for the second time. Susie had been avoiding the park, too weary when she got home to take Mutt for her walk because she was so busy at the office. But soon it wouldn't be necessary to take Mutt to the park at all, she'd be able to race around the yard to her heart's content because Susie was having a fence erected around her house. Not a high, forbidding one but a tasteful construction of white pickets that Mutt would be able to look through but not jump over. Susie thought it would add to the attractiveness of her property, as well as keep the dog confined.

And so it wasn't in the park that she encountered Arthur again. She was coming out of the bank when she saw him, on a Wednesday: Susie had Wednesday afternoons off, in addition to weekends. He was across the street, hands in his pockets, studying the Italian bakery's window display. It so happened that the bakery was the next thing on Susie's list.

As she stood at the corner waiting for the light to change she saw Arthur step back from the bakery window, as if wanting to get a broader view of its contents, and collide with a man who was just getting out of a car. Arthur whirled around, one fist raised, and shouted something at the man — Susie couldn't make out what he said but she saw the anger in his face, dark and possessive. The other man lifted his hands, palms out, wanting no trouble, and Arthur retreated. He took a whack at his own thigh, looking around at the passersby who had stopped to see what was going on, and they quickly dispersed.

Susie hesitated, and missed the green light, and had to wait for the next one. By the time she had crossed the street Arthur had entered the bakery. She hesitated again, then followed him.

"Well, whaddaya know," said Arthur, grinning. He had bought a loaf of French bread. "Long time no see. How about a coffee?"

She had intended to say to him, "What was *that* all about?" But for some reason she changed her mind.

"Fine," she agreed. "But first I need some bread, too."

Susie's favorite was the glistening, creamy fruit flan; she was always looking for an excuse to buy one. Canada Day was coming up soon and Leigh-Anne usually came over to celebrate the holiday: hamburgers and a fruit flan, thought Susie, gazing into the display case. That would be good. And perhaps she would invite her neighbors as well.

But now Leigh-Anne had this boyfriend, this married boyfriend. Would she be free this year?

And if she was, would she be able to stay in the guest room overnight? Susie loved it when Leigh-Anne stayed overnight. They would curl up in the living room, Leigh-Anne on the sofa and Susie in her big red velvet chair, sipping cups of cocoa or glasses of wine and chattering away until one or both of them started to yawn. It hadn't happened for quite a while, the sleepover, and here in the bakery, gazing at the fruit flan, a ribbon of unease twisted through her and she wondered if the next one might be confrontational instead of cozy, because Susie knew she would have to speak her mind about this boyfriend if the affair continued. But perhaps it wouldn't continue. Perhaps it was already over.

She bought a loaf of sourdough bread, and a focaccia, too. She would have to freeze one of them but she

couldn't leave an Italian bakery without buying
something Italian. Was fruit flan Italian? she wondered
suddenly.

They went down the street to the coffee shop and
passed through a huddle of outdoor tables occupied by
smokers. Susie ordered a herbal tea and Arthur stuck
with the coffee of the day, small, black, three sugars.

When they were seated she studied him surrepti-
tiously. Yes, she did find him attractive. It was his
burliness, she decided, his breadth, as if he were a small
building she could hide behind and peek around,
observing threatening aspects of life from a safe haven.
He was somewhat flabby around the middle, as she was,
despite her thinness.

She didn't like being thin, and never had. She'd been
sure that she would retain some of the weight gained
during her pregnancy, but she hadn't. Later — much,
much later — she'd been equally confident of packing
on the pounds when menopause rolled around. But a
slight expansion of her waist was all that happened. Susie
was now resigned to becoming as thin an old woman as
she had been a young and a middle-aged one. But that
didn't mean she had to like it. She wanted not to be able
to see and touch hipbone and clavicle. She wanted more
flesh, to be softened, made cuddleable. Maybe getting
fatter would have infused her with calm, too. Slowed her
down some.

She had long since stopped stuffing herself with
cheeseburgers, french fries, and milkshakes in vain
attempts to gain weight. Gluttony made her feel physically uncomfortable and morally corrupt. And besides, it
didn't work. It had never worked. And so for years now
she'd been eating what she felt like eating, when she felt
like eating it. And although she remained as skinny as a
rail, she was extremely healthy. For her age. There was
stiffness and sometimes soreness and swelling in some of
her joints, now, and there had been that scare about her

heart, and of course her eyesight had deterioriated — but everything else was hunky-dory.

There was a lineup at the counter, and Susie knew that most of them were there to pick up a coffee for the road. She herself didn't drink or eat anything when she drove. She considered it dangerous. Though not as bad as the ubiquitous cell phone. Just seeing somebody driving a car and talking on one of those things made her heart jump.

Where does your friend live?" she asked Arthur. "The one you're staying with?"

"On Triumph. Four or five blocks from here."

"Did he help you get a job, like you hoped?"

"A few things didn't pan out. But I've got another interview tomorrow." He shrugged. "You never know."

"Well, good luck," said Susie.

"I'll need it. The guy said on the phone he's had fifteen applications."

"For what kind of work?"

"Night watchman. They call it security, they gotta do this big security check, but that's all it is, a glorified night watchman. At some computer store. The kind hotshot kids drive their four-wheel into the window of, scoop up all the merchandise while the siren's screaming in the wind, they're gone before the cops can blink. So they figure a human on the premises might be more of a deterrent."

"It sounds dangerous," said Susie.

"Yeah. Maybe they'll give me a gun." He grinned. "I'd love to shoot the bastards' tires out, see them try to make a getaway then." He tilted his head. "If I get the job, *if* I get the damn job, I'll be moving out of my friend's place, getting one of my own. You heard of anything available? A bachelor, that's all I'd need."

Susie had begun shaking her head before he'd finished speaking. "I'll keep my eyes and ears open, though. I'll ask my neighbors. They know more people than I do. I tend to keep to myself."

"I better give you my friend's number, then," he said. "Or you could give me yours, that might be a better idea."

"Yes, sure," said Susie. And she fished paper and pen from her handbag and jotted down her telephone number.

He looked at the paper, repeated the number, folded the paper, and put it in his inside jacket pocket, winking at her as he did so. At that moment Susie didn't find him at all attractive.

Walking home a bit later, she pondered the ludicrousness of an almost sixty-year-old woman finding anybody attractive. But of course she knew it wasn't ludicrous at all. Pathetic, maybe. Frustrating, definitely. But perfectly natural.

When she got home she put her bags on the table and called Leigh-Anne, leaving a message with the school secretary, and occupied herself with busywork while waiting for Leigh-Anne to call back. Hung up her jacket. Put the focaccia in the freezer. Sliced the sourdough, buttering the heels, eating one, giving the other smaller one to Mutt, who loved butter above all else.

When Leigh-Anne did phone during the lunch hour, she said, with no preliminaries, "What's up?"

"Can you come over tonight? Have dinner with me?"

"I suppose I could. Is something wrong?"

"Not really," said Susie. "I just haven't seen you for a while. We need to get caught up."

"Uh-oh," said Leigh-Anne. "That sounds ominous."

"Don't be silly. You'll come by after school, then?"

"Sure," said Leigh-Anne. "I've got some work to do here first. It'll probably be five, five-thirty."

Susie rushed back out to the grocery store for ground beef and potatoes, and prepared a meatloaf and a green salad and baked potatoes for dinner.

She managed to restrain herself until they'd almost finished eating. Then, "Are you still seeing that man? The writing teacher?"

"Yes, I am, Mom. I know you don't approve, and I'm sorry. But Mom — I'm happy. Really. I don't think I've ever been this happy before."

"You mean you're having good sex," said Susie, shocking the both of them.

Leigh-Anne blinked, and tossed her hair. "Well, that too," she said.

She was positively glowing, pulsing with something she would call joy. Susie hardly knew her. The light in her eyes was blinding.

All Susie could do was wait.

Arthur called her a few days later. "Hi," he said.

Susie felt a spurt of anger — with him for assuming she'd recognize his voice even though they had never before spoken on the phone, and with herself for recognizing it. "Who's speaking, please?" she said briskly.

He laughed. "It's Arthur."

"Arthur. Hello."

"I got the job."

"Congratulations," she said. "That must be a big relief."

"Yeah."

Susie held the phone between chin and shoulder and went on drying the dishes.

"So I was wondering, did you ask your neighbors about a place to rent?"

"Yes, I did," Susie lied. "No luck, though, I'm afraid."

"It's okay. I was really calling to tell you not to bother. My friend saw a sign the other day, over on Oxford. So I just came back from there. Rented a basement suite in a big old house. So we're gonna be neighbors." He laughed again, and gave her his phone number.

She hung up and had to sit down for a while before finishing the dishes. She didn't know if this was a thing she wanted or not, Arthur Bentley as a neighbor.

"Oh well," she said to Mutt, who was sprawled in her basket, vigorously licking her private parts, "he probably won't be there for long. He's a mover-on, that one, would be my best guess."

TWENTY-ONE

On a Monday morning in August when Susie was getting milk from the refrigerator to pour over her bran flakes, her eyes fell upon a platter of chicken left over from a barbecue she and her neighbors had had in the backyard two days earlier, to celebrate the completion of her new fence. There was a container of potato salad in there, too. And some lettuce and tomatoes, along with a cucumber.

She rummaged in her handbag for the piece of paper on which she had written Arthur's new phone number, and dialed.

"Oh dear, I think I've woken you," she said, dismayed, when after seven rings he finally answered.

"Yeah, who is this?"

She thought, I could hang up now and he'd never know it was me.

"Susie," she said weakly. "Susie Wilson."

"Susie," he said, his voice husky with sleep. "Hi, Susie. What can I do for you?"

"I wondered if you'd like to come over for dinner," she said. "Nothing special. Pot luck. Leftovers, actually."

Mutt was standing in the middle of the kitchen floor, planted firmly on four skinny legs, watching her intently with what Susie believed to be incredulity.

"Leftovers. My favorite," said Arthur.

"Six o'clock?"

"Six o'clock."

"Welcome to the neighborhood," said Susie when he arrived. "How do you like your place?"

"Good. It's good," said Arthur, handing her a bottle of wine in a brown paper bag. "Suits me just fine." His gaze wandered over the dining area. "I like that stuff on the wall there," he said, gesturing toward the fishing net.

"My daughter did that for me — oh, it's years ago now." She was about to usher him into the living room when he pulled out a chair at the table and sat down. He took a pack of cigarettes and a lighter from his pocket.

Susie found a black plastic ashtray at the back of a cupboard and set it down in front of him. She hesitated for a moment, then joined him at the table.

Mutt, lying on a rag rug next to the china cabinet, growled softly every few minutes.

Arthur tapped the heel of his work boot against the floor; Susie thought he probably didn't even know he was doing it. He lifted the cigarette to his lips with the thumb and index finger of his right hand, squinting against the smoke. Somebody's taught him that, thought Susie, a long time ago. He took a drag, lowered the cigarette to the ashtray, and put it between his index and middle fingers for easier tapping. But when he wanted another puff he picked it up with the thumb and index finger again. Susie found this fascinating.

"When did you start smoking?" she asked.

He looked startled. "Does it bother you? I mean, I can put the damn thing out, no problem."

"No, it doesn't bother me. I'm just curious."

"Jesus, I don't know," he said. He remembered crouching in the weeds behind a billboard with some kid whose name escaped him now. He thought they'd stolen the smokes from the other kid's house. And yeah, that's right, they'd brought along a couple of oranges, too, because somebody had told them that if they ate oranges afterwards nobody would be able to smell smoke on their breath. "I must have been — I don't know, ten, maybe?" he said. "Eleven? Somewhere in there." They'd intended to smoke the whole pack, he recalled. But had barely gotten through one cigarette. They hadn't actually thrown up, but they'd sure felt like it.

He watched Susie run her hand across the tabletop, brushing some grains of salt onto the floor. She was a bit skinny for his taste, and a lot older than the working girls he was used to.

Mutt growled again.

"What's the problem with the damn dog?"

"It's just her way of joining in the conversation," said Susie.

"Does he ever bite?" He couldn't do any real harm, Arthur figured. But it would damn well smart, getting those sharp little teeth clamped on to your wrist.

Susie, looking at Mutt, laughed.

"He didn't growl at me out in the park."

"No. Only in the house," said Susie. "It's her job, after all. Protecting her territory. And me."

"What're we having?" he said suddenly.

"Pardon?"

"What're we eating?" This was another advantage of a female friend, he thought, congratulating himself on making Susie's acquaintance. They always wanted to cook for you.

"Cold chicken," she said. "Barbecued. And a couple of salads."

"How about I open that bottle I brought? We can have a drink while we wait." He stabbed his cigarette into the ashtray, killing it dead, and stood up, tugging at his brown leather jacket, which had crept up in the back.

"Sure," said Susie, and she stood up, too, and preceded him into the small kitchen.

She opened one drawer after another. "I can't remember where I keep the corkscrew," she said, flustered. "Leigh-Anne must've put it away." She was getting angry now, closing the drawers with unnecessary force. "Here it is." She turned, and found Arthur standing within inches of her. Susie moved back, involuntarily, and the edge of the counter pressed against her spine. She was holding her breath, looking him in the eyes, smelling the smell of him, which was leather and some kind of aftershave. She considered pressing her hands against his chest, under the jacket. Would that be to push him away? she wondered, or to caress him and bring him close? She had acquired a sudden intense interest in studying his mouth, but kept her eyes on his eyes, which she thought might be smiling at her.

"So hand it over," he said.

Susie looked down at the corkscrew she was holding. And handed it over. "You'd better take it to the table," she said. "There are glasses in the china cabinet out there."

As she sat opposite Arthur, who was pouring wine, she patted her cheeks. "I must be all red in the face," she said. "It's hot in here."

"It's a hot day," Arthur agreed, handing her a glass.

Mutt offered another growl, which turned into a yawn, and lowered her shaggy head onto her paws.

Susie was struggling with a sensation that was, like nostalgia, composed of longing and regret, but was also something different because it was not linked to a memory. She found it distinctly unpleasant. It threatened to smother her.

"What are we doing sitting in here?" she said stiffly. "We ought to be in the living room."

"I like kitchens," said Arthur.

Maybe it stemmed from memory after all, she thought, studying Arthur, who had suddenly reminded her of Buddy.

He lifted his glass. "To my hostess," he said. "Your very good health." He drank.

Susie hadn't dated a great many men in her lifetime. She could count on the fingers of one hand those she had gone out with more than once since Buddy's departure. Sometimes she regretted this. Mostly she didn't.

She lifted her glass. "And to yours," she said, and drank.

"To good neighbors," said Arthur, and they drank again. "And friends," he said, leaning slightly toward her.

"Friends," said Susie feebly, and took another sip.

Arthur refilled their glasses.

"How's the job?" said Susie.

"It's okay. It's fine. Boring, though." He looked at his watch.

"When do you have to be there?"

"They close at ten, I check in about nine-thirty. Can I have a piece of this bread? Or do I have to wait for the chicken?"

"No, no," said Susie, flustered again. "Help yourself."

She had set the table before he arrived but hadn't thought they'd be sitting here before she'd served dinner. Arthur was sitting in her chair, actually, but she couldn't think of a nice way to ask him to trade places with her. He would look at her with furrowed brow and an otherwise blank expression because why on earth should it be necessary? Except that Susie felt uneasy — nervous, even — with her back to the back door. She wasn't about to tell Arthur that, though.

"I'll only have one piece," he was saying, "so as not to spoil my appetite."

Susie thought, I should have had an appetizer, even some chips and dip would have been enough, I should have realized that he'd be hungry. Next time, she thought. If there was a next time.

"Hmmm, good bread," he said. "Did you get it at that bakery? The Italian place?"

"Yes," said Susie. "It's focaccia." She didn't like it that he was talking with his mouth full.

"Yeah, it's an okay job," he said. "I'm glad of the money, that's for sure. But it's hard to stay awake sometimes."

"You should take a big thermos of coffee," said Susie.

"And a book to read. Or crossword puzzles."

"Oh, I keep myself amused." He winked. "Casing the joint from inside. Working out how to rob the place." Susie's mouth opened in horror, and Arthur laughed. He sat back and reached for another piece of bread. "I'm trying to keep one step ahead of the outlaws, that's all, Susie. I figure that's part of my job. Or it oughta be, anyway."

"Aren't you hot in that jacket?" said Susie. "Don't you want me to hang it up for you?"

He lifted his arms to the sides and looked down at himself. "Yeah. I guess it is a little warm." He stood up and slipped the jacket off and handed it to Susie, who took it into the hallway and hung it on a hook. "I think we ought to eat now," she said, and moved past Arthur into the kitchen.

She knew nothing about him, really, she thought, munching on a drumstick. Absolutely nothing. He was, if she were to be perfectly honest, someone she had picked up in a park. He could have all manner of unsavory events in his background. She liked him — but that was a surface thing. She felt comfortable with him, most of the time, and yes, she found him attractive, too, although she would never have admitted this, to him or anybody else. A TV commercial came to mind in which Burt Reynolds had wiggled black eyebrows (a dramatic contrast to his thick white hair) and made leering references to women who wore nothing but perfume. It had made her shudder — but not with lust. Men, too, then, apparently reached a point beyond which their sexual banter became offensive instead of bewitching. It wasn't necessarily age, of course. Or not entirely age, anyway. But certainly age had something to do with it.

Susie was eating while she thought, and listening to Arthur describe his apartment, even as he scarfed down the chicken and the salads as if this were his last meal, or else his first in weeks.

Mutt lifted her head from her paws and gave an

obligatory growl, then sighed, curled herself up tight, and went back to sleep.

Divested of his leather jacket, Arthur was slighter than Susie had thought. He was wearing a short-sleeved shirt, white with a light blue stripe, and jeans. His arms were pale and hairless. His face was broad, the nose somewhat flattened — in a fight, maybe? He had dark eyes and eyebrows, and wore his wavy dark hair long to his shirt collar and combed straight back; strands of silver glinted sometimes in the overhead light. A pack of cigarettes and a lighter caused his shirt pocket to sag.

Susie wondered how he would describe her, honestly, if asked. Maybe he had mentioned her to his friend, or his new employer; maybe he had told them about the woman he had met in the park.

She didn't know yet how much — if anything — they might have in common. She just knew that she liked him, and felt like confiding in him.

Except of course there was nothing to confide.

Susie kept her car on the street in front of her house. Although she had no garage there was plenty of space in the lane, behind the fence that now encircled her property, but she felt that it was safer to park in front where the street was brightly lit. It wasn't that she lived in a particularly dangerous part of town, but she knew that two of her neighbors whose cars were habitually kept in the lane had been broken into.

When she pulled up in front of the house on this Friday in September she saw that Arthur was leaning over the fence, hanging on to the pickets, and on the other side Mutt was leaping into the air and barking.

"What's going on?" she called.

Arthur didn't hear her — at least he didn't immediately turn around. As she approached the fence he tossed something at the dog, who grabbed it in midair.

"What on earth are you doing?" said Susie.

"Oh, hi," said Arthur. "I'm making friends with your dog."

Mutt was chewing vigorously, her head cocked to one side. She spotted Susie and gave an absentminded wag of her tail.

"Arthur, what are you giving her?"

He opened his hand to show her. "Beef jerky. He loves it, watch this. You finished, partner? Huh?"

Mutt swallowed and started barking again.

"Here you go," said Arthur and threw another piece. "Lookit that," he said as Mutt leapt high and caught the jerky. "He could stay on the ground, catch it just as good. But no, the damn dog wants to jump for it."

"She. Mutt's a she. And you shouldn't be feeding her." She returned to her car and locked it.

"Why not?" said Arthur, watching Mutt happily chomping.

"I don't want her to start taking food from strangers. Dogs get poisoned that way."

"Hey," said Arthur, opening the gate for her, "I'm no stranger. Am I?" He followed her up the walk to the porch as Mutt started barking again. "That was the last one, pal," said Arthur. "There ain't no more."

The dog raced past them up the steps and waited for Susie to open the front door.

"I thought I'd come around, maybe take you out for supper," said Arthur. "Nothing fancy. That Italian place down the street from the bakery maybe," he said as Susie took off her jacket and hung it in the closet.

"I don't know," said Susie. "I don't know if I want to go out. I'm pretty tired." She straightened her bony shoulders and smoothed her hair. She felt herself frowning, exasperated and ill at ease here in her own front hall. "I'm going to make a pot of tea," she said and headed for the kitchen, where Mutt was lapping from her water dish.

"Well? Do you want me to stay, or leave, or what?"

Arthur called after her.

"Do you want some tea?" said Susie.

"Sure." He sat down at the table, unzipping his jacket, which he apparently wore every day of the year, oblivious of the weather.

Susie turned on the cold-water tap and decided she didn't want Arthur there. But she couldn't figure out how to say so without offending him.

She was looking out the kitchen window, which faced the house next door. It was almost exactly opposite her neighbors' bathroom window, which was made of glass blocks. Susie admired the look of this very much. She would have liked to have it in her own bathroom, allowing plenty of light to come in but preventing oglers from ogling. Not that she expected oglers. But you never know.

The tap was running and Susie was leaning on the edge of the sink, looking out the window, thinking about the glass blocks in her neighbors' bathroom . . . I do this a lot, she reflected. Instead of distracting herself with trivialities she ought to march right in there and give the man his walking papers. If I don't want someone in my house, she told herself, I damn well ought to get him out of it. I'm a wimp, is what I am. A wuss.

"So what do you think?"

Susie jumped.

Arthur was lounging against the refrigerator. He rubbed his cheek, producing a rasping sound. The lines from his nose to the edges of his mouth looked deeper today, Susie thought, as if he hadn't slept, or else he'd aged suddenly. She believed this did happen to some people. They looked exactly the same for years and years, then wham! Lines and wrinkles and gray hair and stooped shoulders overnight.

Or maybe it was the observer, she thought. Maybe it's me, not noticing little things, seeing clearly and well only sometimes, only once in a while.

"About what?" she said.

"Supper. You gonna let me take you out?"

Susie turned off the faucet. "Sure," she said. "I'd like that. Let's skip the tea, okay?"

"Fine with me."

Susie went to her bedroom to comb her hair and get a sweater from the closet. When she came out again Arthur was in the living room, gazing out the front window.

"I was married once," he said, without turning around. "A long time ago. I was walking along the street with her one day and these teenage kids came along. Two guys. Looking for trouble." He touched the window. "They bumped into her, like by accident, except it wasn't." He rested his forehead against the glass. "Fucking kids. Stupid fucking kids."

Susie didn't move.

"They brought it on themselves. Probably high on some fucking thing." He lifted his head and turned around, shoving his hands in his pockets. "It's the look of the street out there that reminded me. Something. Maybe that big blue bush over there."

"What happened?" said Susie.

"I beat the crap out of them," said Arthur.

They walked to the restaurant, since it was only a few blocks away. It was a warm evening, with a tinge of autumn in the air. The day had been overcast but the clouds were retreating eastward now and a wide slice of the sky was clear. As the sun lowered itself toward the horizon it burned suddenly gold, and laid garish fingers upon trees and sidewalks and the windows of the houses they passed.

Susie and Arthur maintained a pace that was purposeful but not swift; maintained a distance between them that was circumspect but not disinterested.

TWENTY-TWO

The time had come for Susie to speak her mind. But she was afraid of landing on Leigh-Anne's doorstep and finding her boyfriend there. She didn't know how much time he spent at her daughter's apartment, but surely that was where they would have to meet, the two of them, clandestine as this business was. So when would it be most likely that he would not be there? A weekday evening? A weekend afternoon — maybe Saturday? Or Saturday morning, maybe. Yes, Susie decided. Saturday morning.

She didn't sleep well Friday night and finally wakened for good at six o'clock. She lay quietly for a few minutes, marshaling her thoughts, trying to plan what she would say.

Finally she threw the covers back and got out of bed. Mutt watched from her basket as Susie dressed and pulled back the drapes and raised the blind, letting in the late-summer sunshine. It was a day for walking Mutt in the park. A day for eating sandwiches under a tree. Or cleaning out the attic, with the small high windows flung wide open.

Maybe she and Leigh-Anne would spend the day together, she thought. They might buy popcorn from a street vendor and take on the walk that circled Stanley Park, strolling, avoiding skateboarders and power walkers, watching the sunsparks on the water and listening to the cry of gulls, the lapping of the tide, the shouts of children. She would wear walking shoes, just in case, thought Susie as she dressed and made her bed.

Mutt followed her to the kitchen and banged out into the backyard through the new dog door. Susie opened cupboards and eyed the teapot.

It wasn't even six-thirty yet.

She knew Leigh-Anne liked to sleep in on weekend mornings, but what if today she had plans that called for an early start?

Mutt crashed back through the dog door and padded over to Susie.

"I'm too nervous to eat," she said to her, scooping Kibbles into her dish. She got a can of dog food from the fridge and added half a cup, then some hot water, and mixed it, and put it down on the mat. She watched distractedly as Mutt dug in. "I don't even feel like making tea," she told her.

She sat down in the dining area. If she drove slowly she could make the trip to Leigh-Anne's apartment last maybe half an hour. She couldn't show up there at seven o'clock. That would be ridiculous. And it would alarm the girl, too. So what was the earliest she could get there without feeling foolish and having to make a bunch of excuses? Nine, she decided. Nine o'clock. Susie looked at the clock and sighed.

Then, "I could go to a restaurant," she said to Mutt. "Take along a book to read, have an omelet." She looked at the clock again. "Okay. That's what I'll do."

She waited until Mutt had finished eating and took her out into the backyard, where fifteen times she threw her tennis ball and watched her race off, catch it, and return it. She had on several occasions tried to throw the ball until Mutt decided she didn't want to play any more. But Susie couldn't go beyond thirty-nine throws, it was just too darn boring. And even after thirty-nine throws Mutt still wanted more.

She looked around the yard, which had a narrow walk leading to the back gate and some patchy lawn and a spindly tree of some kind, but nothing more. I could grow things out here, she thought. Sunflowers. Tomatoes. Things that I like. "Oh, the heck with it," she said aloud as Mutt sprinted back with the tennis ball for the fifteenth time. "You don't care, do you," she said to her, "if we have sunflowers or not? That's it," she said, snatching the ball from the grass and holding it high so that the dog couldn't leap up and grab it from her.

She went back into the house and dropped the ball into Mutt's basket, then washed her hands clean of dog slobber and picked up her handbag from the hall table.

"See you later," she said to Mutt, who was noisily slurping from her water dish.

At nine o'clock she pressed the apartment buzzer beside Leigh-Anne's name. She waited, then pressed it again. Still no response. Susie became convinced that her daughter wasn't home, that she was spending the night somewhere with that man, whoever he was. Her eyes prickled with tears.

What would she do with herself all day if she couldn't find Leigh-Anne and say what she had steeled herself to say? There was absolutely nothing else on her mind. She hadn't been able to read while she picked away at her omelet; she'd spent the time readying herself to confront her daughter. And now Leigh-Anne wasn't even here.

She turned around, clutching her purse, looking at her car, parked at the curb. Maybe Leigh-Anne, upon hearing the buzzer, had looked outside and seen Susie's car. Maybe that man was up there right now. Maybe Leigh-Anne was urging him to get dressed and get out quickly, the back way. Susie didn't even know if there was a back way, but thought there must be.

"Hello?" said Leigh-Anne, her voice tinny through the speaker.

"Oh, you're there," said Susie.

"Mom?" She sounded surprised. Susie heard sleepiness, too, and irritation.

"Yes," said Susie, "it's me. Can I come in?"

"What are you doing here? What's wrong?"

"Nothing, nothing," said Susie. "I'd just like to see you, if that's okay." She felt like a petitioner. Which was no role for a mother. "If you have time," she added.

"Sure. Come on up," Leigh-Anne said, and the buzzer sounded.

Leigh-Anne was tying her robe when she answered the door, a long, white terrycloth robe that she'd had for years. The sight of it caused some of Susie's anxiety to subside.

Leigh-Anne gave her a hug. "It's good to see you, Mom. How about some coffee? Or I can make tea, if you like."

"No, coffee's fine."

"Come on into the kitchen and sit down."

Leigh-Anne's West End apartment building, into which she had moved in midsummer, was old but well kept, located only a few blocks from Stanley Park. Her corner apartment was small but adequate.

Susie sat down in the kitchen and draped her jacket over the back of one of the chairs. A large maple tree grew next to the sidewalk. She thought she might be able to touch its branches if she leaned out the window and stretched her arm as far as it would go.

"You sure there's nothing wrong, Mom?" said Leigh-Anne, pouring water into the coffee pot.

"I'm sure," said Susie.

Leigh-Anne took a bowl of sugar from the cupboard and a small pitcher of cream from the refrigerator and set them on the table. "So — why are you here?" she said, taking the other chair.

Her hair was tangled from sleep. She had pulled it back and wrapped an elastic band around it but she hadn't brushed it first. Susie imagined her waiting by the door, wondering what on earth had brought her mother here so early on a Saturday morning, combing her hair back with her fingers, drawing it into a ponytail. She would have thought first of Susie's health, which was excellent but who ever knew what might happen; then probably of Mutt; then household disasters — fire, perhaps, or a tree blown down on Susie's roof. But all the while, surely, in the back of her mind she must have known what had brought her mother here.

"I'm worried about you," said Susie. "That's why I've come."

Leigh-Anne, feigning shock, rested the fingertips of both hands delicately upon her chest and widened her eyes. "Me?"

"I want you to tell me about this man."

Leigh-Anne became not pink but pale, and began shaking her head, slowly. "You're not going to give me grief about him, are you, Mom? Because I won't have it. Really. I won't."

"I don't know, Leigh-Anne, if I'm going to give you grief or not. That depends on what you tell me. But I am your mother, and I will say to you what I have to say to you, whatever that is."

She was smouldering, Leigh-Anne was, it was clear as day. But she was indecisive about this smouldering, not sure whether she wanted to tell Susie here and now to take a hike or hear her out. Susie figured that if Leigh-Anne could hang on to her temper, she'd let her stay.

Susie looked down at her lap while Leigh-Anne worked out what to do. She scratched with a fingernail at a spot on her skirt, maybe dried dog food. She glanced up at Leigh-Anne and saw that her daughter was staring at her, arms crossed, mouth pursed. Susie tried a smile.

"I could point out to you, Mother," said Leigh-Anne coolly, "that *your* choice of a boyfriend doesn't exactly thrill *me*, either."

Susie was flabbergasted. She wasn't *serious* about Arthur. She wasn't in *love* with Arthur. She opened her mouth to say this.

But Leigh-Anne went on. "Okay," she said with a sigh. "I'll get the coffee."

Susie waited silently while Leigh-Anne poured coffee into two big mugs and placed them on the table.

"He's a writer," she said, when she had sat down and stirred cream into her coffee. "I think I told you that."

Susie wanted to comment or ask questions, but she knew that was just because she was nervous. For the moment, she decided, she would keep her mouth shut.

Leigh-Anne wrapped her hands around her coffee mug and shivered a little, although it was really very warm in the apartment. It was so warm, in fact, that Susie would have liked to open the window.

"And he teaches," said Leigh-Anne. "Part time."

She looked beyond Susie as she spoke, as if willing him to materialize there behind her mother. It would be two against one then, and maybe together they could make her understand. Oh, Susie knew what was in her heart, all right. At least, some of what was there.

"He's a good writer, too. And intelligent. But he's also a good person, Mom. Very thoughtful, very sweet," Leigh-Anne said earnestly. "You would like him, I know you would. I know you both, and I am convinced that you would like each other."

She had a compelling need for Susie to acquiesce to this relationship, and Susie, knowing this, struggled to withhold her disapproval. There might be mitigating circumstances, she told herself. Justification. She picked up her mug and drank.

"I'm sure he's everything you say he is," she said. "But he's also married. Isn't he?"

Leigh-Anne leaned back in her chair and tried to produce an expression of forbearance. But it didn't sit well. She knew this, and had the grace a moment later to look embarrassed. "Yes," she said decisively. "He's married. But — well, you didn't stay married either, did you, Mom?"

"That's neither here nor there," said Susie. "When there's an end to something, then there can be a new beginning. Not before." Memories of Buddy wriggled into her head again — this had been happening far too frequently lately — and for a moment Susie felt like oh! such a fraud.

"That's a nice thought," said Leigh-Anne, smiling a little. And the smile angered Susie. It suggested indulgence. It insinuated that Leigh-Anne was tactfully declining to press the advantage of her own worldliness, implicitly labeling her mother unsophisticated — no, more than that: ignorant of significant matters of the heart.

"Do they have children?"

Leigh-Anne had been waiting for this. Susie could see it in her face. And although she probably thought she was ready for it, she wasn't. She couldn't help but flinch, and her face sagged.

Susie said, "How many?"

"Just one," Leigh-Anne said quickly.

Susie laughed. She couldn't help it, shaking her head and laughing quietly. "Just the one," she said. "Oh good. How old is it?"

"I'm not sure," said Leigh-Anne. "Young. She doesn't go to school yet."

"Ah," said Susie. She sat back and spread her hands on her thighs, feeling her thinness. "Does his wife know about you?"

Leigh-Anne flushed. "He'll be moving out, Mom. Getting his own place."

"How long had this been going on before he decided to tell her?"

"I would imagine," said Leigh-Anne quietly, with dignity, "that he waited until he knew it was serious."

"So then, if it hadn't turned out to be serious, he would never have bothered her with it," Susie said coldly. "What kind of a man is this? What kind of a dishonest, cheating person is this?" She looked out the window, at the oak tree whose scattered leaves, brown and brittle, littered the grass and the pavement below, elbowed from its branches by the sprouting of this year's foliage. She felt a great sadness. She turned to Leigh-Anne, who hadn't moved, who hadn't said a word. "You can't trust this man."

"Yes, I can." There was absolute conviction in her daughter's voice. "You're right, Mom. It would have been better for everyone if he'd left her before he met me. I wish he had." She leaned toward Susie, her hands clasped on the table. "Things haven't happened in the right order. That's all."

I want her to be happy, Susie thought, gazing at her daughter. Don't I? I want her to have a family of her own, a life of her own. Don't I?

Leigh-Anne was watching her worriedly, and Susie knew she was hoping for acceptance, if benediction was out of the question.

"He's not going to stop being his child's father, Mom, if that's what you're worried about. He loves her to death. And besides, I wouldn't let him. I wouldn't let him do to his daughter what my father did to me."

Susie's gaze wandered to the living room, where separate photographs of Leigh-Anne's parents sat upon the mantel. She couldn't see them — the fireplace was around the corner — but she knew they were there. A picture of herself taken five or six years earlier, with Mutt, Susie laughing, her head thrown back, arms spread wide, and the dog sitting docile by her feet with her head cocked and her tongue hanging out, so that it looked like Mutt, too, was laughing.

And close to it — not cheek by jowl, for that would have been inappropriate, but nearby — a photograph of Buddy. He was leaning against the hood of an old Ford, wearing jeans and a white shirt open at the throat with the sleeves rolled up. His arms were crossed and there was an expression both patient and quizzical upon his face. Whenever she looked at it, Susie wondered what he'd been thinking while she took that picture. Had he already made the decision that had shattered their family? Or had it been a decision? Or just a collision of planets, or some damn thing? She wished, now, that she had asked him that.

"I don't know," she said heavily. "I just don't know."

Leigh-Anne sat quietly, her head slightly tilted. Susie wanted to wrap her arms around the girl, keep her safe. But she knew that Leigh-Anne was inwardly radiant with joy and confidence, keeping the flame low with an effort so as not to upset her mother any more than was absolutely necessary. It was Susie who needed hugging, Susie who craved reassurance.

"How long have you been seeing him?" she asked.

"It'll be a year in January."

"Oh yes," said Susie softly.

And the moment reinvented itself in her brain, the moment in April when Leigh-Anne in her mother's kitchen had brushed her hair back from her face, revealing her private joy; displaying, unaware, love's transfiguration.

"Oh yes," said Susie. "The writing class."

TWENTY-THREE

It was the following year — a Friday in March — when Eddie Henderson went home from work in a state bordering on elation. She parked in front of her house and walked rapidly up to her front door, hardly even appreciating the primrose paint job or the dark blue trim, and she always did that, always. She loved her little house. It made her smile every time she looked at it. But not today. Today her mind was on other things.

She went straight to her bedroom, where she stripped off her uniform and unbraided her hair. Wearing only her underwear, she grabbed a brush and bent from the waist, brushing her hair until it crackled. Who could she call?

Whom, she corrected herself. Whom could she call, to share her news?

There was her father, of course. But would he be sufficiently delighted?

There was Cindi. But Cindi was a reporter, and might think of it at first as news.

There was Marjorie, who was now working out of the Surrey detachment. But Eddie no longer had her home phone number.

Eddie's euphoria was rapidly deflating. She really had to get more personal people in her life.

She straightened, pulled on sweatpants and a T-shirt and tied her hair back with an elastic band. She slipped into a pair of sandals and hurried out of her house and down the sidewalk to the house next door, where she banged on the door and waited impatiently, her hands in her pockets.

"Hi, Bev," she said when the door opened.

"Hi, Eddie. You'll be wanting Alvin, I guess." Bev McKechnie was taller than her husband but considerably thinner. She wore jeans and a man's shirt, and sneakers on her feet. Her gray hair was short and curly. She had brown eyes behind large glasses with silver frames.

"Both of you, Bev," said Eddie, beaming at her. "I've got news."

"Have you, now," said Bev, amused. She stepped back, and Eddie went inside. "Alvin," she called. "Sit down, Eddie. Alvin!"

The front door led directly into the living room, which contained two easy chairs at angles to the gas fireplace, a long sofa under the window, a rocking chair in one corner, and a large television in another.

Alvin came into the room from the kitchen, drying his hands on a teatowel.

"Eddie," he said. "What can I do for you?"

"She's got news," said Bev, arranging herself in the rocking chair.

"I'm — they've asked me to take over. Temporarily," said Eddie. "From Karl Alberg. He's leaving, you know. At the end of the month."

"Eddie!" Alvin crowed. He came toward her, arms outstretched. "A promotion!" He hugged her. "We've gotta celebrate."

"That's wonderful, Eddie," said Bev, rocking. "Congratulations."

"Well, it isn't permanent," said Eddie. "And it isn't a promotion. That is, I'm still a sergeant."

"But you're gonna be in charge," said Alvin, grinning at her. He made a fist and slugged her gently on the shoulder. "You're gonna be the boss. The big cheese."

"Yeah," said Eddie. "For the time being, anyway."

"You're gonna do such a bang-up job, girlie, they're gonna make it permanent. Eventually. You wait and see. Now sit down, we'll have a drink to commemorate the occasion."

"We'll have one drink," said Bev, "to commemorate the occasion, and then we'll take her out for dinner, is what we'll do."

"Oh no," Eddie protested. "I couldn't let you do that."

"Oh yes you can," said Bev. "But first — Alvin, get out the good scotch."

It was still early when she got home. She closed the curtains against the gathering darkness, got a beer from the fridge and called her father.

"What you're saying is that you'll be filling in until they find somebody they want to do the job, is that it?" he said.

"I guess you could put it that way," said Eddie. "But I'm pretty happy about this, Dad. And I plan to be so damn good at it that they can't help but be impressed."

"I just hope it isn't too big a disappointment," he said, "when you've got to give it up and take orders from the new man."

"I'll live with it," she said, experiencing a whole-body clench.

When she'd hung up she sat in front of the television for a while, thinking about her day, reliving her interview with Alberg, which she would eventually record, cryptically but adequately, in her work diary.

He had called her into his office just before the end of her shift, and had given her the news.

"But I haven't got the promotion yet, Staff," Eddie blurted. She didn't know why she said it, because of course he knew that, he knew that she had just begun the process, which could take up to a year.

He frowned at her. "Maybe I haven't made myself clear. Understand this, please, Sergeant. This is a temporary appointment. You'll be holding the fort until a staff sergeant has been named to the job and can make arrangements to move over here."

"How long do you think that'll take?"

He shrugged. "Could be only a couple of weeks. Or maybe they'll offer it to somebody who doesn't want to come here. So they'll have to look around again. And a year could go by. You never know."

Eddie reached for the beer can on the coffee table and took a drink. She wondered if she would still be acting head of the detachment when her promotion came through. *If* it came through.

Of course it would come through.

And when it did, if she was still doing Alberg's job, would they consider making it permanent? Or would they insist on transferring her?

"Is there a limit, though," she said, "to how long they'll let me do the job?"

"Only if you screw up."

"I guess — I guess that's pretty fair," said Eddie.

He stared at her for a minute. "And sit down, will you, please?"

Eddie realized that she had been standing in front of his desk in review position, stiff, and smart, and staring straight ahead. She felt like an idiot.

As she sat, she saw the photo of his daughters that hung on the wall near his desk. She wondered if she would hang something there — but quickly acknowledged that there was nobody in her life whose photograph she would want to be that close to her all the time. She felt melancholy for a moment, experienced it as a long, lingering scratch on her heart. But then her excitement ballooned: this was going to be her detachment.

For a while, Eddie reminded herself, as the telephone rang. Only for a while.

"Hello."

"Hi, doll," said Alan.

Eddie said nothing.

"You there?"

Eddie didn't reply. Her heart was beating fast and her hands were damp. She wondered if he was calling to congratulate her. She knew there was no way he could know of her news but she thought nevertheless that maybe he did. Perhaps her father had called him. But Alan didn't mention Alberg, or the Sechelt detachment.

"Where are you, babe?" he said. "In bed? Are you in bed? Naked, beneath the sheets? Lonely, beneath the sheets?" There were layers in his voice, his tone. He was seductive, but he was also amused. Having fun.

Eddie, listening, felt her anger growing, and was gratified. She had come to fear him, to cower when she heard his voice, and righteous anger was a nice change. She let him go on for a while, holding the phone away from her ear. Then she swung her feet to the floor and stood up.

"Sorry, Alan," she said, interrupting him, "I was busy doing something else and didn't hear that. Listen, these calls are really very boring. Perhaps you don't realize it, you pitiful hunk of shit, but you are making me extremely impatient."

"You need a good fuck, Eddie," he said.

Eddie laughed. "That's about the only thing you do well, Alan. And you know what? I can live without it just fine." She slammed down the phone. Her face was hot and she knew it would be beet red but at least it was rage that had done it and not embarrassment.

The phone rang again. She snatched it up.

"I wasn't finished, cunt."

"Leave me alone, you goddamn psychopath! Or I swear to god I'm going to report you!" She hung up again.

This time he didn't call back.

TWENTY-FOUR

On a bright Saturday afternoon toward the end of March, Susie took Mutt to the park for the first time that year. The dog strained at the end of the leash while Susie contemplated her life.

Well, a part of her life.

Susie was grateful that she and her daughter had remained close and loving as adults. Leigh-Anne had been precious to her from the day of her birth, and had become more so when Buddy left and there was just the two of them to face the world and its troubles together. Susie had nurtured the relationship from its beginning, determined that they would never grow apart, like Susie and her own mother had grown apart.

The only thing Susie and her mother had in common as adults was being a single parent. Susie acknowledged that this had been much more difficult in her mother's day than in her own. Granted, there was no shame involved — Susie's father had had the good grace to die of a heart attack at an early age, which was infinitely preferable to Susie's situation. (Her mother had never forgiven him for it nonetheless.) But Susie growing up had felt herself to be largely a burden in her mother's life, and was relieved and thankful when her own daughter brought her only joy.

But now Susie suspected that she might have become in late middle age too dependent upon her relationship

with her daughter. She had Mutt, and she had a responsible job that required considerable skill, yet Leigh-Anne
remained paramount in her life. Susie knew that at least
some of her objection to this married person that Leigh-
Anne continued to be involved with had to do with
Susie's fear of losing her.

She also wondered for the first time whether keeping
the truth about her father from Leigh-Anne had been
the right thing to do. Maybe she *ought* to know. Was it
too late for Susie to tell her? Would she hate her mother for having kept it from her? Or would she hate her
for finally telling her?

Susie was walking beneath the cherry trees, whose
blossom-buds were once again beginning to swell. In a
few more weeks a quick press of a breeze would send
them fluttering onto her head and shoulders, reminding
her of the day a year ago that she and Arthur had met.
The petals would pile up on the ground beneath the
trees, pink mounds of them at first unsullied by rain or
the deliberate scufflings of children and dogs.

Brilliantly green grass undulated across the park,
forming knolls here and there, rising in the center to a
hillock that was crowned by several evergreens whose
lowest branches brushed the ground. The grass was
sprinkled with tiny wildflowers, white and blue and
pink. Susie always marveled that after the Parks Board
lawnmower had swept languidly from corner to corner,
cutting the grass and wiping out the flowers as it did so,
they always came back. Until their season was over, and
they decided on their own to depart. They were blooming now, too small to gather and take home for a bou-
quet. They looked like a painting, Susie thought. In fact
the whole park, on this warm and sunny day, looked like
an expressionist painting, the colors of blooming greening things gloriously flourishing, making Susie's eyes
sting and her soul acquire that discomfiting sensation
that was part joy and part pain.

Susie thought this feeling must be something carried over from whatever existence she'd had before she was born. She was uncertain about her developing conviction that she had in fact existed before her actual birth, didn't know where or when it had begun, but she kept acquiring evidence that it was so. Not real evidence; only an inexplicable interest in long-felt mysteries for which she thought solutions might now be found. But if that was in fact where this feeling of pain and joy originated . . .

Susie couldn't take the thought any further. Maybe later, she thought. Maybe in my seventies. An assignment for my old age.

Where was Buddy now? she wondered. He had been out of prison for more than twenty years. He'd written to her often during his first years in jail but she never answered, and eventually the letters stopped coming. She had told him to stay away from them, and he had. Now she wondered what had happened to him. Had he managed to construct a decent life for himself? Or had he gotten into trouble again, and again?

Had she deprived Leigh-Anne of something important by encouraging her to believe that her father had abandoned them? Susie had never once thought so — until now.

Mutt nosed the ground for traces of friends and enemies, looking for an appropriate place to relieve herself; in her jacket pocket Susie had two plastic bags and a twist tie. Several large trash containers were stationed on the periphery of the park, which also sported signs advising dog-owners to clean up after their pets, and to keep them leashed. Susie endorsed this policy because it was a small neighborhood park. Still, what she really preferred was taking Mutt to those areas in Vancouver where dogs were allowed to run free. She hardly ever did this, unfortunately. But her intentions were good.

She wished that Leigh-Anne had a pet. A cat, who could look after itself without having to go outdoors.

Who could even be left alone overnight, if enough food and water was put out for him. A cat would offer companionship. And demand a certain amount of responsibility from his owner.

But why on earth did she think Leigh-Anne needed more responsibility? She took her job so seriously that Susie often worried that she was working far too hard.

No, Leigh-Anne didn't need a pet. She didn't need new information about her long absent father, either.

The bench at the end of the park was empty, and Susie had a sudden need to do her thinking sitting down. She tethered Mutt to the end of the bench and petted her for a few minutes, assuring her that their break would be a short one. Mutt reared up on her hind legs, resting her front paws on the bench, and barked.

"Okay," said Susie.

The dog leapt up beside her and lay down, her front paws dangling over the edge, her ears cocked, her bright eyes scouring the park.

Maybe she ought to meet him, Susie thought. Leigh-Anne's separated but still married boyfriend. After all, they had been seeing each other for fifteen months now. And Susie had approved of every boyfriend Leigh-Anne had brought home, once she got to know him. Maybe this one deserved the same consideration.

Head bent in thought, her elbows resting on her knees, she had been looking down at the concrete path that encircled the park, and now she noticed that the wildflowers spilled right to the edge and over, tiny flecks of pink and white, no blue ones here. They looked like daytime ground-level stars. She felt a lifting in her spirits.

Leigh-Anne arrived in mid-afternoon, as planned. Susie noticed the ring immediately — how could she possibly not? But she said nothing.

She and Leigh-Anne walked up to the bakery, where Susie bought a loaf of French bread and Leigh-Anne, finger to her lips, studied the glass cases intently before deciding upon half a dozen biscotti, half a dozen dinner rolls, and two bruschetti, which she and Susie munched as they made their way down the street to Starbucks.

Susie said, when they were seated, each with a decaf latte with extra foam, "I've decided I'd like to meet your young man."

Leigh-Anne flushed. "What brought this on?"

"You believe this is a serious, permanent relationship, don't you?"

"Yes, of course. I've told you."

"Well, then. It's about time I got a look at him."

"But why now, Mom?"

"I don't know why now, Leigh-Anne," said Susie. She pointed to her daughter's right hand. "Maybe that's why."

Leigh-Anne instinctively covered the ring with her left hand, then withdrew it.

"Is it an engagement ring?"

"No, Mom, of course not, he's still married. It's — it's a token of his love, though. It'll be our engagement ring as soon as he's free. I'll wear it on my other hand then."

Susie considered this to be inappropriately sentimental and, embarrassed, kept her eyes riveted on the ring. It was a large rectangular green stone in a gold setting. A manmade emerald, probably, she thought. Expensive. It suited Leigh-Anne's hand, she had to admit that. Leigh-Anne had large strong hands with long fingers and short, well-manicured nails, bare of polish but buffed to a shine.

"It's beautiful," said Susie, and for the second time that day tears threatened hotly at the backs of her eyes. I'm getting old, she thought peevishly. Or maybe it's something else from my previous damn existence leaking into this one.

Would she ever learn anything useful from these incidents? Or would they remain ineffectual, but become more frequent and unsettling?

Leigh-Anne's blush had faded but there was still a lot of color in her face, and Susie noticed that she was maintaining her weight. The school year was only a few weeks from its close and Leigh-Anne looked as healthy and energetic as she had at its beginning. Susie knew that at least some of the credit for this probably had to go to Leigh-Anne's young man, married though he might be.

"Why don't I invite the two of you for dinner?" said her daughter. "Next weekend?"

TWENTY-FIVE

It was the morning after Alberg's departure, and the detachment seemed completely altered. Eddie had experienced Alberg's absence frequently, of course — when she was on duty and he wasn't. But she had never felt it so massively; never felt it echoing, as it was now. She wondered how much more strongly other people were feeling this — people who had been here, served under him, much longer than Eddie had. For christ's sake, smarten up, she told herself impatiently, standing in the doorway to his office. Which was now — temporarily — hers.

She noticed immediately the pale rectangle on the wall where the photograph of his daughters had hung. But that was the only change she could see. The bulletin board was still crowded with notices, announcements — Alberg hadn't paid any attention to the bulletin board, not that Eddie had observed. It was Isabella who regularly removed outdated material and tacked up new stuff. Would she continue to do this, unasked? Or would Eddie have to make a formal request? The in-tray was full and the out-tray empty, which had often been the case when Alberg sat behind the desk.

She had an hour left before the detachment meeting. She had thought she was ready for it — after all there wasn't a whole lot to say to them — but standing here, now, alone in this room, she felt completely unprepared

for this undertaking. She crossed to the window and
yanked up the blind, letting the sunshine in. It was an
unsettled day, sometimes sunny, the next minute cloudy.
For the moment, sunny. But it was a temporary thing.
Like my job, she thought dryly.

She took off her jacket and draped it over the back of
the desk chair. Then, standing in the middle of the room,
she rested her hands on her hips and turned, slowly, taking in the filing cabinet, the desk, the bulletin board, the
black leather chair. And finally she stepped behind the
desk and sat down. She remembered that there had
always been pieces of paper stuck in the corners of the
blotter, business cards, telephone message forms, memos
— things Alberg had decided he couldn't afford to lose
track of. The corners were empty now. She wondered if
perhaps at this very moment he was sitting behind a
brand-new desk in a brand-new office — a brand-new
PI — and maybe he was a little bit nervous himself
about launching into his new life. She sat back and
opened the drawer. It contained a selection of pens and
pencils in a narrow horizontal tray and was otherwise
empty — except for a piece of paper, folded, with her
name on it. Eddie took it out.

*You're going to do just fine. Call me if you need to. But you
won't need to.*

It was signed *Karl*.

Eddie pulled out her notebook and turned to the
page where she had written an agenda for this meeting.
Her mouth was very dry.

The fifteen Members and their three-person civilian
support staff filled the meeting room and spilled out into
the hall. Eddie stood behind the small oval table and
waited until they had all gathered — all except Isabella,
who was out there manning the phones and watching
the door, but who was still close enough to hear what
was going on.

While she watched them get settled Eddie thought about the list she'd made (one of many) of the Members whom she didn't know as well as she should. She had to do something about that as soon as possible.

Greetings had been exchanged, coffee mugs filled, chairs pulled to the meeting room from offices and work stations: the detachment was assembled, and its faces were turned to her with expressions that were mostly friendly, sometimes curious, occasionally distant.

"Good morning," said Eddie. She made herself relax, let her fingertips bounce lightly on the tabletop. "I've brought you all together first of all to assure you that nothing much is going to change around here in the short term." She clasped her hands behind her, conscious of her straight back, her legs planted comfortably apart. "My job, as I see it, is to make sure that things continue as much as possible as when Staff Sergeant Alberg was running the show."

Cornie Friesen drank from his coffee mug.

Jeannette Peterson moved her intense gaze from Eddie's face to scribble something in a notebook.

"As soon as I'm told who the new staff sergeant will be," Eddie promised, "I'll let you know."

Joey Lattimer, slouched in his chair with his arms crossed over his chest, looked her up and down, managing to appear both sleepy and lecherous.

"Meanwhile," said Eddie, "we'll continue as we are."

"But short-handed," said Cornie Friesen.

"Right," said Eddie. "Temporarily short-handed."

"We can manage," said Frank Turner.

"Yeah, don't we always," said Friesen.

"I need to be brought up to speed on some of the community-based projects," said Eddie. "Victims Services, Citizens on Patrol, Speed Watch, Court Watch. Frank and I met earlier — he's going to be my 2IC. He'll arrange this, over the next few days, with the Members and the civilian reps and give me a schedule of who's seeing me when." She looked around, trying to make eye contact with each of the men and women present. "Any questions?"

"What about the bike patrol?" said Jeannette Peterson. "Is that going to happen again this year?"

"That was your project, wasn't it?"

The constable nodded.

"I don't see why not. But come and see me about it. Anything else?"

"Yeah." Joey Lattimer straightened in his chair. "How long is this gonna take? This hunt for a staff sergeant?"

"Don't know, Constable. Depends on the housing markets, I guess. Anybody else?"

"Because it's kind of a drag," Lattimer went on.

"I don't think it should be," said Eddie, keeping her voice level. "Like I said, my job is to make sure things continue as they are. The changes you seem to be antic-ipating won't happen with me on the job. They'll happen under the new guy."

" 'Guy?' " said Cornie Friesen with a laugh. "Well, that's a relief."

"Jesus, Friesen," said Norah Gibbons wearily.

"One more thing," said Eddie, ignoring this and glancing at her watch. "I'm also going to schedule meetings with each one of you individually. I want to know what you need. Courses, whatever. To do your jobs as well as you can, and to do the kind of work you want to do."

She looked them over again. At least she knew every-body's name, and how long they'd been here, and what Alberg's opinion of each of them had been. That was enough to be getting on with, she thought.

TWENTY-SIX

Susie couldn't accept Leigh-Anne's invitation to meet her married boyfriend after all.

Susie got the flu, taking to her bed with an aching throat and a chestful of cough, every bone in her seriously imperiled body hurting. It was all she could do to roll from her bed to visit the bathroom and feed Mutt; she had never been so thankful for the dog door.

Susie hadn't been so ill in years. Sleep was fretful — nonrestorative — sticky with dream-trash. A springtime storm attacked, and rain clattered against her bedroom window, creating static in her sweltering, over-burdened brain: that night she couldn't rid herself of the unpleasant illusion that someone was flinging handfuls of soft-shelled crabs against the glass.

Her continuing absence from the real estate office alarmed her fellow workers, who began making worried phone calls that soon became a genuine nuisance, since the answering machine beeped continuously.

Her colleagues called more often than Leigh-Anne, who had an almost fatalistic toleration of illness, her own as well as other people's.

And a lot more often than Arthur. He called only once, after which he turned up at her door. It was clear that he had felt somehow obligated to appear in person, even though his uneasiness at the sight of Susie — pale, ill, coughing, clinging breathless to the edge of the door

— was manifest.

"You can't help me," she told him, her voice rasping in her throat. "And I certainly don't want you sitting in my house watching me like this."

"I could make you some tea," he said.

"I'm making my own tea, thank you very much." She would have liked a comforting hug. She would have welcomed his big warm hands on her shoulders, turning her around, propelling her into a comfortable chair while he stripped her bed and put clean sheets on it. Glaring at him from around the door, she almost laughed aloud at the unlikeliness of this.

Leigh-Anne came in midweek, though, and did it for her.

But Susie lay in her newly sweat-drenched bed for another entire week before she finally began to feel better.

Having lost more than three weeks, at work and in life, it took her a while to feel that things were getting back to normal.

Before she knew it spring had passed, and it was summer.

Then Leigh-Anne and her friend went off to Saltspring Island for a month. He made regular trips back to town, Leigh-Anne assured Susie, to see his child. And while he was gone Leigh-Anne worked, preparing for the new school year.

Susie got caught up at the real estate office and spent a weekend painting her year-old fence.

She had become perpetually restless. She was afraid of missing something. She needed to feel purposeful almost all of the time, grew edgy sitting around, felt oddly threatened when she allowed herself to relax too much, to be distracted from what she thought of as life.

Ah well, she would think, shaking her hands until her wrists thrilled with a little ache. Ah well, she would say to herself, and she would look around almost willfully in search of another task.

And so what with one thing and another, it was an evening in August when Susie finally met Leigh-Anne's friend.

"He isn't here yet, Mom," said Leigh-Anne, giving Susie a welcoming hug. There was slightly more color in her face than usual, but then she'd been in the kitchen, hadn't she, making dinner — undoubtedly using the stovetop, probably the oven as well. Her eyes were perhaps a little brighter than usual, too. But her demeanor was calm, her smile affectionate, her hug as firm and warm as a mother could wish.

"How about a glass of sherry? You can sit in the kitchen and watch me toss the salad."

"I could even help you toss the salad," said Susie, but of course Leigh-Anne wouldn't hear of it.

Susie's apprehensions grew as they waited, and Leigh-Anne's friend didn't appear. Was he habitually late, then? Susie considered tardiness a serious character flaw. Or could it be that she'd come early? Gotten the time wrong? When she finally sneaked a glance at her watch she was astonished to see that only ten minutes had passed since her arrival. And there was her untouched glass of sherry sitting there to attest to it.

The buzzer rang as she took her first sip. Leigh-Anne was unruffled as she pushed the button that unlocked the lobby door.

Leigh-Anne's friend Blair had blond hair, blue eyes, and a forehead that was deeply lined. He kissed Leigh-Anne's cheek with circumspection before turning with a hesitant smile to Susie, who held out her hand without rising.

He was a perfectly pleasant man, only a few years older than Leigh-Anne, which surprised Susie; she was disconcerted to realize that she had been thinking of him as some kind of father figure to Leigh-Anne. His hair shone, and his eyes, as if someone had turned up the lights when he stepped into the room.

Susie felt awkward as she watched him light the candles. He was obviously at home here. She expected that she would continue to feel awkward. Excluded. And braced herself for this.

But Leigh-Anne and Blair included Susie without seeming to try. The conversation, which Susie had been afraid would quickly focus on this relationship and her attitude toward it and a discussion of whatever future it might have, was from the beginning wide-ranging. They discussed the housing market. The economy in general. Education. Federal—provincial clashes. The continuing wearying threat of Quebec separation.

Susie watched Leigh-Anne and her friend exchange smiles that were open, not private. She watched them bend discreetly toward each other when passing the salt or the bread basket. She remarked to herself upon the fact that they never touched, beyond the greeting exchanged at the door.

He was a civilized man, Leigh-Anne's friend. Courteous and thoughtful. Quiet. Was he strong? she wondered. For he would have to be, she thought, thinking again of Buddy, in order to relinquish his family. An unrelenting self-centeredness would be needed, she thought, to permanently abandon wife and daughter and establish himself with Leigh-Anne. She wondered, stealing glances at him as she ate her lasagne, if he was up to it.

Not tonight, she decided, appropriating as a sign the ebbing of his brightness as he sat back in his chair, temporarily out of the candlelight, darkness etching his cheekbones and hollowing his eyes.

TWENTY-SEVEN

Golden-eyed, middle-aged Isabella Harbud wasn't at all sure that the RCMP in its wisdom had done the right thing in handing over Karl Alberg's reins to Eddie Henderson, and Eddie knew it. She believed that Isabella, if asked her opinion, would have said that Eddie was too young, and only a sergeant. The gender thing, she would insist, had nothing to do with it.

But Eddie thought it did.

Most people had been reasonably polite so far, but this was because they knew hers was an interim appointment. Eddie had no illusions about that. And she admitted, it was a difficult situation for everyone. She had taken charge — because she had to — just as if she were going to be head of the detachment forever, and the Members and the civilian staff had for the most part accepted this. But she knew they were just putting in time, waiting — some patiently, some not — for the "new guy" to be assigned.

On a day in September she was in the reception area, waiting for Isabella to get off the phone, drumming her fingers on the counter.

Norah Gibbons, Eddie knew, was one of the unhappy campers, although she was struggling not to show it. She had wanted to be named Eddie's second in command. But her promotion to corporal had come after Frank Turner's, which gave him seniority. Eddie was secretly relieved that it was Turner, otherwise it would have looked like the detachment had been suddenly overrun by women.

And we can't have that, she thought dryly, watching Isabella, her exasperation mounting.

"Just a sec, Phil," said Isabella. She put her hand over the mouthpiece and raised her eyebrows at Eddie.

"I'm going to court," said Eddie.

"I know," said Isabella. "The Jefferson thing."

"And then to the school."

"I know," said Isabella. "Career day."

Eddie studied her for a moment. "I'm irritated with you," she said. "But I don't have a real good reason to be irritated. Which makes me even more irritated."

"Sorry, Sergeant," said Isabella. She gave Eddie a wink.

"Have a nice day, Isabella," Eddie said evenly.

Isabella kept her hand over the phone, watching Eddie stride down the hall toward the exit to the parking lot. She shook her head, exasperated. The sergeant was trying, Isabella had to give her that. She'd done what she'd said she was going to do, talking to everybody, more than once, about the Job and how to do it better. She hadn't made a lot of stupid little changes, trying to put her personal stamp on things. She was, as she'd promised, keeping things pretty much as they'd been before Karl left.

But she was still taking calls, for pete's sake, reluctant to delegate anything she thought sounded interesting or important. In this, Isabella had to admit, she was too *much* like Karl.

She heard squawking from the phone. "Yeah, sorry, Phil. I'm here. Go through that again for me, will you?"

In court, which was a dilapidated facility on the floor above a commercial establishment — making transport of witnesses and the accused sometimes tricky, especially if they happened to use wheelchairs — she testified in the case of Harold Jefferson, whom she had arrested and charged with robbery several months earlier. There were witnesses to his thievery and plenty of physical evidence, too — Harold was a rather stupid individual who seemed to get more stupid every time he went to jail — and his trial promised to be mercifully brief.

The sky had been overcast when Eddie entered the courthouse, but she emerged at lunchtime into a brilliant autumn day. She stood for a few seconds next to the patrol car with her eyes closed and her face lifted into the sunshine.

Then she drove to Davis Bay and parked next to the drive-in hamburger stand. Fifteen minutes later she was sitting on the beach across the highway, a diet Coke on the log next to her, devouring a giant cheeseburger.

The day was warm but cool around the edges, the sea was bluer than the sky, the sound of the waves washing upon the gravelly shore was as soothing as a lullaby. Eddie, planted comfortably on the log, thought she had never eaten a more delicious burger and wished she'd ordered fries as well.

She thought about her small house, where the clock would be ticking on the kitchen wall and sunshine would be slanting through the bedroom window. Bev McKechnie would be working in her garden on a gorgeous day like this, raking leaves or digging up dahlias — or maybe it was too early to be digging up dahlias. And Alvin was almost certainly out on the water.

She checked her watch: half an hour to go before she was due at the school. Eddie drank some Coke and finished off her burger, then crumpled the wax paper and tucked it into her pocket so it wouldn't blow away in the breeze.

She slid onto the sand-and-gravel shore and leaned against the log, looking out to sea, shading her eyes with her hand but squinting anyway against the bright sunlight.

A man was fishing from the end of the wharf that stretched maybe sixty yards out from the beach. Far away on the water a tugboat seemed to glide silently upon the surface of the sea, and at the end of a long, long towline an enormous log boom obediently followed.

Eddie sighed, and wondered if there was something wrong with her. Here she was, professionally marooned in this rural backwater, lacking close friends to call her own, with no love life whatsoever — not even a sex life. And how was she supposed to ever acquire a sex life in this place, where she was the very visible next best thing to a chief of police?

She looked again at her watch and reluctantly stood up, brushing at the seat of her pants. She was the damn police chief in a place that didn't even have a decent crime rate.

She picked up her diet Coke and climbed up to the road and across it.

Yeah, she thought as she unlocked the patrol car, there's something wrong with me, all right. She leaned on the roof for a minute, gazing across at the water and the blue and lavender islands in the distance.

Because I'm so damn happy here.

Twenty minutes later she was standing at the front of an elementary school classroom, hands clasped in front of her, feet apart. She was pretty sure she looked calm enough, but she wasn't. This was one of the things about her new temporary job that she didn't like much — talking to groups of any age. The teacher was introducing her and at one point Eddie turned to her in surprise: where the hell had she gotten that kind of information? She was telling the kids about Eddie's commendation. Finally the teacher gestured to Eddie with a smile and squeezed herself in at the end of the front row, much to the chagrin of the boy occupying the seat next to her.

She mightn't enjoy it much but that didn't mean that Eddie didn't prepare for these events. She started with a brief history of the RCMP, then talked about the training program, went on to describe her job as head of the detachment, and finally, with relief, asked for questions.

One of the windows was open several inches at the top, and for several minutes Eddie had been subliminally aware of the far-off purr of a lawnmower. She became conscious of the sound now as it rose over the scuffling of shoes against the tile floor and the giggling of suddenly self-conscious children.

One entire wall of the room was windows. There were blackboards at each end, and artwork and essays were tacked to a bulletin board that occupied the space between two doors on the wall opposite the windows. The children sat on each side of a narrow aisle at long tables, some sprawling, some upright. Eddie thought she could smell them, these children. They were fragrant with sweat and dirt and effort; what specific kind of effort depended on what kind of people they were becoming.

"Come on," she said good-naturedly. "Somebody must want to know something."

"Have you ever shot anybody?" said a boy at the back of the glass.

There was more giggling. Eddie looked them over before she answered, and as the children waited they whispered behind their hands, their bright eyes flitting between Eddie's face and the holster on her belt.

"No, thank goodness," said Eddie. "I've never even had to draw my weapon."

A few of the kids nodded wisely. A few of them offered disinterested shrugs. Some looked disappointed.

"You've arrested people, though, right?" asked the same boy, his chin resting on his arms, which were folded on the tabletop.

"Yeah," said Eddie, and gave him a wide, warm smile. "I've had to do that once or twice."

"Did you arrest them for beating somebody up?" asked a girl in the third row. She had extremely pale skin, light blue eyes, and hair so fair that at first glance Eddie had thought she had no eyebrows or eyelashes. The room grew quieter, and the pale girl absorbed curious glances as if they were blows, her cheeks growing pink, then red.

"Yes," said Eddie, "that's one of the things people get arrested for." She pointed to a boy seated near the blonde girl. "Have you ever been beaten up?"

The boy shrank into his shoulders and looked right and left.

"How about you?" she said to a boy wearing glasses who was vigorously rubbing his head.

He stopped rubbing and looked at her uncomprehendingly, as if Eddie had spoken in a foreign tongue, or burst into song. His sandy hair was now standing straight up in astonished tufts.

"Do you know what it's called?" said Eddie. "When somebody beats on another person? It's called assault."

"Did anybody ever do it to you?" said a blue-eyed girl with long brown hair and a cleft in her chin.

The girl sitting next to her poked her in the shoulder. "Eleanor, she's a policeman. Nobody beats up policemen."

The children's collective gaze swiveled from Eleanor to Eddie.

"Well," said Eddie, "not often, anyway. And I haven't been beaten up since I was just about your age."

The class exchanged glances, and looked at her skeptically.

"How come you wanted to be a policeman?" said Eleanor.

"I wanted to do important things," she said. "And I wanted to be in charge."

The girl looked at her thoughtfully. "Hmmm," she said.

What a stupid thing to say, thought Eddie, furious with herself. How bloody pretentious. How damn — inflated.

"Can we see your gun?" said a big boy slouching in the very back row, his legs extending into the aisle.

As the teacher rose hastily to her feet Eddie smiled at the boy and shook her head.

Somebody always wanted to see her gun.

TWENTY-EIGHT

On that same September day, Susie received a phone call at work.

"Mrs. Wilson? I'm afraid I have sad news for you."

Susie's mother had been found dead by the mailman, who had banged on her front door in Nanaimo, on Vancouver Island, when the mailbox hadn't been emptied two days in a row.

She was lying on the living-room floor, a full cup of cold coffee on the TV tray that sat next to her reclining chair, felled by a heart attack.

Susie's first thought was to wonder if, after forty-eight hours, decomposition would have begun, but she didn't want to ask.

The second thing that happened was guilt, although its sudden appearance offended her and she pushed it to the edges of her consciousness.

"Will you be making the arrangements?" said the woman from the hospital where Susie's mother had been taken.

"Of course," said Susie. "I'll be there tomorrow."

When she had hung up she told her boss what had happened. "I'll need a few days off," she said, and although his dismay was obvious he quickly tried to hide it, assuring her that time off wouldn't be a problem. She had expected no less. The place had no more conscientious an employee than Susie Wilson.

She left immediately, and when she got home, called Leigh-Anne at school. "No, I don't want to leave a message," she told the secretary. "I need to speak to her now. It's an emergency."

While she waited for Leigh-Anne to be fetched from her classroom, Susie picked up Mutt and sat down at the kitchen table with the dog in her lap. She was shaking, her body buffeted by an internal bluster. Although Mutt was lapdog size she didn't have a lapdog's disposition, and she usually tried to jump down when Susie held her. Today she stayed where she had been put, peering uneasily into Susie's face and laying upon her chin licks that Susie just knew aimed to be comforting. Susie stroked her and rubbed behind her ears.

"Leigh-Anne," she said when her daughter had picked up the phone. "Mother has died."

"Oh, Mom," said Leigh-Anne. "I'm sorry."

"She went fast, just like she would have wanted. Heart attack. Died in her own living room." Mutt placed her head on her paws, and Susie rested her hand on the dog's back. She thought she had stopped shaking. She'd know for certain when she stood up.

Leigh-Anne said, "And she lived eighty-five years before it happened. That's a pretty long life, Mom."

"The thing is, Leigh-Anne, I've got to go over there. To make the arrangements. That means deciding, does she get cremated or buried? If buried, where? Will there be a funeral? And all things like that."

"Do you want me to go with you?"

"No, thank you, dear. I think I ought to do this by myself. But what I *would* like is for you to come over here and help me make these decisions before I leave."

"Maybe she left something behind," suggested Leigh-Anne. "A will, or some kind of a document that will tell you what she wanted. People must start thinking about these things by the time they're eighty-five, don't you think?"

"She certainly didn't ever *talk* about dying," said Susie. She could feel Mutt's warm breath on her thigh, even through the fabric of her dress. "She could have written it down, I guess. But you'd think she would have told me."

"I'll come over after school," said Leigh-Anne.

Susie hung up the phone. She started thinking about what she could make for dinner. Leigh-Anne would be hungry, even if Susie wasn't. Was there something in the freezer? she wondered. A couple of chicken breasts, maybe? She felt herself to be suddenly weightless, sitting there. Weightless and aimless and without resolve.

After a while she put Mutt on the floor and stood up. Not a bit of a tremor did she feel. Her strength had returned.

That evening she and Leigh-Anne worked out a plan of action.

And the next morning Susie took the ferry from Tsawwassen.

She stayed in her station wagon for the entire crossing because she didn't want to leave Mutt alone down there on the car deck, which was no more than a big echoey garage with window-sized openings in the side of the hull through which seawater splashed when the weather was stormy.

It wasn't stormy today, though. There was a bit of a wind, but the sun shone steadily from a cloudless sky and the Strait of Georgia was relatively calm. This was Susie's favorite time of year, partly because it could usually be depended upon to bring a succession of sunny days to B.C.'s south coast before winter settled in, and partly because Susie had always associated autumn with the beginning of things. As she waited in the car she made lists, striving to bring good management to what she knew would be a difficult and painful task, that of bringing her mother's life to an orderly close.

She went first to the house, to which she had a key. It was on an acre of land several miles out of town. Her mother's old Chevy sat at the end of the drive, in front of the garage, and Susie wondered when she had last taken it out. It must have been several years ago, when her eyesight had begun to fail. She couldn't have known that it would be the last time, though, or she would have put the car in the garage, wouldn't she?

When she turned her attention to the house, guilt reappeared, shouldering its way from the shadows of the wings to center stage. The place had become positively ramshackle. How long had it been since Susie had visited? Her mother had been relentlessly fastidious. Susie was appalled to recognize how much of her energy had been exhausted, for the place to have become so run-down, so dilapidated.

"My eyesight isn't what it used to be," she would tell Susie on the phone. "I don't do so much, anymore. I'm conserving myself," she would say, quite comfortably. "Getting other people to do things for me. Letting things slide a bit."

But Susie hadn't realized just how much things had been allowed to slide. She should have listened more closely. She should have visited more often.

She got out of the car. "Come on, Mutt."

Mutt jumped out and lifted her face into the wind, sniffing energetically.

The house was secluded from its neighbors by high hedges of rhododendrons and surrounded by a weedy lawn with large bare patches; it looked like it had some kind of skin disease, Susie thought. Her mother had once grown vegetables in a large plot beside the house, and roses in a south-facing garden. Susie saw no sign of either now. She didn't remember how important these things had been to her mother — the vegetables, the roses. She only knew that if she had been upset when she could garden no longer, her mother had not confided this to Susie.

Disposing of the house and its contents seemed an insurmountable task. Her mother had occupied the house for sixty years. Susie had lived here herself, from the age of ten until she moved to the mainland, soon after her eighteenth birthday.

She found herself unwilling to go inside. Key in hand, she tentatively approached the front door.

In the interior silence she realized how much sound existed outside, created by birds and breezes and the occasional vehicle trundling past. She stepped back out onto the front steps and called to Mutt, who had been intently investigating one of the bare patches in the grass.

"Get over here," she demanded, because she needed companionship, and Mutt reluctantly acquiesced.

Susie closed the door behind them and leaned against it for a moment, cautiously testing, with antennae she hadn't known she possessed, the house's aura. Mutt crossed the kitchen, her toenails click-clicking against the linoleum, and disappeared around the corner that led to the living room.

There were a few dishes in the draining rack. A bottle of plant fertilizer sat on the counter next to an empty pitcher. Lined up beside the sink were four small vials containing medications.

Susie decided that the ambience she felt was benign, and was soon able to move from the door. She opened the fridge: two apples in the fruit drawer, four baking potatoes in the vegetable drawer, some eggs, some moldy cheddar, a quart of milk that smelled bad, a half-eaten casserole, some bread. She'd have to clean out this fridge. She'd have to clean out the whole house.

Mutt barked from the living room, and Susie joined her there. The dog had jumped onto the recliner and was standing on her hind legs, her front paws on the back of the chair, barking at something through the window. Birds. Crows. A swarm of them (a gathering? thought Susie. Or is that ravens?).

She turned and folded her arms protectively across her chest, looking down at the floor, imagining the mailman coming in here with a bag of letters slung over his shoulder. Of course he wouldn't have brought his bag with him — he'd have left it in his truck — but that was the image in Susie's mind. One look at her mother lying there dead and he'd have flung up his hands and the bag would have slid from his shoulder and fallen to the floor, spilling mail every which way. So vivid was this image in Susie's mind that she glanced involuntarily left and right, looking for scattered envelopes.

She had expected to feel at least wistful, if not nostalgic, standing again in what had once been her home. But it had been home too long ago. Her former bedroom had decades earlier been transformed into her mother's sewing room. There was no longer anything here that felt to Susie like home.

Soon she made her way upstairs. The carpeting on the stairway was soiled. The paint was chipped. The wallpaper in the hallway had begun to peel back from the edges. There were layers of dust, and cobwebs in most of the corners. But in the first room she entered, Susie discovered that Leigh-Anne had been right.

The room was a small office, dusty and obviously not recently used. Susie looked in desk drawers and shuffled through folders in a filing cabinet, and soon found a folder marked *SUSIE: FOR AFTER MY DEATH*.

Dear Susie, said the letter inside, which was dated three years earlier. *My will is with Bill Sampson. Please don't bury me. I want to be cremated, and then maybe you'd scatter my ashes where my rosebushes used to be. I don't want to have a funeral because although I started off in this life as a religious person I've changed my mind about a lot of things along the way. And I don't want to have one of those memorial services either. Just put a dignified announcement in the paper that says I've died.*

I don't have much to leave you — only the house, and what's in it. I expect you'll sell the place.

I love you, and I wish I'd seen more of you and Leigh-Anne. But I've been happy here. I have no regrets.

Mutt was barking again, still trying to chase away the crows.

Susie folded the letter and put it in the pocket of her dress. She would go directly to the hospital now, and then to the funeral parlor, and then to Bill Sampson's office.

She was very grateful to her mother, and left the house with a heart that was almost light.

"These things can be done quite quickly, as it turns out," she said that evening on the phone to Leigh-Anne. "I'll be able to scatter the ashes in a couple of days."

Mutt was at the door of the motel room, looking patiently from the door to Susie and back again.

"But the house," Susie went on. "That's going to take longer. I plan to clean out the fridge tomorrow and run a dust rag and the vacuum cleaner over the place. But I find that I don't want to sort through all her belongings. Not yet. I'm just not up to it."

"Don't do it, then," said Leigh-Anne. "There's no hurry. Go back when you're ready. Maybe I'll be able to go with you."

"Yes," said Susie, relieved. "That would be good, Leigh-Anne. That's what I'll do."

"I want to be there when you do the scattering," said Leigh-Anne.

"Good heavens. Why?"

"Why? For god's sake, Mother, she was my grandmother."

"I know, but —"

"It doesn't matter that I hardly knew her. She was my grandmother. You and I, we're all she's got."

Susie, watching Mutt, who was now scratching impatiently at the door, felt a cool stroking upon her forehead. She held her breath for a moment, concentrating. Then, "You're right, Leigh-Anne," she said. "Come tomorrow."

Two days later Susie and Leigh-Anne stood in the backyard of Susie's mother's house. Susie was holding a cherrywood urn. They were both dressed for the occasion, Leigh-Anne in a gray suit that Susie had always admired, and Susie herself in the closest thing she owned to something black, the blue dress with narrow white stripes.

Mutt was inside the house, because Leigh-Anne had been afraid the dog would chase the ashes when they were scattered, getting them all over herself.

The once lush rose garden had become a parody of itself, consisting mostly of dead but still thorny stalks. Two bushes struggled to survive; most of their leaves had fallen to the ground, and those that remained were covered with black and yellow splotches.

"It must have been beautiful, once," said Leigh-Anne.

Houses had pressed up against the property from both sides. When Susie was a child there had been woods there, which she had spent hours exploring with her best friend. They had found trilliums in the spring, wild strawberries in the summer, autumn apples in an abandoned orchard.

And once, a nest of kittens in a hayloft in a deserted barn: Susie still remembered it vividly. A shaft of sunlight fell through the opening high in the wall, creating a warm pool of radiance in the hay, and in it the kittens pounced and played and languorously stretched, while from a distance, in the shadows, their mother kept a watchful eye on the kittens and on the two children who huddled together at the top of the ladder.

Susie's father had died two years earlier. It was this moment with the kittens that persuaded her that although that loss was indeed a tragedy, and her life would indeed never be the same again, it would not be less than it had been — only different. That she would continue to experience joy as well as grief; wonderment and wisdom and understanding, as well as bitterness and confusion. That between Life and Death there was a benevolent collusion that Susie couldn't yet comprehend. She knew all that, looking at the kittens awash in the golden sunlight.

"Mom?" said Leigh-Anne, a gentle prompting.

"She always wanted to be a teacher," said Susie, gazing at the lamentable roses. "That's what she told me, anyway."

"Why didn't it happen?" said Leigh-Anne.

"Her parents couldn't afford to send her to university. Or normal school or whatever it was." She had been sent to a secretarial school instead. "I was always disappointed that she showed no interest in your work. I thought she'd be proud that her granddaughter had done what she had wanted to do."

Leigh-Anne shifted her bag higher up on her shoulder. She was becoming impatient. Susie, too, wanted to get the scattering over and done with; she didn't know why she was putting it off.

"What did *you* want to do, Mom?" said Leigh-Anne.

"I wanted to be safe." Having said this, quickly, without reflection, Susie looked at her daughter in astonishment, and blinked.

They were facing each other across the old rose garden. Susie wanted to reach over the misshapen blooms, the diseased bushes, and clasp Leigh-Anne's hand tightly. But it was too far. And Leigh-Anne wouldn't welcome the gesture, anyway, Susie saw this in her face, which had become remote.

"Did you call Grandmother on the day Dad left?"

Susie felt ambushed. Her mind scrambled to find an escape. Looking helplessly at her daughter, she finally accepted defeat — but even as she did so she saw a way out and squirmed toward it, a tiny opening in this dreadful situation. She could get out of it. Yes. Of course she could. She could lie her way out.

She clung to the urn with both hands, turning it in her palms, warming it, or perhaps it was warming her, she wasn't sure.

"No," she said. At first her voice was hardly there. It was less than a whisper, smaller than a murmur. But as she continued to speak it became stronger. "No, I didn't call her. I waited until the next time she called me. And then I told her. She said she wasn't surprised." Susie rubbed her arms and listened for a moment to the birds chuckling in the cedars at the bottom of the yard. "I can't tell you why he left. But you asked me once about the day he left. I can tell you that."

"Yes," said Leigh-Anne. "Please."

Susie put the urn down on the grass and brushed her hands together, ridding herself of that day even as she prepared to give a mendacious account of it. "It was mid-afternoon. You were asleep, sick with the mumps. I went into our bedroom for something and found him sitting on the edge of the bed."

She recited this like it was something memorized, and sounded to her own ears like an automaton.

"His head was bowed. I hadn't known he was there. I think I hadn't even known he was in the house. I was startled to see him, and I said, 'What's wrong, Buddy — is something wrong?' "

She was suddenly so nauseated she thought she was going to vomit. But I'm already vomiting, aren't I? she thought. Puking up a bunch of lies to tell my daughter . . . She glanced at Leigh-Anne, whose expression, though apprehensive, was also rapt.

Susie went on. "He looked up at me. And there was such absolute bleakness in his face. 'I can't do it,' he said, and tears started rolling down his cheeks." Well, that part was true, anyway, thought Susie grimly, and she struggled on. "'Can't do what?' I asked him. He didn't say anything for a long time. Then he got up and came over to me, moving like he was very old, or very ill, and he was neither, and he put his arms around me and whispered in my ear, 'I can't be married. I can't be a father.'"

Susie discovered that she was weeping. Good god, what have I done, she thought. And then Leigh-Anne was next to her, rummaging in her shoulderbag for Kleenex. She tore out several tissues for Susie and several more for herself.

"Don't go on. I'm sorry, Mom."

"Well, I'm not," said Susie, wiping her face. "Let's get this show on the road." And she picked up the urn.

The ashes of her mother fluttered in the breeze, some landing in the old rose garden, the rest going every which way.

TWENTY-NINE

A month later, Susie sat at her kitchen table with the morning paper spread out in front of her.

"Police have identified Donna Theresa Decker as the victim of a fatal car crash that occurred Friday morning in North Vancouver.

"Decker, 36, died after her vehicle was struck head-on by a car driving the wrong way on Highway 1 near an area referred to as 'the cut,' west of the Second Narrows Bridge, RCMP said. The driver of the other car was taken to hospital with injuries not considered life-threatening. Police said the investigation continues."

"He was drunk," said Leigh-Anne on the telephone.

It was October. Eighteen months had passed since Susie and Arthur had met; almost two years since Leigh-Anne and Blair Decker had begun seeing each other.

"The guy was drunk," Leigh-Anne repeated.

The item was one of a row of brief stories that took up one vertical column: a series of small black eruptions, Susie thought, brusquely rolling down the page. Body found in dumpster. Man robbed at knifepoint. City church vandalized. Accident victim named. Susie was surprised that she'd noticed it. But she had, and it had caused her skin to prickle. She had read it over several times — and had finally registered the last name and connected it with Leigh-Anne's boyfriend. Yet it was a common enough name. Why had her skin prickled? Had she known, somehow, who the victim was?

"She was just out doing some errands," said Leigh-Anne. "She liked to drive. Blair says she said driving helped her think."

Leigh-Anne was crying, Susie realized. This didn't seem appropriate. They had never met, had they?

"There was nothing wrong with the road," said Leigh-Anne. "Or the car. Or the weather. There was just this — this criminal, this — jerk."

Susie glanced at Mutt, dozing in her basket. Susie's head was aching badly, and she had to move slowly, stiffly, so as not to make it worse.

"Blair is beside himself," said Leigh-Anne.

Susie mouthed the words: "Beside himself. Beside himself."

"Absolutely beside himself," said Leigh-Anne. "Oh, what's he told Samantha?"

Who? thought Susie. Told who?

"What's he going to do, Mom? What will he do now?"

Susie looked down at the newspaper. Her head was pounding relentlessly. She didn't remember the beginning of this headache. Maybe if she'd felt it coming on she could have taken something. But it was too late now. Ah — skullcracking pain. She narrowed her eyes against the morning light.

"And how can I help him?"

Listening to her daughter, Susie thought of the ragrance and succulence of ripe tropical fruit. Leigh-Anne's generosity to her lover, she knew, would be spontaneous and abundant.

She flattened her fingertips on the page of newsprint, smoothing the paper surrounding the announcement of Blair Decker's wife's death, not letting her flesh touch the words "Accident Victim Named." She was experiencing an extraordinary blend of grief and fear.

"Well, I don't know, Leigh-Anne," she said eventually, speaking over her daughter's muffled sobs. "I don't know what he's going to do."

Susie studied the sympathy cards in the grocery store that afternoon while doing her weekly shopping, picking them up one by one, reading their messages. She wouldn't send one, of course. She had met the man only once.

She wondered how much he was suffering. There must be some grief there, surely, even though they had been separated, about to divorce. Always, a residual tenderness existed between people who had been married, who had had a child together. Wasn't that true? Unless, of course, whatever had existed between them had turned to hatred. Susie hoped this hadn't been the case for Blair and his wife. She picked up another card, read it, replaced it. Even if she had been tempted to send him condolences, none of these cards were satisfactory.

She could write him a note, of course.

But she wouldn't. That would be inappropriate.

There was a funeral several days later that Leigh-Anne at first thought she might attend. "I could just stand at the back, I thought," she said to Susie. "Nobody else would know I was there. To give him my support, Mom."

"Don't be ridiculous," said Susie, cold and sharp like a trap snapping shut on Leigh-Anne's greedy fingers. "Leave them alone, for god's sake. He won't be the only one mourning her. How would they feel — her relatives, her friends — if they knew her husband's mistress was hanging about the funeral parlor?"

Leigh-Anne hung up without saying goodbye. Susie thought she had probably made her daughter cry. She imagined Leigh-Anne staring into her mirror, holding her reddened cheeks and watching tears trickle from her swollen eyes.

She didn't want to see Leigh-Anne these days. She was reluctant even to talk to her on the phone. Susie sensed an impatience in her daughter that made her uneasy. Yet when they did talk, Leigh-Anne was constrained enough.

"I've met her several times," said Leigh-Anne a few weeks later, "over this past summer. Samantha, I mean. She's a charming child, Mom."

"I'm sure she is," said Susie. "How did you meet her?"

"Oh, when Blair had her for weekends, sometimes I would go with them. To McDonald's. Or the park."

"How did he introduce you?" said Susie curiously.

"As a friend," said Leigh-Anne shortly.

"Hmmm."

"She's very bright, too," Leigh-Anne went on. "She's in kindergarten, and doing very well. But now she's very sad, of course. She misses her mother very much."

"Of course," said Susie. "She would."

"Do you think you'd like to meet her, Mom?"

"This is not your child, is what I think," said Susie grimly. "I think you're being extremely presumptuous, is what I think."

THIRTY

The day that was the beginning of the end was a beautiful day in late winter. A day that suggested spring. A day brimful of possibilities. And it should, in fact, have been a day of great joy.

Leigh-Anne had called Susie the previous evening, Friday, asking if she'd like to accompany her to Maple Ridge, where Leigh-Anne had an errand to run. Susie accepted eagerly, and with some relief. Leigh-Anne hadn't spent much time with her in the months since the death of Blair's wife, and although she was a dutiful telephoner her calls lately had been brief and distracted — a necessary concomitant to being in love and making plans for the future, Susie thought.

"Whose car shall we take?" she had said, but she was only being polite; they both knew what she thought of Leigh-Anne's driving.

On Saturday morning they set off, following Hastings Street east to the Barnet highway. The sky had been swept almost entirely clean of clouds by a strong, mild wind, except for the ones that were caught in the mountaintops on the northern and eastern horizons — mountaintops gleaming with snow that was backlit by a bright winter sun. The highway rolled and curved, and through the bare branches of the deciduous thickets that flanked the road, the deep blue wind-furrowed waters of Indian Arm flickered.

Susie regarded the landscape happily through her sunglasses. She loved wearing sunglasses. She felt enigmatic and provocative behind them, as if her head held many mysteries that a gleam in her eye might inadvertently divulge.

She glanced at Leigh-Anne as they drove through the town of Port Moody. "You're awfully quiet today," she said.

"Not really," said Leigh-Anne, looking out the side window.

"Let's have lunch somewhere," said Susie, "when you've done your errand."

"Sure," said Leigh-Anne.

Soon they were on the Lougheed Highway, which in this area was not much more than an endless succession of malls and car dealerships and fast food outlets. They passed Coquitlam Centre, and a couple of giant supermarkets, and when they reached the Pitt River Bridge Leigh-Anne said, "Turn off here, Mom. Let's go the back way."

The meadows held quivering pools of rainwater. The manes of grazing horses were tossed by the wind. The mountains were nearer now: Susie imagined that she could hear them breathing, and wondered, if she was to climb one, would she feel the beating of its heart beneath the soles of her sneakers? Fields of blueberry bushes stretched into the distance, their redness so pronounced that a rosy flush seemed to rise into the air above them and hover there trembling. It felt to Susie like spring.

"Pull over, Mom, will you?" said Leigh-Anne suddenly. "There, by the dike."

Susie pulled over obediently. It didn't occur to her to ask why — she just did it, pulled the car into a small parking area, which was empty except for a pickup truck, and turned expectantly toward Leigh-Anne. Who was sitting on her hands, staring out the windshield.

"Do you want to get out?" said Susie. "Walk along the dike?"

"I'm pregnant, Mom."

Swift as the swiftest bird, Susie uncoupled her seat belt and embraced her daughter. She pulled Leigh-Anne's head to her shoulder and rocked her, and stroked her cheek. "Are you all right?" she whispered.

Leigh-Anne nodded.

After a while she sat up and smiled at Susie, but her face was wet. Susie found a tissue in her jacket pocket and wiped Leigh-Anne's tears away, taking great care, patting her cheeks dry. Then she rubbed gently at the faint lines on Leigh-Anne's forehead and the brackets around her mouth. They were etched just below the surface of her skin. Ineradicable. But Susie had to try.

"My goodness," she said after a while. "My goodness," she said, wonder in her voice.

"Let's get out and walk," said Leigh-Anne, opening her door.

They climbed to the top of the dike and looked down upon a large pool of blue water, runoff from the Alouette River, that held quivering reflections of the leafless trees that clustered at its eastern border. The water was surrounded by a golden growth of dead weeds and grasses. A series of paths wound around the pond, disappearing into thick brush that stretched into the distance; beyond it, out of sight, flowed the Alouette. Far away, cultivated fields sprawled toward purple hills that were nudged from behind by white-crowned mountains.

"We should have brought Mutt," said Leigh-Anne, whose hair was whipping in the wind.

Susie adjusted her sunglasses. I'm going to wear these all the time, she decided, shivering.

They trudged on, Leigh-Anne's hair flying behind her. Then the wind tripped on itself and reversed direction, and her hair wrapped around her head, obscuring her face. She took hold of it and pulled it back behind her head, stuffing it down inside her jacket. She led Susie down from the dike onto a path that meandered through shoulder-high scrub. Susie didn't know what it was, but admired it anyway, some of it red like the bark of arbutus trees, some of it golden like wheat.

"When is it due?" she asked.

"August," said Leigh-Anne.

"A summer baby." Susie began to feel a thrillingness like nothing she had experienced before. She grabbed Leigh-Anne's shoulder and turned her around and threw her arms around her, hugging her fiercely.

Leigh-Anne's face was flushed and her eyes were so bright Susie thought she probably wouldn't have been able to look right at them if she hadn't been wearing her sunglasses.

"But Mom," said Leigh-Anne. "I can't do it."

"Can't do what?"

"Have a baby."

Susie stepped back. "Can't . . . Why? Is there something wrong?" She moved close to Leigh-Anne again, touching her arm. "Is something wrong with you? With the baby?"

"It isn't a baby, Mom," said Leigh-Anne querulously. "It's barely even a fetus. It's an embryo, is what it is."

Susie clasped her hands in front of her. She looked hard at Leigh-Anne, waiting for clarification. But Leigh-Anne was silent, shivering, her arms wrapped around her.

Susie removed her sunglasses and put them in her jacket pocket. She looked up the path, beyond Leigh-Anne, and back over her shoulder, in the direction from which they had come, but saw nobody else. She wondered where the driver of the pickup was. She wondered where the children were. This place ought to be crowded, she thought, on a Saturday, with adults in winter jackets, and children running on ahead, and dogs on leashes.

"I'm going back to the car," she said abruptly, and turned, heading for the parking lot.

She walked hurriedly, trying to put distance between herself and Leigh-Anne, trying to ease the sudden exacting ache behind her ribs. She thought Leigh-Anne began to speak but by then Susie was far away and the wind was sweeping her daughter's words, whatever they may have been, toward the eastern horizon.

Susie climbed back up to the dike, scurried along it and down into the parking lot. She was breathless by the time she reached her car.

She sat behind the wheel and waited for Leigh-Anne, trying to calm herself but unable to do so. Things were clashing in her head. She wanted to cry out, like a befuddled figure in a fairy tale . . . Where on earth had that notion come from? she wondered, dazed, as Leigh-Anne got into the car and slammed the door.

They sat in silence for several moments. Wind occasionally buffeted the car. The clouds caught in the mountaintops had freed themselves and were scudding giddily across the sky. On one of the posts holding up a barbed wire fence that angled across one side of the parking lot someone had tacked a sign that read, Border Collie LOST on New Year's Eve, and a telephone number.

"This has been a devastating time for Blair, Mom," said Leigh-Anne, and Susie almost jumped, so unexpected was the sound of her daughter's voice. "He just isn't ready to commit again. Not yet."

"Commit?" said Susie, incredulous.

"We're going to get married," Leigh-Anne went on doggedly. "But this isn't the way to start off together. He's already got one child. And she needs him. Very much."

"There are people," said Susie, struggling, "lots of people, I believe, looking for babies to adopt."

Leigh-Anne sighed and looked out the side window, and said nothing.

After a while Susie started the car and drove them home.

THIRTY-ONE

Susie didn't go to work on the day of Leigh-Anne's abortion. She took the time off for what she described to her boss as personal business and stayed home, waiting for the hours to pass. Sometime during the evening, when she knew Leigh-Anne would have returned from the hospital, she would phone her to confirm that the awful thing had really happened. But all day long she waited — she couldn't help it — she waited for *Leigh-Anne* to call *her*. "It's me, Mom," Leigh-Anne would say. "I didn't go. You're right. And I changed my mind."

Susie imagined this conversation so often she could almost believe she wasn't making it up but recalling it.

As the day passed she also found herself praying, or rather, whispering to the god in whom she did not believe — making promises, trying to cut a deal. "Please," she said, aware of her lips moving, aware of the word escaping from her mouth in almost soundless puffs, "Please . . ."

Leigh-Anne had been adamant. Blair wasn't yet ready to marry again, and she wasn't about to endure pregnancy and childbirth only to give her child away to strangers.

Susie had offered to raise the baby herself, and wouldn't soon forget the expression of impatience and distaste that had winkled then across Leigh-Anne's face. "Don't be ridiculous, Mother" is what she'd said. "You don't want to be a single mother twice in your life."

"Well, what about you?" said Susie. "I did it. Your grandmother did it. You can do it, too, if you have to. You don't have to be married to have this child."

"I don't *want* to, Mother. It isn't something to be *proud* of, you know, bringing a child up alone. It isn't a *good* thing, to grow up without a father. I have no intention of thrusting any child of mine into that situation."

Susie knew it wasn't a human being yet, the tiny creature growing in Leigh-Anne's smooth, flat belly.

She had for years been a proponent of abortion. She believed absolutely in a woman's right to choose. And now she was ashamed that her point of view had shifted so radically, simply because it was her grandchild that was about to be refused life.

She had struggled mightily with her dilemma, trying to reconcile her philosophical conviction with her personal circumstances. But she couldn't. And finally she had given up.

Yes, she believed that every woman had the right to say, "No, I do not want this child." And yes, this included Leigh-Anne. But Susie would nonetheless do everything possible to change her daughter's mind. She argued. She cajoled. She pleaded. She demanded. She became angry. Shamelessly, she even wept.

"Stop it!" Leigh-Anne shouted into the phone. "I can't take this any more. Please. I do *not* want to *have* this child, why can't you get that through your head?"

She stopped taking Susie's calls then, and began refusing to buzz Susie into her apartment.

And still Susie didn't give up hope. She reviewed in her head the arguments she had presented, some of them informed by logic, some by passion. Perhaps one of them had taken root after all, in Leigh-Anne's mind, or heart. She would have to wait and see.

She decided that when the day came she would spend the time doing something useful while she waited. She could give the kitchen a good cleaning. Wash the living-room curtains. Or winnow through her closet, creating a pile of clothes to be given away.

In the end she sat at the kitchen table, or on the sofa, drinking endless cups of tea, doing nothing, with the television on for company.

Outside, the world was gray and sodden. Mutt ventured through the dog door only twice, and each time came quickly back inside, where she shook herself vigorously, scattering raindrops, before jumping back up on the sofa to snuggle uncharacteristically close to Susie.

"Please," said Susie again, to her indifferent deity. "Please . . . I'll do anything."

Sometime during that long, long day she thought again of Buddy. Would he have sided with her? Or with Leigh-Anne? She couldn't remember whether they'd ever discussed abortion, she and Buddy.

She had gradually come to believe that it was time to give Leigh-Anne the facts about her father, and why he had left them. Leigh-Anne had Blair now. He could help her hear the painful truth, and learn to accept it. And Susie's mother was dead now. That had something to do with it, too.

Susie felt good about this, for now, along with the bad thing, she could tell her daughter all the other truths about Buddy. The things that had caused Susie to love him in the first place. The things that had caused Leigh-Anne, treasuring her few memories of him, modest and blurry though they were, to stubbornly love him in absentia.

She had been sitting in front of the television set for some time before she realized that her tea was cold and the room was dark. She got up to turn on some lights, pull the curtains closed and deposit her teacup in the kitchen sink.

She fed Mutt, and decided that Leigh-Anne must be home by now. She was holding the telephone receiver when there was a knock on her front door.

Mutt raced into the hall, barking, and Susie put the phone down.

She remembered this later, very clearly — remembered shifting the receiver in her hand and placing it back in the cradle, then stroking it with her fingertips as if reluctant to relinquish it. It was a black phone with rows of gray buttons. If she hadn't answered the door, she thought later; if she had ignored the knocking and kept on doing what she had been doing, which was telephoning Leigh-Anne, maybe everything would have been different.

She went to the door, shushing Mutt, who was still barking, and opened it.

Blair Decker stood on her porch. Susie looked past him, but he was alone, and the car parked under the streetlamp in front of her house was empty.

"Mrs. Wilson. I'm so sorry."

Susie hung on tightly, her right hand clasping the knob, her left clutching the doorframe. Slowly, she shook her head.

"I'm so terribly sorry. Something went wrong." His voice trembled, like rain in the wind.

Susie shook her head again, and closed her eyes.

"She died, Mrs. Wilson. They said — It's called angioedema. If she'd waited at the hospital a little longer . . . May I come in?" He stepped inside and closed the door.

Susie took several steps backward, then turned and retreated down the hall. Blair Decker followed, with Mutt snuffling at his trouser legs.

In the living room, Susie sat on the edge of the sofa.

"It would have been treatable," he said, "if she'd stayed at the hospital. It's a thing — it's rare, very rare."

"What happened?"

He was still standing, his hands hanging loose at his sides. "I took her home. I was going to stay with her, overnight, to make sure she was okay."

"What happened?"

"Her tongue started to swell. We didn't know what to do. I phoned the hospital. She — she was having trouble breathing."

He spoke quietly, almost with resignation. Like some kind of detached official type person, Susie thought.

"They told me to take her back there right away." He stopped talking, as if there were nothing more to say, or he'd run out of words. Then he went on. "We didn't get there in time." He stopped again.

Susie, looking at her hands clasped tightly in her lap, waited.

"The swelling got worse and worse." He looked at her pleadingly. "It was horrible." Again, he hesitated. "She suffocated."

"Where is she?"

"She's still there. At the hospital. I thought — I assumed that you'd want to make the arrangements."

"It might be a mistake," said Susie, fingering the hem of the yellow tunic she wore over a long denim skirt. "It could be a mistake. She might have recovered. After you left."

"No," said Blair Decker. "I'm sorry."

He was still standing awkwardly in the middle of the living room, dripping rain upon the carpet. Susie thought he looked like he ought to be holding a hat, turning it around and around in his useless hands.

"I can't believe this," said Susie. Mutt abandoned her investigation of Blair Decker's shoes and jumped up onto the sofa. "It can't be true."

But she knew it was. She knew that later, in the dark, lying in her bed, she would go over and over this day in her mind, trying to identify the moment at which it had happened, the moment when her lovely, pliant daughter had been lost to her.

"I'm so sorry," said Blair Decker once more.

Susie looked at his face, searching. She found nothing. "Why wouldn't you marry her?" she said.

He flushed. "I — it wasn't . . ."

"If you'd been married, she would have had the baby." She was unaware of her tears. "What was wrong with her that you wouldn't marry her?"

And as long as she would live, Susie would never forgive herself for those words.

"If there's anything I can do," said Blair Decker quietly, after a moment, "please call me." He took a business card from an inside pocket of his jacket and held it out to her.

Susie watched him walk slowly toward the hall. "You never did leave your wife, did you," she said.

He stopped, but didn't turn to face her.

"Did you tell Leigh-Anne you'd left her?"

He shook his head. Susie couldn't tell if this was disavowal or confession.

She stayed where she was until he had driven away. Then she closed the door and went to the telephone. She couldn't get through this alone.

One week later Susie and Arthur were sitting on her sofa, side by side. Her head was on his shoulder and he was stroking her hair. Leigh-Anne had just been buried, in a sprawling cemetery in Burnaby. Susie didn't know if she would have wanted this or not. It had been suggested to her by several people, including Arthur, that Leigh-Anne might have preferred cremation.

But Susie needed to be able to go to a place where Leigh-Anne was. And so she had buried her. There would be a brass plaque that would have her name inscribed on it, along with the dates of her birth and death. Susie wouldn't be able to plant anything there, like a rose bush or a lilac tree, but she could put cut flowers in a vase that would be embedded in the grass next to the grave. And kneel there, and have imaginary conversations with her daughter.

She thought she must still be in shock. It was certain that she was inhabiting a hostile landscape, bleak and cold. Was this to be permanent? she wondered. Had she moved forever from a reasonably benevolent world, a world with Leigh-Anne in it, into this desolate society? She must have said something to this effect aloud, for Arthur responded.

"You lived before Leigh-Anne came along," he said, stroking her hair. "You were happy then, weren't you?"

Susie grappled with this concept. "I can't remember."

Arthur shifted slightly, causing Mutt, lying in her bed, to lift her head and growl. "That damn dog," said Arthur, and right away he gave Susie's shoulders a quick squeeze. "You'd think he'd be used to me by now," he said, by way of apology.

"She," said Susie. "Mutt's a female dog. How often do I have to tell you that?"

They sat like this a little longer, Susie resting quietly. Her body rested, that is. Her mind didn't. It continued to work hard, trying to put the world to rights again.

"You should go see him," said Arthur.

"See who?"

"That Blair guy. The one who's responsible."

He had sent flowers, but he hadn't come to the funeral. He hadn't wanted to intrude, that's what the card had said.

"I never want to lay eyes upon that man again," said Susie. She heard the sharpness in her voice, and the steel, and wanted to transform her words into a weapon and drive it through his heart.

She wished she hadn't let him into her house, the day he came to tell her that Leigh-Anne was dead. She wished she'd made him spew out that ugly, unimaginable message while standing on her porch, shivering, with rain dripping down the back of his neck. She hated the idea that he had stood right here, in her living room, contaminating her environment with his presence, with his breath.

"You should make demands," said Arthur, absently kissing her hair. "He owes you."

"He owes me what," said Susie bitterly. "A daughter?"

Two weeks later, Susie pulled up in front of her house after work. She turned off the engine. She removed the key from the ignition. She collected her handbag from the passenger seat. And then she noticed that her front gate was standing open.

She swept her gaze across the street and saw Mutt standing in a neighbor's yard. Susie got out of her car and started to cross the road. "Mutt!" she called. "Mutt, come!"

The dog turned to look at her, cocked her head as if considering the situation, then began running toward her. Susie, who was now on the sidewalk in front of the neighbor's house, almost directly across from her own, clapped her hands encouragingly. But when Mutt came near, she suddenly swerved and ran into the street, where she stopped and faced Susie again, her forelegs flat on the pavement, her back end high in the air. It looked to Susie as if Mutt were laughing at her, black eyes gleaming from behind errant chunks of hair.

A car was coming, and Susie screamed at Mutt, who started trotting toward her.

"Go home!" Susie shouted.

But Mutt, bewildered, stopped in her tracks.

The car struck her in the hindquarters and kept on going. Mutt staggered, fell, then got up and weaved across the street and into Susie's front yard.

She collapsed on the grass, and looked up at Susie with clouded eyes.

"No!" said Susie sternly, crouched next to the dog, weeping. "Mutt, no!"

But Mutt, disobeying, died.

"He owes you," Arthur had said.

"He owes me what?" Susie had replied. "A daughter?"

Yes, she decided that night, lying sleepless in her bed, lying dry-eyed in her bed, Mutt's empty basket on the floor next to her.

Yes.

Blair Decker owed her a daughter.

PART THREE
THE PRESENT

THIRTY-TWO

It was very early on the day after Samantha's disappearance. Eddie Henderson was at her desk in the office that had been Karl Alberg's, and the black leather chair that Sid Sokolowski used to sit in was occupied today by Frank Turner. Norah Gibbons had dragged a metal chair in from the interview room.

Norah said, "Man, I knew there was a good reason I never got married." Her face looked folded in on itself, etched with weariness. "You have kids, then you gotta worry about this kind of shit happening to them."

The window was open, and the venetian blind had been pulled as high as it would go. Eddie's stomach was grumbling but she couldn't have eaten anything. "When does the air search get under way?" she asked Frank.

"They said first light, so they'll already be at it." He leaned forward, resting his arms on his thighs, and gave his head a shake. "Jesus, I'm tired. Must be getting old."

"No," said Eddie. "You wouldn't be tired if we'd found her." She was holding a mug half full of dark, thick coffee that had gotten cold. There were grimy streaks around the interior. Eddie set it down on the desk, next to the blotter, and pushed it away from her.

"Okay," said Frank dully. "What now?" The scar that zigzagged across his forehead and halfway down his left cheek looked whiter than usual against his already pale, freckled skin.

Eddie flicked back to the first page in her notebook. "This was a regular, routine thing, right? The kid going to the library."

"Almost a daily occurrence," said Norah. "Early afternoon. Right after the lunch dishes."

"She's been here, how long?" said Frank, looking up from the floor. "A couple of weeks?"

"Two and a half," said Eddie.

"And she's almost six. Thinks she's a big girl. She knows the place now, she can find her own way." He glanced at Gibbons. "I've got kids. Three of them." Eddie watched as he touched his scar, tracing it delicately with a fingertip. He did it again, and again. "She's doesn't even think about whether it's safe out there. She knows it's safe. Nothing bad's ever happened to her."

"Her mother died," said Norah.

"That's different."

"What's your point?" said Eddie.

"Somebody's snatched her."

"Yeah," said Eddie. "Somebody has." She remembered sitting in the black leather chair watching Alberg make stick men out of paperclips. She glanced at the desk blotter, where a column of inch-high stick men marched in perpetuity completely around the edge. A second column, inked-in just below the first, covered the top and halfway down one side.

"We already knew that," said Norah.

"Not for sure," said Eddie. "But we know it now, because we haven't found her." Teams of officers, on- and off-duty, had been joined by civilian volunteers to scour Sechelt street by street, lane by lane. They had done so throughout the night and into the tender light of the new day's beginning. "We would have found her," said Eddie, "if she'd just been lost." She knew that the wider search being conducted now was more likely to find the child dead than alive. "And why do kids get snatched?" she said.

"Sex," said Frank.

"Money," said Norah.

"If some pervert's got her," said Turner, "he'll use her and lose her. Dump the body somewhere. Maybe take the trouble to bury it. Eventually it'll be found. But it might take a while."

"But if she's been taken for ransom, we're going to know soon," said Eddie. "They might want to wait until the search is over, let the relatives suffer for a while, so that when they're told she's still alive they'll be so grateful they'll want to cooperate. But they'll be in touch within forty-eight hours, I bet."

"The guy's not rich, though, is he? How much could he raise?" said Norah.

"Not much." Eddie thumbed through her notebook. "The sister says if they gave him time to take out a second mortgage —"

"Jesus," said Frank. "Dream on."

"— he could probably come up with a couple hundred thousand in total."

"Huh," said Frank. "Well, there's plenty of people out there desperate enough to snatch a kid for two hundred thousand bucks."

"It doesn't seem likely, though, does it?" said Eddie. "You're right, they're not going to give him a lot of time. And if they researched how to grab the kid, they also researched her father. They'll know all about his finances."

"When's he getting in?" asked Norah.

"About five this afternoon," said Eddie.

"Maybe we'll have some news for him by then," Norah said.

Eddie pushed back her chair and went to the window. The sky was the clear blue of a robin's egg. A straggly row of yellow tulips bloomed valiantly along the chain-link fence that encircled the detachment parking lot. The breeze drifting through the window was already warm, and she lifted her chin slightly, encouraging it to stroke her cheek. "So we've got both land and air searches in progress," she said.

"And Lattimer's got a team checking the water," said Turner. "Boats in the area, people on the beaches who might've spotted something."

"Right," said Eddie. "And house-to-house interviews have been done. And the child's picture's gone out to all the news outlets, here and on the mainland and on the Island. Right?" She went back behind her desk, standing in front of the chair, drumming her fingers on the desktop.

"Right," said Gibbons.

"And the ferries've been covered, too," said Frank. "Trouble with that, of course —"

"Yeah, don't say it," said Eddie. "They could have gotten her on a ferry before anybody ever knew she was missing. She could be anywhere by now. Shit." She sat down. "If she's off the peninsula, it's out of our hands. I think we should assume she's still here. Somewhere."

"Alive?" said Norah, doubtful.

"Alive," said Eddie firmly. "And you know why? Do you?"

They shrugged.

"Because if we don't, then we've got nothing to do but sit around twiddling our damn thumbs until somebody somewhere finds the kid's body. And I don't know about you guys, but that certainly doesn't appeal to me." She opened her notebook to a blank page. "Abduction for abuse, ransom, or nurture. Find out who on the peninsula lost a baby recently, or was refused an adoption," she said, scribbling.

"That'll be me, I take it?" said Norah. "Being the woman and all?"

"We've got no time for that kind of crap, Norah," said Eddie.

"Yeah. Okay. Sorry."

"And, optimist that I am," said Eddie to Frank, "I still have a little bit of hope that she's just lost, and we missed her last night, because she was sleeping under some damn bush. I want the route she took hit again. The residences, too. Maybe she crept into somebody's crawl space."

"Got it."

"And we're going to widen the house-to-house around the Murchison place and the library," Eddie went on.

"I'll take care of that, too," said Frank.

"I don't want people asked only about yesterday," said Eddie. "I want to know if anybody's noticed anything unusual — anything at all — over the past two or three weeks. Because if this was a planned abduction, he must've been scouting her."

"Maybe in West Van, too," said Turner. "I know the boys over there checked out the house, but maybe we should get them to talk to the neighbors."

Eddie nodded. "Couldn't hurt. Why not?"

"Sure," said Norah, stretching her arms above her head. "She might turn up there. I mean, dogs find their way home, after all." She looked from Eddie to Frank. "Just trying to lighten things up."

Eddie closed her notebook. "I'll talk to the father as soon as he gets here. See if he knows anything that can help us. Find out if he'll do a public appeal with the mainland TV stations. And I'd like to talk to the other kid again, too — the cousin." She sat back. "Okay. Get your guys launched, then grab yourselves something to eat and a few hours' sleep. And let's get together this evening to compare notes."

They stood up, their chairs scraping the floor.

"It's probably a make-work project, all of it," said Norah. "But what the hell."

When they had left, Eddie closed her eyes and slumped in her chair. She sat quietly for a few moments,

letting the faint sounds of a spring morning that drift-
ed in through the window take precedence over everything else, trying to identify them, constructing expla-
nations when she had to. Bird chatter was easy. Passing
traffic, too. Then there was the sudden wail of a young
child — but it could also have been a dog howling,
thought Eddie, who had little acquaintance with either
children or dogs. Next, a curious noise that was both
fast and labored — somebody cycling, hard, along the
sidewalk?

She sighed, opened her eyes and linked her hands
behind her neck. Tendrils of a headache were gathering.
Readying for an assault she figured would occur directly
behind her forehead. She needed to go home for a while.
Brush her hair. Have a shower. Change her clothes. Eat
something. Maybe by the time she had showered and
changed she would actually *feel* like eating.

At home, she pulled the bedroom curtains closed,
stripped to her panties, and dropped into bed.

Three hours later she was woken by the ringing telephone, but when she answered it, there was nobody
there. She called the detachment.

"Did you just phone me?" she asked Isabella.

"Nope."

"Any news?"

"About the missing girl, you mean? No. But they're
still looking, aren't they?"

"Of course they are." Cautiously, Eddie moved her
head from side to side. No pain. Sleep had dispelled the
fragments of headache. "I'll be in about noon. Maybe a
little later."

She freed her thick hair from its braid and brushed
hard, bending from the waist, then stepped into the
shower.

Lathered, scrubbed, and rinsed, her freshly sham-
pooed hair coursing down her back, she lingered for a

while under the stream of hot water, turning slowly, until she felt stroked and burnished.

Then she rebraided her damp hair and settled on the living-room sofa with a glass of orange juice and her work diary, which needed bringing up to date.

GIS — the General Investigation Section, headquartered in Vancouver — would have to take over eventually. She knew this. And by the time it happened she would be glad of it — she knew this, too: they were the experts, after all. But Eddie devoutly hoped they would end up not needing them. She wanted the men and women in her detachment to bring the matter to a close — a successful close — all by themselves. She noted all this in her diary, then put the pen down and shook her hands, trying to loosen the tension that was causing her to write jerkily, the words on the page sprawled and splayed instead of placed there neatly by a person fully in control of her pen and her world.

She thought about the child a lot. She would try to imagine where she might be. She would imagine her looking from a window somewhere, and hope that the sunshine was bringing her solace.

She started wondering again what condition Samantha was in. She summoned the child's face . . . and there it was, in close-up, there were tears on her cheeks, her eyes were squeezed shut and her mouth was open and Eddie thought she was screaming.

Eddie dropped the diary and went to the window. She put her clenched hands in the pockets of her pink terrycloth robe and took several slow breaths, standing straight and tall, breathing deeply, until she was slightly dizzy, until she was aware of the blood coursing through her veins and she felt strong again.

Kidnapping for sex, for money, or for nurture, she thought. We've got it covered. We're doing all that can be done. Shape up, for chrissake, she told herself. And get back to work.

After replacing the diary in her night table, Eddie tossed laundry into the washing machine and loaded up the dishwasher that had been a Christmas gift from her father. She had thought it an unnecessary luxury at the time — but no longer. Then she dressed in a fresh uniform — navy pants with the yellow stripe down the leg, short-sleeved light brown shirt, the belt with all the paraphernalia — locked up her house and drove away, catching in the rearview mirror a glimpse of her primrose yellow house with the blue trim.

At the beachside restaurant that was by default her favorite, Eddie ordered an omelet with fries and opened her notebook. As she ate, she made notes for the upcoming interview with Samantha Decker's father.

THIRTY-THREE

"I've told him everything you've done," said Harriet Murchison when Eddie arrived at the house late that afternoon. "Everything everybody's done. How you've looked everywhere for her. How people brought food." She was wearing the same clothes she'd had on the day before. Her face looked pale, and her eyes were puffy. "They did that when Richard died. My husband. Everybody brought food." She looked over her shoulder and lowered her voice. "At least it's good that — that nobody's found her body. That's a good sign, isn't it?"

"Of course it is," said Eddie warmly. She reached out to squeeze Harriet's hand. "Hang in there."

Tears leapt immediately into the woman's eyes but she ignored them and stepped back so that Eddie could enter. "Blair," she called. "Sergeant Henderson's here."

They began their conversation in the living room. Harriet sat in the rocking chair, listening. Eleanor was nowhere to be seen. Eddie wondered if she was still at school — and remembered why the child had looked familiar: she had been one of the kids in the class Eddie had talked to in the fall.

Blair Decker was full of questions that Eddie answered patiently, waiting her turn. He paced incessantly. Eddie craned her neck trying to keep him within view. He walked up and down the living room and sometimes through the doorway into the kitchen and back, and sometimes out into the hall, and then he disappeared entirely. Harriet, catching her eye, gave Eddie a rueful shrug.

Finally, "Mr. Decker. Mr. Decker?"

He emerged from the hall, still pacing, his hands behind his back.

"Let's go for a walk," said Eddie, standing up.

He looked startled, then relieved, and headed instantly for the front door.

"We won't be long," Eddie told Harriet.

"I'll put on some coffee," said Harriet. "Or I've got a jug of iced tea in the fridge."

"That'll be great," said Eddie, following Blair Decker.

He was halfway to the gate and once through it, began power walking up the street.

Eddie stopped and watched him. "Hey," she called. He turned, surprised to find her so far behind. "Slow down a bit, okay?"

"Sorry," he said.

His face was deeply lined. It looked to Eddie like crumpled sandpaper. His feet and hands were in constant motion. Even ostensibly standing still, waiting for her to catch up with him, he was lifting his feet and swinging his arms, moving helplessly and without purpose. He wore an expression that was equal parts grief and bewilderment. As she approached him she noticed that his clothes were loose, that he'd had to cinch his belt smaller than when it was new: the man had lost weight, too much for it to have happened in the last twenty hours.

Blair Decker put both hands through his hair, watching Eddie but not really seeing her. Seeing something, though. Eddie didn't know what, but it was nothing good.

"Sorry," he said again as she joined him, notebook in hand.

"Tell me about your daughter, Mr. Decker," said Eddie, establishing a pace that was neither fast nor slow.

A woman wearing a large straw hat was weeding a flower bed in a front garden. She sat back on her heels and watched as they set out. Eddie moved into her head for a moment, to see what she was seeing: a tall, well-built policewoman wearing her cap on her head and a holstered 9mm automatic on her hip, walking down the block accompanied by an obviously distracted man clad in Hawaiian shirt and surfer shorts. Ah well, she thought — Sechelt has probably seen odder sights.

"She's — she's five years old," said Decker. "Almost six. She's — uh — got short hair, blonde, and blue eyes. She's chubby, you know, like a, like a little, little girl." He stopped and lowered his head, pressing his fingertips into his forehead. "She could still be lost, couldn't she? Harriet said you looked everywhere. But did you? Are you sure?" His voice was deep and husky, probably made huskier by exhaustion and anxiety.

"We're still looking, Mr. Decker," said Eddie. "But I'm afraid that if she were just lost, we would have found her by now."

He took her by the shoulders, gently, almost apologetically. Eddie permitted him to do this. But she was aware of an unforgiving strength in his grip. "Who's got her, then?" he said. "And why?"

"That's what we're trying to find out, Mr. Decker."

He was staring intently into her eyes. Eddie could feel — and smell — his dusty, musty breath on her face. Two teenage boys throwing a football back and forth down the middle of the street stopped to watch them. Eddie stepped back, and Blair Decker's hands dropped to his sides.

"What can I do?" he said. "Oh, christ, there must be something I can do."

"You can tell me about her," said Eddie. "It might help us to find her. What does she like to do?"

"Read. She likes to read." He wiped his face with his hands and started walking again. "She learned to read this year. She got *The Wizard of Oz* for Christmas. I read it to her twice, the babysitter read it to her twice, finally neither of us ever wanted to see the damned thing again. I told Samantha, if you learn to read, you can read it to yourself, over and over, whenever you want to."

A scattering of neighbors continued to watch them pass, from porches and front yards. They recognized Eddie and had probably drawn the obvious conclusion about the man beside her.

"And any book in the library, too, I told her," he went on. "And so she did. She learned to read." He was striding along with his head down and his hands in his pockets. Eddie slowed her pace until he noticed that she had fallen behind. "Sorry," he said once again, and waited for her.

Eddie said, "What else does she like to do?"

He gave her a glance. "I haven't been paying much attention, I'm afraid."

"Well, when you get home from work, what's she usually doing?"

"I don't — I work at home. I'm a writer. Freelance. But Samantha spends most of her time with the sitter." They had reached the end of the block. He hesitated, looking left and right, his arms raised and fluttering. "Which way?"

"Let's go this way," said Eddie. She took his elbow, guiding him around the corner. "When did your wife die?"

There was no sidewalk on this street and to Eddie, waiting for him to answer, the sound of their feet crunching in the gravel at the edge of the road seemed very loud.

They were walking west, toward the sun, which although still high in the sky had begun to descend. Eddie hated the thought of the day ending, and another night beginning.

But she refused to believe that the child Samantha was dead. She wouldn't believe it until she was confronted with a body.

"In October," said Decker finally. "My wife was killed. In a car crash."

"Does Samantha understand about death?"

"You mean, would she go off looking for Donna someplace?"

"I guess that's what I meant, yes."

"It's an interesting idea, Sergeant. But I don't think so. Not Samantha. Besides, even if she did, she wouldn't look here. We never lived here. Samantha's only been in Sechelt a couple of times before." He suddenly stopped. "Has somebody checked my house in West Van? Has somebody called the babysitter? Patsy?"

"We've checked the house, yes. Let me have the sitter's full name and phone number, and we'll call her." He gave her the information and Eddie recorded it in her notebook.

Decker again combed his hair with shaking fingers. "She's only five. I don't see how she could get over there all by herself. But maybe she started, started walking down the highway, and somebody picked her up . . ." He leaned against a telephone pole. "I can't stand this," he said, sounding amazed. "I really don't think I can stand it."

"That's one possibility," said Eddie calmly. "That somebody abducted her, either deliberately or on an impulse. Another is that she's been kidnapped, and you'll soon get a ransom demand." Which was beginning to sound like a better idea all the time, she thought grimly.

"If she was abducted," he said, "what will they do to her?"

"I don't know, Mr. Decker."

"I can imagine. I can imagine." He turned and wrapped his arms around the pole. "Oh, jesus. I'm sorry. I'm sorry. It's too late. But I am so fucking sorry."

Eddie touched his shoulder. "Let's go back to your sister's house now." The heat from his body burned through his cotton shirt and into her palm. She wanted to withdraw from him, as from someone infectious. But she left her hand where it was until he let go of the pole.

They headed back the way they had come, Blair Decker trudging slowly now, his hands in his pockets, eyes fixed on the gravel beneath his feet.

"Why didn't you take Samantha to Hawaii with you?" said Eddie.

He stopped walking. "I thought — I was becoming afraid," he said, enunciating carefully. "I thought it might help. To go away. For a while. To a place . . ." He looked blankly down at the ground, then back at Eddie. "Where she had been happy. We had been happy. My wife and I."

"What were you becoming afraid of?"

"Of dying." He looked up the street and started walking again.

"Are you ill?"

"No."

They walked along quietly for a while. Then Eddie said, "Have you any thoughts about who might have taken her for money?"

"Christ, no. Everyone who knows me knows I'm not rich, for god's sake. But they also must know that I'd do anything, sell everything . . . If these bastards are willing to settle for what I can raise I'll pay a ransom, my god, of course I will." They had reached the corner. He swept around it rapidly. Maybe they had called in his absence. Maybe a note had come. Eddie could see this hopefulness speeding him on.

"Will you do a television appeal?" she asked.

"Of course. I'll do anything. Anything you think might help." He was almost running now, Harriet's front gate beckoning to him from near the end of the street. Eddie followed, abandoning her questions, just keeping up. When they reached the house he was panting, and he stopped on the porch to catch his breath.

"Why did you say you were sorry back there?" said Eddie. "What have you got to be sorry about?"

He was leaning over, his hands supported by his thighs, breathing quickly. His hair was disheveled and his shirt had come untucked. He looked up at her in disbelief. "Are you kidding? I lost them, for god's sake." His breathing was shallow and ragged. "I lost all of them. You couldn't bloody *invent* a more heedless — *evil* — sonofabitch than me." He straightened and opened the screen door. "Are you coming in?"

Eddie shook her head.

"Please let me know if there's any news," he said and went inside.

Eddie leaned against the patrol car and folded her arms, studying the Murchison house, thinking.

After a while Eleanor slipped through the door. She didn't acknowledge Eddie's presence, but skipped down the steps and picked a pansy from the garden under the window, then climbed back up to the porch and sat on the top step.

Eddie waited a bit longer, then she went through the gate and up the steps. "May I talk to you for a minute?" she said.

Eleanor shrugged. She was wearing shorts and a T-shirt, twirling the stem of the pansy between her fingers.

Eddie knew she should knock on the door and ask Harriet Murchison to join them. But it wasn't an interrogation, she told herself. Not really.

She sat down. She took off her cap and placed it between them. Eleanor shifted a few inches away, twisting her body slightly, almost but not quite turning her back on Eddie. The sun put golden glints in her brown hair, which fell to her shoulders.

"We've met before, haven't we?" said Eddie. "Well, sort of. You were in the class I talked to last September."

Eleanor didn't reply.

"You asked me why I decided to become a police officer," Eddie went on. "I remember because I didn't like my answer much. I thought it sounded kind of pompous."

Eleanor was studying the pansy intently, as if she were soon to be asked to draw it from memory.

"Do you know what pompous means?"

"It means full of yourself," said Eleanor.

Eddie winced, and laughed. "Yeah. That's close enough."

Inside, the telephone rang, and for a few moments Eddie waited, listening. Then she said, "Tell me about Samantha."

Eleanor began stripping the petals from the pansy. "She's pretty young. Only five. Almost a baby, really. She doesn't know much." Her voice was high and clear and confident.

"I wonder what's happened to her," said Eddie.

"Well, you're supposed to find that out, aren't you?" Eleanor reached over to drop the petals, one by one, back into the flower garden. "Isn't it your job?"

"Can you help me?"

Eleanor scooted to the edge of the porch and leaned against the wall, facing Eddie. She drew up her legs and hugged her bare knees. "My mom wouldn't let me."

"I don't mean help me look for her. I mean, help me figure out what might have happened to her."

Most of Eleanor's face was hidden. Only her eyes and her forehead were visible above her knees.

The phone rang again. Eddie glanced through the screen door. She heard Harriet answer, in the kitchen, and waited.

Eventually she turned back to Eleanor, who was rocking back and forth on her bum, staring at Eddie over her knees, twirling a strand of her hair in the fingers of her right hand.

"Uncle Blair's gonna search for her," she said. "He might find her. He knows her better than anybody, I guess."

"I'm sure he does." Eddie leaned back on her hands and stretched her long legs out in front of her, resting her feet on a lower stair. "But you must've gotten to know her pretty well, too. Living in the same house with her."

"I don't *live* with her. She's only *visiting*." Eleanor let go of her knees and got to her feet. "I've gotta go in. I'm supposed to set the table."

"Your hair's very pretty like that," said Eddie. "Down, I mean. Mine gets all frizzy when I try to wear it down." She picked up her cap. "I'd like to come back and talk to you again, Eleanor. Meanwhile, you think about what I said, okay? I'm sure you've got a lot of useful things to tell me." She stood up and offered her hand, smiling at Eleanor, who slid her own hand briefly into Eddie's before running into the house.

THIRTY-FOUR

Samantha was standing at the window, looking down at the old people who'd locked her up in this room. They seemed to be having an argument. She wondered if they were arguing about her, about what to do with her. She thought the old woman was the boss of the two of them, because although the old man yelled a lot he only yelled at Samantha, never at his wife. She wondered if they had any children of their own. Maybe they didn't, and that's why they'd stolen Samantha. She started crying again, thinking this way.

She watched the old woman shake her finger in the man's face, then poke him in the shoulder. Then the woman marched away, down the driveway, toward the road. Samantha was horrified. Her tears fell faster and harder and she wiped them away with the back of her hand. Where was she *going*, what was she *doing*, leaving Samantha here with that angry old man?

She heard the man shout something — it sounded like a name, but Samantha couldn't make it out, the sound was too muffled. She saw the woman shake her head, and the man shouted again, and started after her. Now the woman stopped, put her hands on her hips, and turned around. The man hurried up to her and draped his arm around her shoulder, but she shook it off. The man stepped back. Samantha could see that he was talking to her very seriously.

Suddenly he glanced up at Samantha's window. She wanted to duck out of sight but she couldn't, it was like she was frozen there, staring down at them. The man looked back at the old woman, whose gaze was on the driveway. She moved her foot back and forth, rubbing at the ground — Samantha could just barely see her sneaker under the long dress she was wearing. Dust rose up in little poofs, making an ache in Samantha's chest: she could almost feel the dust in her throat, and smell the grass.

She remembered — was it only one day ago? — sitting on the grass in Aunt Harriet's yard looking at the pansies in the garden. She had stopped crying for a few minutes but now she started again. Samantha turned from the window and made her way across the room to the bed and lay down, her face in the pillow.

Down on the driveway, Arthur said to Susie, "It was only a thought."

"It's a thought that's been in your head all along, isn't it?" said Susie, her arms folded across her chest. She felt that she was huddling, and knew why. She was thinking that she needed to protect herself from certain aspects of this man, and wondered why on earth she hadn't seen this before.

"We might as well try to get something out of this situation you've managed to botch the hell out of," said Arthur. "Why not, for god's sake?"

Susie started back toward the house.

"Think about it, just give it a damn thought," said Arthur, following. Inside, he grabbed her arm. "We could set ourselves up for life, Susie."

Susie pulled away from him. "I'm set up already," she said, opening cupboards, taking out bread and peanut butter. "I've got a house, I've got a perfectly good job, I'm doing just fine, thank you very much."

"Well, I'm not," said Arthur loudly. "I've got a crummy basement apartment and a crummy night watchman's job. I'm not doing just fine, thank you very much."

Susie put the peanut butter jar down hard and turned to him. "This isn't about you, Arthur. It's about me." Her face was burning. "I want him to hurt. So much that he can't breathe. And I want to see it. And that's all I want." She pulled two slices of whole wheat bread from a plastic bag. "I can still have that, even though it hasn't worked out the way we planned. And if you don't want to do it my way, you might as well go back to Vancouver."

Arthur leaned against the refrigerator. "You've become one cold woman, Susie."

Susie spread peanut butter on one slice of bread and honey on the other. "Yes, I guess I have." She cut the sandwich in half and put it on a plate. "Here. Take this up to her."

Samantha heard the footsteps coming up the stairs and knew it was the old man: the woman walked faster, and made less noise. She grabbed a tissue from the box and quickly wiped her face while the key turned in the lock. But he didn't even look at her, just came in, put the tray down, and went out again. Maybe he'll forget to lock the door, she hoped. But of course he didn't.

Samantha hadn't eaten her breakfast, except she'd drunk the glass of milk. She pulled the sandwich apart to see what was in there. And sighed. Samantha hated peanut butter almost as much as she hated asparagus. She was getting so hungry, though, she might have to eat it. She would chew it up fast, and swallow it while holding her breath so that maybe she wouldn't really taste it.

She wandered to the window and rested her forehead against the glass. She wondered if God was watching her in this room. She wondered if He was going to get her out of there before another night came.

Last night had been awful. At Aunt Harriet's house she had missed her father and her own room and her own bed, but last night she had missed Aunt Harriet and the guest room. She had even missed mean old Eleanor. There was nobody in this awful big old house to listen to her prayers, or tuck her in, or leave a nightlight on.

She had thought a lot about her father in the night. And her mother. And had wondered why these terrible things had happened, her mother dying, her father always going away, and now this, somebody stealing her.

The old woman had come into the room while it was still light, to collect the tray. She had given Samantha macaroni and cheese for dinner, and a slice of toast, and another glass of milk. But Samantha hadn't been able to eat any of it.

"I really need to go home now," Samantha had told the old woman. "Will you please take me home?"

"Nobody's going to hurt you."

"But I have to go home," said Samantha, beginning to cry again.

"After a while you can go home," said the old woman. "Good night."

That was a promise. *"After a while you can go home."* And it had made Samantha feel a little bit better.

But not for long, because it had been getting dark. There was no lamp in the room, only a bulb in the middle of the ceiling. It had no shade, and the light fell upon Samantha like she imagined an X-ray machine's light, cold and sharp. When hours and hours had passed she saw the moon through the window, and she turned off the ceiling light then to let kinder moonlight drift into the room.

Samantha had climbed onto the bed, on top of the covers with her shoes on, which wouldn't have been allowed at Aunt Harriet's house. The moonlight crept farther and farther into the room until finally it reached the end of the cot.

Samantha had been sitting up, leaning against the pillow that she had propped against the headboard. But now she wriggled down until she was lying flat, then craned her head up to peer at her legs — and yes, they were in the moon's light now, looking like they were made of silver. Samantha scrambled to the end of the bed and crouched there in the moonlight. Now her whole self was made of silver.

She must have fallen asleep, although she didn't remember doing it. When she awoke in the morning she hadn't known where she was for a moment. And as soon as she did remember she started to cry again. Not too loud, she didn't want the old man to shout at her. Because of the box of tissues on the dresser, Samantha thought they had expected her to cry. But they didn't like hearing it. At least the old man didn't.

Samantha, looking out the window, reminded herself to stand here when it started to get dark, so that she could make a wish on the first star. She hoped she wouldn't still be here when it started to get dark. But if she was, she would wish hard that she could go home tomorrow.

She heard the old woman coming up the stairs. She came into the room carrying a glass of milk, and when she was inside she took an apple from her pocket. "You don't like macaroni and cheese. You don't like toast. And apparently you don't like peanut butter and honey, either," she said, eyeing the sandwich.

"I don't like peanut butter."

"Do you like tuna salad? Egg salad?"

"No, thank you. Please can I go home now?"

The woman put down the milk and the apple and picked up the tray. "Not yet. Soon."

"How soon? When?"

"That depends on your father."

"But my father . . ." Samantha felt a surge of panic. "He's not here. He's in Hawaii."

The old woman didn't answer; she just went to the door.

"He's not here," said Samantha, beginning to cry again.

The woman turned around and put a finger across her lips. "Shhh," she said, backing out of the room, closing the door.

Susie put the tray on the kitchen counter. "She doesn't like peanut butter. I don't think I've ever met a child who didn't like macaroni and cheese and didn't like peanut butter, either."

"You're going to regret it later, Susie. Trust me." He was still harping on the money.

Susie dumped the sandwich in the garbage under the sink. At least the child had drunk the milk.

"When're they gonna get the letter?" Arthur asked.

"Not before tomorrow. They'll probably get it tomorrow."

"And then what? You got any bright ideas yet, to replace the old ones?"

Susie rinsed the plate and the glass with hot water, dried them, and put them away. "I've had a couple of thoughts," she said.

"Do you plan to let me in on them?" He was straddling a kitchen chair and he sounded as belligerent as he looked.

"Of course I do, Arthur." She leaned against the kitchen counter. "I'm going to do a tub of laundry. If you've got anything you want washed, let me have it."

"Susie." He was looking at her speculatively, sizing her up: Susie felt that she was being literally weighed and measured.

"What?"

"I'm damn curious here. Don't you *care* that the kid's seen us?"

"Of course I care. That's what I'm thinking about. I'm trying to think whether there's anything we can do about it."

"Like what?"

Susie moved away from the counter, from Arthur, toward the hall that led to the laundry room. "I've got to get that washing done."

"Do you think you could kill her if you had to?"

Susie stopped. She turned and looked at him, shocked. He had said it almost casually.

"No. Of course not."

Arthur shrugged. "Me neither, probably. It was just a thought." He looked at his watch. "I'm going into town. Get me some more beer."

THIRTY-FIVE

Susie woke abruptly the next morning and found herself staring at the wall. Her throat was throbbing painfully, as if she had been trying not to weep.

She had dreamt about Leigh-Anne. In her dream they had been together on the dike again. Her daughter's long luscious hair was whipped by the wind into a rippling stream, and Leigh-Anne was laughing. There was love and laughter in her face — not like when she was really on the dike, telling Susie about the baby she wasn't going to have.

Susie shoved the covers aside and sat on the edge of her bed — a rented bed, in a rented house. This took all the strength she possessed. She would have to stay where she was for a while, sitting there, not moving, until energy returned. She must have used it all up in her dream.

But how? What had she, Susie, been doing in the dream? She had no recollection of that, nor did she know what had been the cause of Leigh-Anne's delight.

Had Leigh-Anne really been as beautiful as she remembered? Or was it Susie's love that made her so, in Susie's eyes?

And what kind of a baby would she have had if Blair Decker had allowed her to give birth? A girl baby, with laughing eyes like Leigh-Anne's? A boy baby, with Buddy's stubborn chin, or Buddy's fine straight nose? Was it a girl baby who had died with its mother? Or a son?

There was a perfunctory knock on her door, and it opened. "The kid's crying again," Arthur said.

"Well, what do you expect?" said Susie, rubbing her thighs through her cotton nightgown. "She's only five years old. She's frightened. She wants her father."

"Things are gonna start happening today," said Arthur. "Once that letter lands on their stoop. Oh yeah." He entered the room and sat down on an old wooden chair that creaked as it accepted his weight. "Have you changed your mind about the money yet?"

"No," said Susie. "I told you. I don't want his damn money." She shivered, although at just past seven o'clock it was already warm, and stood up, feeling even older than she was, pain pinging in her joints, crackling in her spine, troweling itself inside her head. She went to the window, moving uncertainly, doubtful that she would be able to make the trip across the room without incident: either my legs will give out, she thought, or a hole will appear in the floor and drop me through it. But she got there. She raised the open window still wider and turned to Arthur, her hands on the windowsill behind her, bracing her. "Let me try to explain this to you once and for all," she said.

"Fire away," said Arthur, folding his arms.

"I saw a picture once," said Susie, "in a magazine. It was a photograph of a painting. In the painting, a man's arms are roped to one horse, and his legs to a second, and other men are riding the horses, steering them in opposite directions, going at a gallop." She looked intently at Arthur, wanting the image to be as vivid and terrifying in his head as it was in hers. "While you're looking at this painting, you know that in just a few seconds this man is going to be ripped apart."

"Kind of a weird thing to do a painting of," said Arthur uneasily.

"Get out of here now, Arthur," said Susie. "I want to get dressed."

But she found that she didn't yet have the energy to get dressed, so she sat down on the edge of the bed again.

Arthur got to his feet, but instead of leaving the room he sat next to her. "This was a well-planned operation, Susie."

He was very close, but not disrespectfully so. Susie wanted to lean to the left, to rest her head on his shoulder.

"I admire you for putting it all together," he said.

Susie wanted to weep, now, and at the same time she was feeling a not unwelcome hunger for his body.

"So it took a wrong turn there, when we grabbed her. I know you're putting your mind to that, gonna work it out," he said, rubbing her back slowly, long slow strokes with his strong broad hand. "And meanwhile," he went on, "it seems a shame not to give the guy all the pain he deserves. Not just the emotional stuff, but hitting him in the pocketbook, too. Which is probably where he'd feel it the most anyway."

Susie's desire vanished. She wanted to laugh. What a situation.

"Go on now, Arthur," she said, quite gently, leaning forward slightly, away from his massaging hand. "Let me get dressed."

He got up, reluctantly, and went to the door. "Think about it," he said, and there was a curtness in his tone that caused Susie to look up at him. "We're in this together," he went on. "I've been with you all the way. In fact, it was almost my idea. Right?"

"You set me to thinking about it," said Susie carefully. "That's right."

"So I've got a stake in the operation. Or I should have. It's only fair."

Susie's mouth was suddenly dry. She reached for the glass of water on the bedside table.

"I want you to consider what I've said very seriously," said Arthur. He waited until she nodded. "I'll go put some coffee on." He went into the hall and closed the door.

This room had been crowded with furniture when they moved in. Susie had carried most of it out into the barn. All that remained were the bed, the night table, the wooden chair, a worn easy chair by the window, and a small dresser.

She got up, slowly, and crossed back to the window, where she sank into the easy chair. Had she misjudged Arthur? Miscalculated her authority over him? She remembered watching from across the street while he almost came to blows with someone just because he'd accidentally bumped into him — it had been a gentle bump, too, nothing harsh or threatening. But Arthur's response had been harsh and threatening. Oh yes.

She had lain awake night after night imagining Blair Decker's agony, too consumed with grief to wonder why Arthur was so willing to help her.

He would probably come to her aid if she were attacked, Susie reflected. Like he had come to the aid of his wife, taunted by a couple of stoned teenagers. But he had done this because he enjoyed it, not because he had loved his wife. In fact he had stopped loving her by then, he had told Susie. Stopped loving her years before.

So she could count on him for violence, if violence were required. But violence wouldn't be required.

And why should he be willing to help her anyway, now that she had messed things up by letting the child see them? He should be on his way, Arthur should. Surely he knew that she would never identify him to the police. Surely he knew that.

The sun was shining upon another warm spring day. Susie closed her eyes and breathed in the fragrant breeze. She didn't think she could deprive the child of another such a day.

She had thought he had genuine affection for her. She had thought he was doing it for friendship's sake.

Maybe even for love. But all along, he was doing it for money.

Susie twisted the green ring on her finger. She had slipped it from Leigh-Anne's hand in the hospital. She hadn't asked anybody's permission, she had just taken it. And had worn it herself, ever since.

So much for friendship, she thought, twisting the ring. So much for love.

THIRTY-SIX

It was late afternoon. Sunlight spilled through Eddie's office window, spreading a bright carpet on the floor. Eddie wanted to curl up there like a cat, letting the sun warm her through and through, dispelling fatigue, dissolving hopelessness.

"So you're telling me," she said, "that nobody saw anything."

"Not a damn thing," said Frank Turner, flipping through the pages of his notebook. "I mean, nothing useful. A woman was out on her backyard deck planting petunias or something, she saw Samantha go by, on the path through the bush. She didn't know who she was, but she recognized the photo. But she didn't see anybody approach her. She didn't see any adults at all."

The door was slightly open. They heard the phone ringing in the reception area and the murmur of Isabella's voice as she answered it.

"How about other kids?" said Eddie.

"I don't know. Could be. They use it as a shortcut. I didn't ask about kids, Sarge," Frank said patiently. "Only about adults." He looked like he hadn't slept in a week, although his uniform was crisp and clean.

"They might have used another kid, though," said Eddie. "As bait. Don't you think?"

"Shit," said Frank irritably. "It's possible. Sure. I'll check back with her."

"Anything else?" said Eddie.

"Nothing. No results from the air search. Nothing on the water. And we did the house-to-house again, around the Murchison place, and the library. Everyone's real eager to help, but they just didn't see anything."

"Norah?"

"I'm still working on the nurture aspect. We got names from the hospital of women who lost their babies — three in the last year. Is that going back far enough?"

Eddie looked at Frank, who said, "Maybe not."

Norah shot him an exasperated look. "Fine. Okay. I'll tell them add another what, year? Two?"

"Two," said Frank. "Just to be sure," he added politely.

"And we've started to check them out," Norah said. "I don't have the info yet on people who might have been refused adoptions. Should get somewhere on that today." Her light brown hair was coming loose from its ponytail and her eyeliner was smudged. Eddie hadn't realized that Norah wore eyeliner.

"West Van canvassed around the father's house for us," said Frank. "Nothing there either. But one of the neighbors suggested we talk to the babysitter." He paged through his notebook.

"Patsy McDonough," said Eddie. "That's right. Damn. I forgot. The father mentioned her."

"Yeah, Patsy McDonough," said Frank, reading from his notes. "I've got a phone number here. Bill Cleaver in West Van offered to do it. What do you think?"

"Decker gave me her number. I'll do it," said Eddie. She stood up and stretched. She ached all over. "And give me that woman's name and address, too. The one planting the petunias. I'll do her as well. You and Norah find out who's moved into town in the last month. Renting, not buying. Including motels and B and Bs."

In the reception area, the phone rang again.

"Will do," said Norah. "But I gotta go home first. Have a shower. Change."

Turner tore a page from his notebook and handed it to Eddie. "Every time the damn phone rings," he said grimly, "I think it's going to be somebody who's found her body."

They waited.

"Well," said Eddie finally, "not this time, anyway."

The woman who had seen Samantha pass by had been planting miniature roses, not petunias. When Eddie arrived to talk to her, having called first, she had made a fresh pot of coffee. The two of them sat in lawn chairs on the woman's deck and admired the roses while Eddie asked her questions.

An hour later, Eddie pulled up once again in front of the Murchison house. She sat in the patrol car for a few minutes, thinking. Then she walked to the front door.

"No news," she said quickly to Harriet Murchison, who had materialized behind the screen. "I'd just like a few words with Eleanor. Is she home?"

"Yes, sure. Come in, Sergeant," said Harriet, opening the door.

"No, thanks," said Eddie. "I'll wait out here."

Across the street a man was mowing his lawn, and Eddie smelled the pungent aroma of cut grass. She linked her hands behind her. She could hear Harriet speaking sharply. Eddie couldn't make out the words. A few more minutes passed.

"What do you want?" said Eleanor sullenly.

Eddie turned around. The child was still inside, looking through the screen.

"I think you know, Eleanor," said Eddie softly.

Eleanor hesitated, glancing back over her shoulder. Then she opened the door and slipped through. "No, I don't."

"Come on," said Eddie. "Let's sit on the step."

"I haven't finished my dinner," said Eleanor.

Eddie smiled at her. "Maybe you'd sooner come down to the detachment," she said. "Your mother would come too, of course. We could talk there instead of here, if you like."

Eleanor looked at the patrol car, then at Eddie. Finally, she sat down on the top step, as far to one side as possible.

Eddie sat next to her, about three feet away. "You know that path through the bush? The shortcut?" she said.

Eleanor looked straight ahead, her hands tucked between her knees. She was wearing jeans and a pink T-shirt, and sneakers with white socks.

"There's trees and brush on both sides," Eddie went on. "But one side slopes up. And halfway up, there's a house. In the middle of summer you probably can't see the path from there, because of all the trees. But now, before all the leaves have fully opened, you can see it pretty well."

Eleanor didn't move.

"The woman who lives there was out on her deck on Monday afternoon. She saw Samantha going along the path."

Eleanor was so still, so rigid, Eddie thought if she poked the child in the shoulder she might shatter into pieces.

"And she saw you, too," Eddie said quietly. "Behind her. She thought you were playing a game. Because you were hiding behind trees, running from one tree to another."

Eleanor moved her head slightly to the right, away from Eddie.

"She had to go inside then. Her phone rang, I think she said. And when she came out again, about twenty minutes later, you were both gone."

Eddie waited. She looked down at her legs, the dark blue pants with the yellow stripe, and tucked her hands

under her buttocks. Her forehead was wet under the
sweatband of her cap, and her underarms were damp.
She wanted a shower in the worst way. She watched the
postal truck pull up. The driver jumped out, shoved a
handful of envelopes into the box attached to the fence,
and drove away. Eddie wanted to call out to Harriet to
come check the mail, but then Eleanor spoke.

"I didn't see much," she said. Her voice was so clear
and sinless that it startled Eddie, who had expected to
hear suffering and guilt. "Nothing bad."

"Tell me what you saw," said Eddie, keeping her voice
gentle.

"An old lady," said Eleanor. "She was looking for
something in the bush."

She freed her hands and turned around to lean against
the porch wall, pulling up her knees and peering over
them, like she had the last time. Eddie wanted to grab
her and shake her until her teeth fell out of her head.

"So Samantha helped her, I guess."

"What do you mean, you guess?" said Eddie, struggling for patience.

"Samantha talked to her, I guess she asked her what
she was doing, and then she started looking, too." She
shrugged, her blue eyes flashing. "So I came home."

It's none of my business, thought Eddie, why this kid
hates her cousin.

"Tell me about the old lady," she said. "What did she
look like?"

Eleanor shrugged again. "She was old, that's all."

"Was she tall? Short? Fat? Thin?"

"I don't know if she was tall or short. She wasn't fat."

"Did she have long hair? Or was it short?"

"It came about to here," said Eleanor, indicating just
above her shoulder.

For a moment Eddie could see her entire face. In that
instant, she realized that Eleanor was terrified. She
reached out and put her hand on the child's knee.

"You're helping me very much, Eleanor," she said softly. "Please go on."

Eleanor began to cry.

"Shhh," said Eddie. "It's all right. You can make it right, now, by telling me every single thing you can remember about her. Okay?"

Eleanor nodded. She lowered her knees and swung her feet over the edge of the porch. "She had a dress on," she said. "A long dress. I think it went all the way to the ground." She swiped at her nose with her hand. "And a ring. A big green ring."

Harriet came out onto the porch. "Excuse me," she murmured, slipping between them, and she went down the steps and along the walk to the mailbox.

"That's excellent, Eleanor," said Eddie, very quietly. "This is a big help to me. What else can you remember?" Her voice remained warm, but she was furious with the kid, who could have yelled, shouted, hollered, and kept her cousin safe.

Harriet, thumbing through the mail, coming slowly toward them, gave a muffled cry. She stopped. The rest of the envelopes and flyers fluttered to the ground as she tore open a letter. Eddie got quickly to her feet.

Harriet looked up. "She's alive!" she said, waving the letter in the air. "Oh dear god, she's alive!"

THIRTY-SEVEN

She *wasn't* a cold woman, Susie reflected, watching the mail truck bustling along the road. Arthur was wrong about that. Quite wrong. It wasn't coldness he sensed in her. Not at all.

She had dug an old lawn chair out of the pile of rusting junk that continued to clutter the driveway and placed it on the small patch of weedy grass in front of the rented house, and she was sitting there now, under the willow tree, sipping from a glass of iced tea into which she had dropped a slice of lemon.

It was distance. She had become distant. It was a requirement of her situation.

The mailman honked the horn and stuck his hand out the window to wave at Susie over the roof of the truck. She waved back.

She wondered what Buddy would have to say about what she was doing. She had become a person no better than he was, that's what he would say. And of course he would be right.

It was worth it, though.

They would have received the note by now. They would be relieved, because it said, in effect, that the child was still alive.

But how frustrated, how angry, how — how *impotent* that man must be feeling. Susie's toes curled up involuntarily inside her sneakers, she yearned so badly to stand, to walk, to run all the way to his sister's house. She ached to peer through the windows, to see it for herself, craving to feast on Blair Decker's suffering like an addict craves a fix.

She felt a presence stirring in the grass and glanced down, expecting for just an instant to see Mutt curled up at her feet. This happened often. She would sense the dog there, at her feet, or behind her, curled up in a chair.

It had been even worse at home. Mutt's spirit was everywhere in that house. Susie had thought she'd seen her in every room. Again and again she had heard Mutt's toenails clicking on the linoleum, and the whap of the dog door closing behind her.

She never sensed Leigh-Anne's presence. But she sometimes forgot that her daughter was gone. In Susie's dreams she was alive. And when Susie first woke in the morning she was alive. Every single morning Susie's grief was new. She thought that once this business was over, maybe then the stubborn part of her that refused to accept Leigh-Anne's death would weaken.

And it would be over soon.

Fronds of the willow tree brushed her shoulder, nuzzled her hair, as Susie imagined his sister — Harriet — gathering the mail from the box by the front gate. She might even be doing it at this very moment.

As Harriet walks back toward the house she leafs through bills and flyers and letters, and she sees the one addressed to her brother, the printing shaky and uncertain, as if done by someone very old.

She starts to run now.

She bangs through the screen door into the house, calling his name.

She doesn't tear open the envelope herself because it isn't addressed to her, but she'll hover at his shoulder while he does it, she'll read the letter with him.

And when they've read it, Susie thought, they won't know what to believe, what to do.

Susie had considered cutting words out of a selection of magazines and pasting them on a sheet of paper. But this idea made her uncomfortable. She hadn't wanted to get caught — of course not — and had known that deception and camouflage were necessary. But she resented feeling sly and deceitful. So in the end she had compromised, printing the words with her left hand, so that it was her own writing, and yet it wasn't.

She printed: *We have your child. We are going to keep her. You will never see her again.* She had done it at the kitchen table, which was made of wood, and the grain insinuating itself upon the paper from below made the letters look even more shaky. She had done it days before the kidnapping, soon after she and Arthur had arrived at the house.

She had worn plastic gloves when she handled the paper and the envelope, the kind available in grocery stores, to wear when cleaning silver or mixing up meat for hamburgers. And even though things hadn't gone as planned she had mailed it anyway, as soon as the child was safely ensconced in the upstairs bedroom, with Arthur on guard in the hall.

Susie had driven all the way to Powell River to mail it. It was only about forty miles, but there was a ferry trip between Earl's Cove and Saltery Bay, so that she was gone almost three hours altogether.

When she got back Arthur had the TV on, loud, because he said the kid had been screaming. Susie went right upstairs to check on her, and found that she had fallen asleep on the floor, curled up against the wall.

Now she considered taking the child outside for a while, letting her have some fresh air and sunshine. But that was fraught with hazard. Arthur would say so, and he would be right. Susie drank the last of her tea, the green stone in Leigh-Anne's ring winking in the sunlight.

She imagined encountering Blair Decker on the street, accidentally. At the post office, perhaps. Or in a café.

"Mr. Decker." She would sound surprised. "What are you doing in Sechelt?"

"I might ask you the same thing," he might say back.

"I know people here," Susie would lie. "I'm staying with them. On their boat. Having a few days' holiday."

And then he would tell her about Samantha.

And she would be horrified, and sympathetic. "Is there anything I can do? Anything at all?" she would say, beginning to worm her way into his troubles.

The lines in his face would be deeper, now. She remembered a boyfriend she'd had when she was in her teens. He was only seventeen, yet he had faint but unmistakable lines on each side of his mouth. She had found them extremely sexy in his young face. Evocative of something wise and sensual. But they were not sexy, she thought, on a truly aging man.

Arthur watched her through the wonky living-room window, jingling change and car keys in his pocket. He knew by now that she wasn't about to change her mind. She wasn't going to demand money for the kid's safe return. What a waste, he thought. What a goddamn waste.

He went outside, banging the screen door, stomping down the front steps.

"I'm gonna drive into town," he said. "You want anything?"

"I don't think so," said Susie.

She was so damn calm — he couldn't figure it.

"Why are you going into town?"

"I'm bloody restless," said Arthur. "And sick of that kid's whining."

"She's bored," said Susie. "Get her some more comic books."

"So how long is this gonna go on?"

She took off her sunglasses and squinted up at him, shading her eyes with her hand. "I don't know, Arthur. Why don't you go home, for heaven's sake? I'll be okay on my own now."

"Okay to do what?" he said, frustrated. "Are you just gonna set the kid loose? She'll tell them what you look like. What I look like. What she could see from the god-damn window. Don't you think they're gonna find you?" Jesus, she was driving him nuts, this bloody woman.

"I told you, Arthur," said Susie wearily. "Please. Go home. If they find me, I will not identify you to the police. The child doesn't know who you are. And I won't tell them who you are. That's a promise." She put her sunglasses back on and faced the road again, away from him. "As for me — I don't know if I care what happens to me."

Arthur scurried around to stand in front of her. "And that's the problem," he said furiously. "That's the whole fucking problem."

He was going to have to take matters into his own hands. That was clear. Well, he thought, looking grimly down at Susie, I'm up to it.

He stalked toward his four-wheel-drive, climbed in, slammed the door, and sped off down the driveway, spewing dust.

Susie, watching him go, felt an overwhelming urge to stand up and walk away, leaving the house, the child, and Arthur behind.

"Kidnapped! No! I can't believe it," wailed Patsy McDonough on the phone to Eddie. "I just can't believe it. I mean, it can't be true. It *can't* be!"

Eddie arched her back and plucked at her damp shirt where it had stuck to her skin.

"She's such a sweet kid, really, and smart, too," said the babysitter, who had told Eddie she was twenty years old. Eddie could barely remember being twenty years old. "She's *far* too smart to let somebody kidnap her! Couldn't she just be lost?"

Eddie, peering into her empty coffee mug, opened her mouth to reply, but Patsy McDonough went on.

"You've got woods there, haven't you? And mountains? So maybe she went up there and fell off a cliff. I mean, maybe that kidnap thing, maybe it's just a hoax."

Eddie imagined her as being about five feet tall with short fluffy hair, light brown, and brown eyes. "We don't think it's a hoax, Miss McDonough," she said firmly.

"Oh my god, I can't believe it."

She was probably physically sturdy, thought Eddie. And genuinely fond of the child. "I'd like to get your help, here, if you don't mind," she said.

"Oh sure. Yeah. Okay. But what do you mean? How can I possibly help you find her, from over here?" Patsy sounded on the verge of tears. Eddie could easily imagine her wringing her hands. Except she was hanging on to the phone with one of them.

"You might be able to help a great deal," she said, trying to inject warmth and calm into her voice. "For instance, have you been around to the house since Mr. Decker and Samantha left? You've got a key, I think."

"Yeah, I've been watering the plants." Eddie heard a hard, quick inhalation. "Oh god."

"What's the matter?" said Eddie.

"I forgot, I was supposed to do it yesterday. Oh god. Samantha'll never forgive me if any of those plants die. I better get over there — I can do it today. Now. I can do it now. It's the *least* I can do!" she cried.

"Miss McDonough," said Eddie loudly. "Please. Not now. Talk to me first."

"Oh yeah. Okay. Excuse me for a minute."

Eddie heard sniffling, and a nose being blown.

"Uh, what was your question?"

"My question was, have you been to the Deckers' house, and I believe you told me you have. Right?"

"Yeah, I was pretty good the first week, went there every two or three days, it's just lately, just recently, I've got another job, you see, just temporary, until Mr. Decker's back, but —"

"When you got there," said Eddie, raising her voice
again, "when you got to the house, Miss McDonough,
did you notice anything out of the ordinary? Any sign
that someone had been inside? Broken in, maybe? Or
tried to?"

Patsy McDonough took a moment to think about
this. Eddie rested her elbows on the desk and rubbed her
forehead and the back of her neck with her free hand.

"No," said the babysitter finally. "I didn't see anything
like that." She sounded reasonably certain.

"Okay," said Eddie. "Now I want you to think back
to before Mr. Decker went to Hawaii and Samantha
came over here to Sechelt. Did you notice anything or
anyone unusual?"

She looked again at her coffee mug. She drank too
much coffee anyway, she told herself. Maybe she ought
to get one of those water bottles in here, try to switch
from coffee to the cool clean water that came from
underground springs, or undefiled lakes, or pristine
streams. Yeah. Sure.

"I don't know what you mean," said Patsy unhappily.
"I don't know how to answer you."

"Okay." Eddie settled back in her chair. "Let's do it
this way. Tell me about you and Samantha. What kinds of
things did you do together?"

She took Samantha to kindergarten every morning,
said the babysitter, and picked her up at noon. In the
afternoons they went to the library, or if the day was
nice, to the park. Sometimes to a movie.

"Could Samantha have met somebody at kindergarten — an adult — without you knowing about it?"
said Eddie.

"Well, we knew all the staff, of course. And they
didn't change, during the year. Nobody left, nobody new
came. Sometimes they'd have people come in to teach
the children special things, or demonstrate. Like they had
a cellist once, I remember. And I guess all the kids met

them. Well, they would, wouldn't they? I mean, that was the point. That artists and scientists, they're people like anybody else."

"Okay, now did you meet anybody new at the park, or the library?" said Eddie, feeling slightly desperate. "A stranger who was friendly to Samantha, maybe? Or did you notice that somebody — someone you didn't know — had started showing up frequently when you took her places?" Eddie looked at her watch. She was expecting Frank Turner and Norah Gibbons within the next fifteen minutes. And this interview was going nowhere. She wondered if she'd be able to get more out of the woman if she talked to her in person.

There was silence at the other end of the phone.

"Miss McDonough?"

Eddie heard a sigh.

"Miss McDonough. What's on your mind?"

"Not Samantha," said Patsy McDonough reluctantly. "It's probably nothing. I hope it's nothing."

"You hope *what's* nothing, Patsy?"

"Somebody made friends with *me*. I met her at my gym. Oh god — you don't think . . . ?"

The skin along Eddie's spine moved, slowly, shifting itself.

"I don't know yet, do I?" she said.

She felt time slowing, the better to help her concentrate. At the same time everything around her was louder — brighter — crystal clear: each of her senses was flexing its individual muscles; they were all working together for a change.

She pulled her notebook closer. "I'm sure lots of people make friends with you," she said, clicking open her ballpoint pen. "You sound like a very outgoing, friendly kind of woman. So what makes you remember this particular person?"

"She was very interested," said Patsy, slowly, "in my job. She didn't have any children, and she said she'd always wanted them." Her voice trembled, reminding Eddie of the patty-pat spatular sound of raindrops falling upon the green leaves of summer. "And so she was very interested . . ."

"Yes," said Eddie softly. "Go on, Patsy."

"In the fact that I look after Samantha. Oh my god."

"Patsy. Her name. What's her name?"

"She reminded me of my mother."

"Patsy. Patsy? Her name?"

"She said it was Elizabeth. Elizabeth Munson. But if she — if she was planning this — if she was going to kidnap Samantha, then she wouldn't give me her real name, would she?"

"Probably not," said Eddie. "Which is why I now want you to tell me what she looks like. And everything else you can remember about her."

"Oh, boy, that's a break," said Frank Turner.

"Are you gonna get the ident boys over there, get a drawing done?" said Norah.

Eddie nodded. "It's in the works." She took a bite from a cinnamon-orange muffin. "Thanks for this, Frank," she said, gesturing with the muffin, and managing to include the large paper cup of coffee that sat on her desk blotter. He had brought three coffees and lots of cream and sugar and three muffins and several pats of butter to the meeting.

"No problem," said Frank, stirring cream into his coffee.

"So it's definitely the same woman the kid saw? The cousin?" said Norah. She broke open a muffin and slathered butter on with a plastic knife. "Anybody else want this?" she said, holding up the knife.

"No, thanks," said Eddie. "Yeah, it's the same woman. Right down to the big green ring."

"But there's got to be somebody else involved," said Frank. "This is an old woman we're talking about. I don't think an old woman could pull it off by herself."

"Maybe," said Eddie.

"I think he's right," said Norah, brushing crumbs from the front of her shirt. "They'd have to wrestle Samantha into some kind of vehicle. And I don't see an old broad managing that without some kind of help."

"Okay, so look at this," said Eddie, eating the last of her muffin. She picked up the copy of the note that was sitting on her desk. "They're telling him he's not going to get her back." She looked at Frank and Norah. "Why? They don't want money. So why bother telling him anything? Why not just keep her?"

"They want him to know she's alive," said Frank. He leaned across the desk. "That printing's damn wobbly. Because she's old? How old are we talking here, anyway? Or is she trying to disguise her handwriting?"

"Either. Maybe both. I agree with you," said Eddie. "They want him to know she's alive. So what have we got here, a compassionate kidnapper? Or a seriously grim pervert?"

THIRTY-EIGHT

Susie stood in the upstairs hall listening at the child's door, but all was quiet. She had thought she'd heard Samantha crying again. Maybe she had cried herself to sleep. Susie wondered why she wasn't moved by the child's tears. Had she really managed to distance herself so successfully that she couldn't even sympathize with the fear and sorrow of an innocent five-year-old?

Of course Susie didn't really know she was innocent. It was assumed that all children were innocent, but that wasn't necessarily true.

Samantha was a very small child, thought Susie, tip-toeing away from the door, so small that Susie could probably have tucked her under her arm like a rolled up newspaper.

Oh god, the whole damn business had turned out to be a disaster. Susie shuddered, remembering.

Arthur had parked the Jeep Wagoneer in the brush and Susie had set out reconnoitering once again, intent on spotting something unobserved until that very day — something that would suggest a perfect opportunity for seizing the child. She hadn't been hopeful, though. She was beginning to accept the fact that the child's aunt was not going to let her out of her sight even for a moment. (Which was truly sad, Susie reflected. Imagine, living in a town this small and still not being able to trust the cit-izenry.) She was reluctantly concluding that they would have to perform the night-time abduction, the plan that Arthur so enthusiastically supported.

Then suddenly, out of the blue, just as Susie had warned herself to get off the path — because they'd be coming soon, the two of them, and she mustn't let herself become a familiar figure, someone the aunt would remember later — just as she was about to step into the brush, there she was. Samantha.

Alone.

Susie had not been wearing her disguise. The disguise sat in a drawer in her bedroom: blue jeans, a long-sleeved plaid shirt, a big scarf to tie around her hair, huge round sunglasses with twinkling rhinestones embedded in the frame, and a large straw hat with a wide droopy brim.

And there was no blindfold in the Jeep. No gag. No rope.

But she had gone into action anyway. Instantly. Automatically. Searching the underbrush, calling for Mutt.

And as she did so she thought to herself, I should have been an actor. She came close to convincing herself that Mutt was truly there, mislaid, and that Susie would find her any minute now, crouching behind a tree, or hiding among some tall weeds. She was experiencing genuine panic by the time the child came near. Her tears were real, and so was her disquiet. No wonder she had been so thoroughly convincing.

"Mutt? Mutt! Where are you, you bad dog!" she called as the child approached. "Mutt — come!"

Samantha stopped to watch her. "Who're you calling?" she said.

"My dog," said Susie. "Have you seen her? She's gray, she's about this big," she said, holding her hands about two feet apart. "Her name is Mutt. And I'm afraid she's lost."

The child, of course, had offered to help her look. Susie, searching frantically, had led her gradually through

the bush to the Jeep — and to Arthur, who, watching
them incredulously as they advanced toward him, became
red-faced and bug-eyed. Susie had thought he might not
ever move, he seemed so firmly planted there, next to the
Jeep, staring at her and at the child. But when Samantha
lifted her head and spotted him he sprang into action,
grabbing her and shoving her into the backseat. Susie
slipped in from the other side and took the child firmly in
her arms, stifling Samantha's wails in her lap.

This part she had hated. She had wrapped her long
scarf around Samantha's head, gagging her, and held her
down. Her hand over the child's mouth became warm
and damp as Samantha squealed and tried to cry out.
The child's body clutched to hers jerked and flailed,
shocking Susie, who hadn't been prepared for Samantha
to struggle, at least not so hard, and for so long, her small
body growing hotter and hotter, until Susie became
alarmed, and worried. She had looked out the window
and pretended to be calm, in case anyone was watching
as they trundled rapidly through the village and off into
the countryside. But she had been far from calm.

She hadn't intended it to happen that way, not at all,
thought Susie, going outside, making sure not to bang
the door.

She walked slowly across the weedy lawn and aim-
lessly down the driveway. She was immensely lonely.
She wondered if she would be this lonely in prison. She
looked back at the rented house, wishing she were
home in Vancouver, standing in front of her very own
little bungalow. She wished that her mother still occupied the family home outside Nanaimo. She wished
that Leigh-Anne still lived in her West End apartment
and that there was still a Mutt to slam in and out of
Susie's house through the dog door. She wanted to
weep, but couldn't.

A yellow automobile appeared around the bend in
the road, moving rapidly, trailing a small cloud of dust. It

slowed as it approached the entrance to the driveway, signaled, and turned in. Susie removed her sunglasses and put them in the pocket of her dress. She folded her hands in front of her and waited.

The car rolled to a stop. "Hello, Mrs. Williamson," said Joanna Leery through her open window, smiling broadly, her eyes concealed behind a pair of sunglasses much larger than Susie's. "I'll bet you thought it was never going to happen. But I'm here to tell you you're wrong."

Susie couldn't think of a single word to say. She opened her mouth and closed it, looking intently at the real estate agent.

Who suddenly snatched away her smile and replaced it with an expression of intense earnestness. "I'm terribly sorry that it's taken so long. I can't *believe* that you've been moved in for, what is it, two weeks? Three? And . . ." She looked through the windshield and waved a hand in the direction of the house. "That junk is *still* littering the yard. I can't *imagine* what you must think of me."

Susie, slightly crouched, was squinting at her, narrowing her eyes against the sun's reflection in the car windows. She cleared her throat. She struck the base of her throat lightly several times, as if to loosen her vocal cords. "Oh, we've gotten used to it, actually."

"It's extremely generous of you to say so," said Joanna Leery. "You can expect the truck tomorrow morning. Two men. They'll have the driveway cleared in no time." She beamed at Susie.

"Actually, that won't be convenient," said Susie. She stood straight and took her sunglasses from her pocket and put them on, settling them with both hands over the bridge of her nose, smoothing her hair over her ears.

"Oh dear," said the agent. "Oh dear. Why not?"

"Well, it just won't," said Susie. She kicked at the ground, creating a small swirl of dust. "We like our privacy, you see. We don't like to be disturbed." She looked at Joanna Leery disapprovingly. "You *had* said it would be cleared away before we moved in. Now — well, I guess it's just going to have to stay there."

"Oh," said the agent. "Oh." She was looking longingly up the driveway at the pile of rubbish sprawling comfortably between house and barn. "It's a dreadful eyesore, though," she said.

"That may be," said Susie, who had begun to sweat. "But we don't mind it, as it turns out."

"Well. I see. Well. All right, then." Joanna Leery offered Susie a semblance of a smile. "I guess I'll be on my way. I'll just get turned around first."

She hesitated, though. Perhaps she was hoping to be invited to stay for tea, thought Susie. She stepped back, with a graceful gesture, granting Joanna permission to proceed up the driveway.

The yellow bug drove up to the house, circled the patch of lawn, and headed back toward Susie. Susie wondered if Samantha was watching from her window. Joanna gave Susie a wave as she passed, and Susie waved back, and continued to watch until the car had turned onto the road and disappeared around the curve.

She walked back to the house and sank into the lawn chair. Another glass of iced tea would be nice, but she needed to sit a while first — the real estate agent's visit had rattled her. But it was a good thing she had come. Susie certainly didn't want a truck and two possibly curious laborers mucking about the place.

She rested her head against the back of the chair and closed her eyes. The sun was warm on her face and bare arms, and calming. Again she considered bringing the child outside for a while. She remembered watching her playing on the swings in the park with her babysitter. Those days had often been cold and rainy, but the two of them had seemed oblivious to the weather.

Susie went into the house, listening for a moment at the bottom of the stairs, and poured herself another glass of tea from a pitcher in the refrigerator. She went back out to the lawn chair.

She had asked her employer for time off, without pay. He didn't want to give it to her. He said they depended on her too much, she was the glue that held the place together. Susie thought he was probably right. But she had to have the time, she told him, and if he couldn't give it to her, then she would have to quit. He didn't want her to quit. They would find a way to get along without her, he said. Temporarily.

Susie then sat in her car down the block from Blair Decker's house day after day for more than a week. It was a wonder, really, that none of the neighbors ever demanded to know what she was doing there. Whenever Blair left home, she followed him. She followed him to Dundarave, where he would go in and out of his favorite grocery store, or a book store, or a stationery store, or one of several restaurants. During this period Susie became quite fond of West Vancouver, whose residential districts tumbled merrily down the mountainsides and onward to the seashore.

But he hardly ever took his daughter with him when he went out. And so she soon stopped following him and turned her attention to the babysitter. Whose name, she eventually learned, was Patsy.

Patsy McDonough lived in a basement suite in North Vancouver, about fifteen minutes by car from the Decker house. She owned an elderly VW Beetle that was painted red and speckled, so that it resembled an enormous ladybug. She looked after Samantha five days a week, arriving at eight o'clock and often not leaving until eight at night. On weekends she worked out at a local gym, met girlfriends for dinner or a movie, shopped for groceries, sometimes visited a hairdresser.

Susie signed up for six months at the same gym and made Patsy's acquaintance immediately by asking for her assistance in adjusting the speed and tension on the stationary bike. She had observed while following the babysitter that Patsy had an amiable, outgoing personality. Striking up a friendship had been easy. Soon they were meeting at the gym every Saturday, often going off afterwards for coffee and bagels. Susie reminded Patsy of her mother, who lived in Saskatchewan. Susie told Patsy that she herself had no children, but had always wanted a daughter.

By the time a month had passed Susie had the information she required.

And now what? she thought. She removed her sunglasses and rubbed her eyes. She laughed to herself, shaking her head. What on earth was she going to do now?

She had suspected from the beginning that she wouldn't be able to get away with it. Patsy, when she heard about Samantha's kidnapping, would of course think about the woman who had befriended her. Quite possibly some of the neighbors would come forward — Susie might have been observed by any number of people, sitting in her car outside Blair Decker's house. And there would be all kinds of police investigation techniques used against her that Susie wouldn't even be aware of.

She had accomplished what she set out to do: the child was here, with Susie — a prisoner. And the child's father was suffering.

It couldn't last. She hadn't expected that it would last.

She just hadn't thought about how the end would unfold.

The telephone rang in Harriet Murchison's kitchen, and Blair Decker picked it up.

"I want fifty grand," croaked a male voice.

"What?" Blair turned to his sister, who was preparing a chicken for the roasting pan. "What?" he said again.

"You heard me. You want your kid back, you gotta cough up fifty thousand dollars."

"Oh jesus," said Blair, standing up abruptly.

"What is it?" said Harriet. "Oh — is it them? Is it them?" She rushed to him and clutched at his arm, but he shook her off.

"Yes," said Blair into the phone. "Of course. But is she okay? Is my daughter okay?"

"Get the money. I'll call you again tomorrow, around noon. Tell you where and when to do the delivery."

"Is she okay?" Blair shouted. "If you've hurt her, you bastard —"

"Watch yourself, fella. You just watch how you talk to me."

"I'm sorry. Yes. But I've got to —"

"The kid's fine."

"I want to talk to her," said Blair. "Put her on."

"I can't do that, goddamnit. There's no phone where she is. I'm at a pay phone."

"Then how am I supposed to believe you? How do I know you've even *got* my daughter?"

"Oh, I've got her, all right."

"Prove it," said Blair. "Prove it!"

He listened, grasping the receiver with a clammy hand. "Yes," he said a moment later. "Okay." He hung up. "He says she's okay," he told Harriet. "I think I'm going to explode. He wants money."

He dialed the RCMP detachment and asked for Eddie. "I just got a call," he said to her. "He wants fifty thousand dollars."

"He?" said Eddie. "A *man* called you?"

"He's going to phone tomorrow at noon to tell me where and when."

"*How* much? Fifty thousand?"

"Sergeant — what does it mean? Is she alive? Do you think she's alive?" Harriet clutched his arm again, and this time he let her.

"I don't know, Mr. Decker. I hope so. Do you have to go over to the mainland to get the money?"

"Yeah. I'll need to talk to my bank manager. I don't have that much cash."

"I'll ride to the ferry with you. We can talk on the way."

THIRTY-NINE

Samantha could tell by the light that it was getting near the end of the day. She had now been in this room for two whole days and part of another one. Except that this morning the old woman had taken her to the bathroom, which was down the hall. When she was in there she had thought about trying to climb out the window, but it was a long way to fall.

She was very sad. Yesterday she had wished for books, and a television, and a computer with some games in it. Today she didn't feel like doing anything. She wondered if she might be getting sick. Surely if this happened they'd have to call a doctor for her, and the doctor would take her away, back to Aunt Harriet. And maybe her father would be there, too.

He hadn't paid much attention to her lately. Patsy had been taking care of her almost all the time. But Samantha was pretty sure he still loved her. He just missed her mother. And Samantha missed her, too.

She worried a lot about her mother. Because although it was true that she missed her — there was a big ache in her body where she used to love her, and where she used to know that her mother loved her too — sometimes Samantha couldn't quite remember what her mother looked like. At Aunt Harriet's it hadn't mattered, because Samantha had a picture that she kept in the drawer next to her bed. She took it out every morning and every night and kissed the glass that covered the photograph. And so of course during the day she had the picture to remember.

So just try to remember it now, Samantha told herself.

She was curled up on the high bed, facing the window, where sunshine was pouring in, making the room hot and stuffy. She was very tired. She wished she had Eeyore with her, something to put her arms around.

In the photograph her mother was leaning against the big tree in the park with the swings in it. It was an old maple tree that her mother said had got bent sideways when it was growing and after a few years it got unbent somehow and started going straight up like it was supposed to, so there was a wide part that was like a bench. And that's what her mother was leaning against, with her arms crossed, and her ankles, too, and she was smiling, almost laughing. It was Samantha's father who took the picture and so it was him that her mother was smiling at, but whenever Samantha looked at it she felt like her mother was actually smiling at her.

In the picture she was wearing a pair of jeans and a pink sweater with a V-shaped neck. Her hair was light brown, almost blonde like Samantha's. It was medium long and it curled under a little bit and she had bangs. And her eyes were blue. Samantha remembered this not from the picture but from looking into her mother's face. She could see the blue eyes, all right. She just couldn't remember how the other parts of her face fit together.

And now she didn't have the photograph to remind her. Pretty soon she would have forgotten her father's face, too. And even her own: she hadn't looked into a mirror for days and days, the one in the old lady's bathroom was too high up on the wall. Tears squeezed out of her eyes but Samantha tried hard not to cry again. Maybe it was all this crying that was making her so tired.

Susie picked up the empty glass from the lawn and headed for the house. She put the glass in the kitchen sink and went upstairs, taking the key from the pocket of her dress. She unlocked the door and went inside.

The child was lying on the bed. She turned to look at Susie. "Am I going home now?"

"No," said Susie. "But I thought you might want to go outside for a while. What do you think?"

"I want to go home," said Samantha.

"Not yet," said Susie. "Soon. But not yet."

"When?"

Susie looked at the window, smeared and smudged, and through it. "I think tomorrow."

The child began to weep. "I don't want to be here in the night again."

"Come on," said Susie briskly, holding out her hand. "We'll go outside. It'll help pass the time."

The girl climbed reluctantly off the bed. "You should have a TV," she said.

"I do," said Susie.

"Can I watch it?"

"We'll see," said Susie.

The child's hand slipped into Susie's. They went out into the hall, down the stairs, and out the front door.

"We'll go this way," said Susie, heading to the left, away from the driveway. "There are some horses in that field over there."

She held tight to Samantha's hand and was reminded of taking Mutt to the park, holding her leash, never trusting her not to suddenly bolt and tear the leash from her hand. Bolting was a game to Mutt. Like disregarding Susie's calls in the last moments of her life had been a game to Mutt. Susie gripped Samantha's hand more tightly, causing the child to give her a fearful glance.

"Sorry," said Susie, relaxing her hold.

They walked to the edge of the pasture and leaned against the wooden fence. Susie pointed to the shelter in which the horses could huddle if it was windy or raining.

"But where are they now?" said Samantha. "I can't see any horses."

"They must be over that hill," said Susie. "Behind it is the house where the people who own them live. Maybe they're riding them today."

"Maybe they're sick," said Samantha. "Or somebody took them."

Susie looked down at her and saw that the child's hair needed washing, and her clothes were limp and soiled. She had gotten scratches on her legs while helping to look for Mutt. They were healing well but there were streaks of dirt there, and on her arms. "You need a bath," she said.

Soberly, Samantha examined herself. "Yes, I do," she agreed.

They heard a car approaching, and both turned to face the road, where Arthur's Jeep was just about to turn in to the driveway. Susie thought about scurrying indoors with the child, and was in fact surprised that she didn't do this.

So was Samantha, who kept looking nervously from the Jeep to Susie and back again. "I don't like him," she said, her voice quivering.

"Shhh," said Susie sternly. "I don't want you to cry. Do not cry. Do you understand?" She squeezed Samantha's hand.

"Yes."

Arthur pulled up in front of the house in a small cloud of dust. He looked disbelievingly through the windshield, then hopped out of the Jeep. "What the hell do you think you're doing?" he hollered.

"The child needed some fresh air," said Susie, pleased that she sounded unruffled. Inside, she was definitely ruffled, as she tried decide what to do next. Several impulses were at work in her, and she needed a bit of time to figure out which one should prevail. "Come on, child," she said to Samantha. "You have to go back to your room now."

Samantha protested, but managed not to weep.

Susie ushered her upstairs. "Stay here for now," she told her. "And maybe you can watch television later."

Samantha stood in the middle of the room with her mouth half open and her smooth forehead suddenly furrowed.

Susie closed the door, and locked it, and put the key back in her pocket.

Arthur was still outside, standing under the willow tree, his arms folded, looking out toward the road.

"I'm going to take her home tomorrow," Susie told him.

What was buzzing around in Arthur's head was how he was going to collect the money from Blair Decker the next day. He had acted on impulse, phoning the guy, he hadn't had any real plan in mind. He didn't have to go through with it. But, jesus, it would be good to have some real money for once.

"Arthur? Did you hear me?"

The guy would have told the cops. So Arthur was trying to figure out a way to get the money without being seen by the goddamn Mounties. And then how to avoid being ID'd by the goddamn kid. It had occurred to him to get rid of her, of course, but he'd never done anything like that before. Sure, there were times when his temper got the better of him. But he had never killed anybody. He had hoped for a while that Susie would do it — he thought she'd been mad enough, and cold enough. But he knew now that that wasn't going to happen. And so Arthur was desperate, because his brain, though adequate in most situations, wasn't as sharp as he was afraid it needed to be to get him out of this predicament with his pockets full and no cops on his trail.

"Yeah, I heard you," he said.

He was hoping to grab the money and get the hell out of the province, start up new maybe in Calgary. There was no way he could stay here. He liked Susie, he admired her — but he couldn't trust her, not with his life. Which he was not about to spend in the goddamn slammer.

He had decided he'd better get himself a whole new identity. He wasn't sure how to go about this, but he thought he knew somebody who could help him. The problem was, he really should have done this first.

He'd been sure that he could persuade Susie to go for the big bucks as well as for revenge. But in order for that to happen they both would have had to keep their damn faces hidden from the kid. Which had been the plan. Until Susie had screwed everything up.

So, "Fine, fine," he said now, desperately trying to think things through. "You're letting her go tomorrow. Fine."

Susie wouldn't go along with him getting a ransom, and he knew she wouldn't let him take the kid anywhere, not on his own, so a straightforward swap was out of the question.

It occurred to him that he might be able to get Susie to return the kid at the same time as he was picking up the money. Now that — that had possibilities.

"How are you gonna do it, exactly? Let her out at the edge of town?" he said, trying to sound calm and only mildly interested. Behind him, he heard Susie sink into the rickety lawn chair.

"I'll probably drive her to the end of her street," she said, "and let her walk from there."

Arthur whirled around. "Susie," he said, through clenched teeth. "You are so goddamn stupid. For a clever woman you can be so goddamn dumb." He took in a big breath. "There's probably a *cop* there, for god's sake. In the house. Or sitting in an unmarked car out in front. And *neighbors*, for god's sake. *Watching*."

"Well, what would you suggest, Arthur?"

"You don't want to get caught, right? And don't for godsake do not tell me again that you don't care. Okay?"

He shook his fist in her face, severely tempted to whack her one. "Because *I* care. *I* bloody well care. I want time to get the hell away from here."

"So *go*, for heaven's sake," said Susie. She sounded exasperated, but Arthur could tell he'd flustered her. "There are two more ferries today, maybe three. I told you, I don't need you any more."

"Jesus christ." Arthur flapped his arms, reminding Susie of an enraged crow, his face darkened with fury, hair askew, as if electrified. "I can't believe how you've screwed it up. After everything . . ."

Susie looked at him curiously. "After everything what? Everything you did? What have you done, exactly?"

"I've been with you every step of the way. I've made it possible for this to happen, for chrissake."

"You've got a mighty inflated sense of your own importance, Arthur. Who did the research? Who made friends with the babysitter and found out the child was coming here? Who trailed her and her aunt around Sechelt day after day?"

"But I started it," Arthur shouted. "I — I ignited the whole thing!"

Susie remembered the long black night in which she had heard the words over and over: *"He owes you, Susie." "Owes me what? A daughter?"*

And she supposed that he was right.

"I opened the bloody gate!" he shouted.

Susie looked at him blankly.

He looked back at her. She'd pushed him into this. She was *such* an infuriating woman.

"What gate?" said Susie.

He hadn't done it on purpose. He'd gone through the gate and thought he'd closed it behind him. But he hadn't.

"What gate?" She stood up. "Mutt. Is that what you mean?"

The damn gate swung open, the damn dog came tearing around from the back of the house and spotted it and before Arthur could have done a damn thing about it, the dog was out of the yard and racing across the street. Arthur had gone home then, not wanting to be around when Susie showed up.

When the damn dog ended up getting himself killed, Arthur had known that his daydream could come true.

"It was a wonderful moment," he said. "As soon as you told me about Leigh-Anne, and that her boyfriend had a kid, there was this plan, full-blown, in my head."

"But you knew you couldn't count on me," said Susie slowly, "unless I had nothing left. Nothing more to lose."

Arthur bowed his head, taking credit where credit was due.

"You're kidding," said Blair. He began driving too fast. "Oh my god." He pulled over to the side of the road.

Norah Gibbons, who was following in a patrol car so she could give Eddie a ride back to the detachment, pulled in behind them.

"You recognize the description?" said Eddie.

Blair was clinging tight to the steering wheel, staring out the windshield. "I might not have. Except for the ring."

"What's her name, Mr. Decker?" "Elizabeth Munson" hadn't led them anywhere, as they had expected.

"Susie Wilson."

Eddie wrote this in her notebook, and the address that Decker gave her, too.

"Has she got a boyfriend? Any men friends you know about?"

Blair shook his head. "I don't understand about the money," he said.

"What do you mean?"

"She wouldn't want money."

Eddie gazed at his profile. "Then what?"

"I can't tell you."

"For god's sake," said Eddie, exasperated. She took a moment to calm herself. "What is your connection with this woman, Mr. Decker?"

"I — I knew her daughter. Leigh-Anne." It floated from his mouth, a fragile whisper.

"Tell me about Leigh-Anne."

He shuddered. "I can't. I can't. I've got to think."

Eddie watched him, her teeth clenched behind lips pressed firmly together. "Stay here," she said. She turned off the engine and took the keys from the ignition. "Don't move." She got out of the car and walked quickly to the driver's window of the patrol car. She tore the page from her notebook and handed it to Norah Gibbons. "Get on the radio, get Vancouver to check this out now," she said. "I think the kid might be there. And have somebody check Motor Vehicles, find out what this woman drives."

She returned to Decker's car and opened his door. "Move over," she said. "I'm going to drive you to the ferry. And while I do, I want you to tell me everything you know about Susie Wilson."

It wasn't much, as it turned out. He had met her only twice, he said.

"Then please explain to me," said Eddie sharply, "why you think she kidnapped your daughter, this woman you knew so slightly?" She glanced across at him. His head was bowed, his hands gripped his temples. "What's it got to do with Leigh-Anne?"

But he wouldn't. He only shook his head. "I've got to think" was all he would say.

Eddie was frustrated and enraged by the time they neared the terminal. As they sped down the hill she saw that the ferry was already approaching. But the lineup wasn't a long one: he would have no trouble getting on.

"Lane twenty-three," said the attendant in the booth.

Norah Gibbons, behind them, turned off, heading for the foot passenger drop-off point.

"You've got to tell us what's going on here, Mr. Decker," said Eddie, entering lane twenty-three. "How do you expect us to get your daughter back if you won't tell us what you know? Do you understand me?"

In her peripheral vision she saw him nod.

"Think about it. And then call me. Tonight," she told him, "as soon as you get home."

There was no response.

Eddie drew up close to the last car in lane twenty-three and switched off the engine. She turned to Blair. "You got that?"

"I've got it. I'll call you."

"You think you can get yourself onto the ferry all right?"

He nodded.

"Okay." Eddie opened the door and got out. "It's all yours." She watched him slide back behind the wheel.

"Thanks."

"Don't mention it," said Eddie, and wended her way through the waiting vehicles to Norah Gibbons's patrol car.

That evening, after dark, Susie and Samantha were in the kitchen doing the dishes. Susie had made scrambled eggs and toast, and they had had ice cream for dessert. Samantha had eaten two helpings of everything, much to Susie's relief. She was now telling Samantha about her mother's house, the house in which Susie had grown up, which would soon belong to somebody else.

"When did your mother die?" said Samantha, carefully drying a bread and butter plate.

"Last September."

The plate was a thick white one with a thin blue ring painted around the rim. Samantha clutched it to her chest with one hand and wielded the teatowel with the other. "My mother died in October."

"I'm very sorry about your mother, Samantha."

"I'm sorry about yours, too."

Susie put a tentative hand on the child's hair, newly washed. She had had a bath, too. But had insisted on putting her own clothes back on, politely declining to wear anything of Susie's.

"Oops," said Susie. "Soapsuds." She tore a piece of paper towel from a roll on the counter and dabbed at the top of Samantha's head until they were gone.

"Is he coming back?" said Samantha. She put the plate on the counter and took another one from the draining rack.

"My friend, you mean?" Susie hesitated, as if listening for footsteps. "No. He won't be back."

"But he might be," said Samantha. She was watching herself drying the plate, making sure it didn't slip from her hand and fall to the floor. "Is he really your friend?"

"Well, he used to be. And no, he won't be back. He'll be on the ferry by now," said Susie, emptying the sink.

"Have you really got a dog?" said Samantha.

Susie wrung out the dishcloth and wiped the counter, then the sink, then the splashboard. She wrung it out again and folded it and draped it over the divider between the sink's two compartments. She turned around and leaned against the counter, her hands in the pockets of her dress. "Not any more," she said. "But I did have a dog, and her name was Mutt, and she looked just the way I told you she looked."

Samantha slid the second dried plate onto the first. "My daddy says I can have a pet," she said. "At the end of the summer. A dog or a cat. I don't know which one I want."

"It's a hard decision," Susie agreed. "Just leave the frying pan to drain dry."

Samantha nodded. "Yeah. It's too heavy." She picked up a handful of cutlery.

Susie opened a drawer. "That goes in here."

"Can we watch TV after this?"

"Depends on what's on. What are you allowed to watch?"

"I don't know. Maybe anything I want." She dried each fork, knife, and spoon separately — there were only two of each — and put them in the appropriate sections of the drawer. "Mostly I like to read. That's where I was going, to the library, when — when . . ."

"When I kidnapped you," said Susie.

"Why did you do that?" said Samantha, looking down into the drawer.

"It was very bad of me."

Slowly, Samantha closed the drawer.

"Maybe we can find you something to read," said Susie. "I found a box of books here, and some of them are children's books."

It was much cooler in the basement, which was only half the size of the house and had no windows. The walls were crumbling and the floor was damp in the corners. There were several boxes, neatly packed with things Susie had removed from the upstairs rooms. Brandishing a large flashlight, because the bulb in the ceiling light had burned out, she pulled open the tops until she found the one containing the books.

"Here we are," she said, aiming the light into the first opened carton. "Take a look."

"They're really old," said Samantha, poking through the box. "And they smell funny."

"They're musty," said Susie, "from being packed away for so long. *Heidi.* That's probably a good one. *Lassie Come Home.* I don't know. That might be too old for you. *Poor Little Rich Girl.*"

Samantha laughed. "Poor little rich girl?"

"Shhh," said Susie, looking up at the ceiling.

Samantha looked up, too, from her crouch upon the floor. "What's the matter?" she whispered.

"I thought I heard something," Susie whispered back. "I'm going to turn off the flashlight." She reached across the box of books and took Samantha's hand. "Don't be frightened."

She heard it again, louder now because it was dark — the slow squeak of the front door, opening. The thick thud as it closed. Now, someone walking through the house. Arthur, she thought. Her heartbeat had quickened.

Or maybe it was the police. Maybe Arthur had gone to the police.

Or someone unseen had spotted Samantha outside in the yard and summoned them.

But then she heard him calling her name.

"Susie? Susie, where the hell are you?"

The child whimpered.

There was no way out of the basement except through the house. Susie turned the flashlight back on. "Don't worry," she said to Samantha. "Really, there's nothing to worry about." She let go of the child's hand and loaded several books into her arms. "You can stay up all night reading, if you like. And tomorrow, like I told you, I'll take you to your Aunt Harriet's house." She led the way to the stairs, and back up into the kitchen.

She ignored Arthur, whose expression registered guilt, defiance, and indignation at the sight of the child, and took Samantha back to her room. "I'm going to lock the door again," she said, putting the books down on the cot. She smoothed Samantha's hair and smiled at her. "I'll bring you up a snack."

In the kitchen, Arthur was drinking a beer. "I couldn't let you finish up by yourself," he said earnestly. "I just couldn't."

"I have nothing to say to you." Susie got an apple and some cheddar cheese from the fridge and began cutting the fruit into quarters, removing the core.

"I'm truly sorry about the damn dog," said Arthur.

Susie put the apple pieces on a plate and cut several chunks from the cheese.

"We'll finish it together," said Arthur, "like we started it together. And then we'll go our separate ways. If that's what you want."

Susie got a box of crackers from the cupboard and added them to the plate.

"What time do you figure to take her back?" he asked casually.

Susie poured a glass of milk and put the glass and the plate on a tray.

"I want to know how early to get up in the morning," said Arthur. "Come on, Susie, for god's sake, what time?"

Susie mounted the stairs, unlocked the door, and took the tray into Samantha's room.

The child was sitting up on the bed. "I can't decide which one to read first," she said.

"Try *Lassie Come Home*," said Susie, putting the glass of milk and the plate on the table next to the bed. "Maybe it'll help you decide whether you want a dog or a cat. It's a pretty sad book sometimes," she warned.

"But it'll end happily, right?"

"I wouldn't ordinarily tell you a thing about the end of a book," said Susie. "But, yes. It ends happily."

Arthur was in the hallway. She was conscious of his size, of the breadth of him, and of his anger, which he would like to have concealed. The hall was only dimly lit and his face looked to Susie like a collection of darknesses, a sinister effect created, she knew, by shadows, and by the fact that he hadn't shaved for several days.

"In the morning," she said quickly. "I'll take her in the morning. Not too early. But before lunch."

FORTY

Susie rose early the next morning. She had a long shower and washed her hair, then went outside to let it dry in the sun.

Arthur was in the living room, nervous and fidgety. He sprawled for a while on the sofa and she heard his omnipresent brown leather jacket squeaking as he squirmed. Then he bounced to his feet to peer again through the window, as if he were expecting someone to advance upon them up the driveway. Susie hadn't slept much and she knew that he hadn't, either; she had heard the television murmuring to him all night long. It had become quiet, finally, only when she emerged from her room and turned on the shower.

When her hair was dry she returned to the house and prepared breakfast for Samantha: cereal with brown sugar and cream, brown toast, strawberry jam, orange juice, and a glass of milk. She delivered it on a tray and allowed the child to go to the bathroom before she ate. She locked Samantha's door before getting dressed, another admission that whatever relationship had once existed between herself and Arthur had now deteriorated into nothingness: she didn't trust him around the child.

But she made breakfast for him, too, nonetheless. It was a homely but ritualistic way of finishing with him. She made fried eggs, sausages, and whole wheat toast.

"That was excellent, Susie. Thank you," he said when

he'd eaten, and she was reminded of why she had been attracted to him. There was a sly, confident courtliness in his manner that cheered her. And he had allowed her to feel his admiration for her, too — physical, as well as friendly. That was no small thing when you'd reached her age. Yes, she hadn't been an absolute dope, she thought, gazing at him. Even though she was now relieved to be getting shut of him.

"What ferry do you figure to get?" he asked.

Susie, clearing the table, said, "Mid-afternoon."

Arthur nodded. "Good. Good. Well, I'll meet you there, then. On the ferry. In the cafeteria?"

"Sure."

He urged her to wait until early afternoon to release the child. "Or even suppertime," he said. "Or evening. Let the bastard suffer as long as possible."

They agreed upon one o'clock.

And he bustled away in his Jeep Wagoneer.

It was then about ten in the morning.

"Her house in Vancouver is empty," said Norah Gibbons. The three of them — she, Frank Turner, and Eddie — were once again meeting in Eddie's office.

"Damn," said Eddie.

"Did the guys talk to her neighbors?" said Frank from the black leather chair.

"Yeah, of course," said Norah. "The people next door said she went away about three weeks ago. They don't know where, or for how long. She asked them to keep an eye on her place."

"Does she work? Do they know who for?" said Eddie.

Norah set her coffee mug down on the edge of Eddie's desk and turned a page in her notebook. "Some real estate place in Burnaby."

"Okay, good. So we get a list and hit the phones," said Eddie. "Find out which one, talk to the staff."

"I'll take that," said Frank.

"Good. And Norah. Have you got the neighbors' phone number?"

"Yep. Right here."

"Give them a call. Ask if they know anything about Susie Wilson's daughter. Leigh-Anne. Don't know her last name. She'll be grown up, could be married. But check the phone book first, obviously, in case she isn't."

"Sure, boss."

"And don't call me boss."

Norah grinned. "Sure, Sarge." She headed for the door.

"Wait a minute," said Frank.

"What?" said Norah.

Frank drew up his long legs and leaned forward, his notebook in his hands. "Can we take stock first?" he said to Eddie. "Go through it again?"

Eddie nodded. "Sure. Good idea." She took hold of her braid and pulled at it, trying to loosen it. "Sit down for another minute, Norah, okay?"

Norah sat, heavily.

"Okay," said Eddie, tossing her braid back over her shoulder "What do we know?"

"There's at least two of them," said Frank. "A thinnish woman who wears long dresses and a ring with a large green stone, and a man. She isn't young. Probably late fifties, early sixties. So him too, probably. We're assuming they've got a vehicle." He turned to Norah. "Did you get anything from Motor Vehicles?"

"Give me a break, Turner," said Norah peevishly. "There hasn't been time yet."

"So?" said Eddie, cradling the back of her head in her hands.

"Well, there may be a difference of opinion between them," said Frank. "The note says one thing and the phone call said another. Maybe they've had a falling out."

Eddie stood up and went to the window, raising the venetian blind, lowering it, raising it again. She returned to her desk and sat on the edge. "Okay. Say you're right.

They've had a falling out. Or at least, they're working at cross purposes. Where does that get us?"

Frank sat back in the chair, causing the leather to sigh.

Norah finished her coffee and put the mug back on the edge of the desk.

Eddie stood up and went back to the window. Her office, she thought, seemed to get smaller every day.

"Another thing," said Turner. "If the guy intends to exchange the kid for the money, that means she's got to be here, on the peninsula."

Eddie nodded. "What do you have on people new to the area, Norah?"

"We're still checking the rentals, the motels, the B and Bs. I've got a list of names as long as your arm. But nothing jumped out at me. Mostly it's families with kids."

"Check again," said Eddie. "Concentrate on couples the right age. Never mind what else — kids, pets, whatever. Maybe they lied."

"I think I'll drag Friesen in on it," Norah muttered. "Get his butt off his chair for a change."

Eddie sat behind her desk. "Okay. Susie Wilson. She lives in Vancouver, works in Burnaby. She met Blair Decker only twice. His connection with her is through her daughter. Now he doesn't want to talk about that, for some reason. But you know what? It's not on. He's going to *have* to talk about it." She scowled at Frank, then at Norah. "He insists she wouldn't have done it for money. I wonder what the hell he did to her, or what she *thinks* he did to her?"

"So has he been in touch?" said Norah. "When's he getting back?"

Eddie checked her watch. "He was going to catch the ten-thirty ferry."

"Has he come up with the cash?" asked Frank.

Eddie nodded. "He called his bank manager last night. It's not a problem."

"How do we even know this guy's the one who

snatched her?" said Norah, rubbing her forehead where the sweatband of her cap had creased the skin.

"He described her accurately, according to her father," said Eddie.

"Yeah, but that description's been circulated all over the damn place."

"But we kept back the scar on her knee. A small half-moon-shaped scar she got when she fell on a board that had a nail sticking out of it. When she was three."

"So assuming he calls Decker again, like he said he would," said Frank, "this will be our chance to get at least one of them. When the money's handed over."

"Right," said Eddie. "And I want you to organize that, Frank. Decker will call us the minute he hears from the kidnapper. You take the call, decide how you want to handle it, then check with me."

"Gotcha," said Frank.

"Meanwhile," said Eddie, "we've got to keep trying to find out where the kid is. Get that list of Burnaby real estate agencies and divide it up. Somebody at her place of work must know something that'll help us."

"I'll get Friesen going on the rentals," said Norah, grabbing her coffee mug and heading for the door. "Look Leigh-Anne Wilson up in the phone books. And then I'll ask the neighbors about her. For what it's worth."

"Where will you be, Sarge?" said Frank, standing up.

"Decker should be here soon. I'm going over to the Murchison place to talk to him." She looked up at Frank, who was slouched in the doorway, his red hair disheveled, the scar prominent on his forehead and cheek. "I've got to persuade him to tell us what the hell's going on here."

"Get something to eat first, Sarge," he said gently.

She gave him a fleeting smile. "Okay. I will. Thanks, Frank."

Eddie went home to grab a quick bite to eat. She made herself a tomato and cucumber sandwich and was standing by the kitchen window eating it, looking out at the backyard, where Max was mowing the lawn, when the phone rang. She gulped down her mouthful of sandwich and picked it up.

"Hi, doll," said Alan.

Eddie went to replace the receiver, then changed her mind. She didn't reply but she didn't hang up, either. She pushed the button on the answering machine that would record the call.

Why hadn't she done this months ago? she thought.

She listened closely. He was even more offensive than usual. His language was foul. There was a savagery in his tone that made her shudder.

When he paused for breath, she put down the receiver and waited. He didn't call again.

She removed the cassette from the answering machine, wrote the date and time on an envelope and slipped the cassette inside.

Samantha was absorbed in *Lassie Come Home*, but as soon as Susie opened the door she put the book aside. "Is it time to go?"

"Not yet," said Susie. "But you can come downstairs if you like. Bring the book."

The child climbed off the bed, holding two fingers in the book to mark her place. "When will it be time?"

"We'll go right after lunch."

"But I only just had breakfast," said Samantha, dismayed.

Susie ignored her and cleaned up the kitchen, and soon the child settled onto the sofa, reading.

Time passed unutterably slowly. Susie glanced at the clock on the kitchen wall so frequently that the hands seemed never to move.

She sat at the kitchen table and ran her hands back and forth over the grain in the wood, thinking about the note she'd sent, wondering how she could ever have done such a thing, thinking about Leigh-Anne, and Mutt, and betrayal, and revenge. She shook her head wearily.

Finally, just before noon, she could stand it no longer. She got up and went into the living room. "We'll go now," she said.

Samantha's eyes grew wide. Susie saw her catch her breath and hold it.

"Come on," said Susie.

"Are you fooling me?"

Susie shook her head.

The child turned over the corner of the page she'd been reading, put the book down on the sofa next to her, and scrambled to her feet.

"Take it with you, if you like," said Susie.

Samantha picked up the book. "Thank you."

They went out the back door, because Susie's station wagon was parked there, and Susie put Samantha in the front passenger seat and made sure she did up the seat belt. Then she climbed in behind the wheel and started the motor.

"We have to let it warm up," she told Samantha. "For one minute." It felt good to be in her own car again, driving her own car again. She gave the dashboard an affectionate pat.

Neither of them said much on the way into town. Susie had thought about blindfolding the child but she didn't have the heart.

Inside the Murchison front door Eddie took off her cap and stood with her feet apart, gazing at Blair Decker. "I want to know why Susie Wilson has it in for you. It's got something to do with her daughter, hasn't it?"

Decker pressed his lips together and shook his head. He was standing next to the archway that led into the dining room. He was stiff and straight — there was something unyielding in him, something so indifferently stubborn that she wanted to hit him.

The house was somnolent; blameless. Morning sunshine slanted through the living-room windows and arranged itself in a broad swath upon the hall floor.

Harriet had tiptoed through the kitchen and out the door into the backyard when Eddie arrived, and Eddie thought this was because she was looking so grim. She must look grim, because that's how she felt.

"What's your relationship with her?" she asked. "How can I reach her? We've got to talk to her, surely you must see that."

Blair Decker shook his head, slowly, looking at the floor.

Samantha sat quietly, holding the book in her lap. Occasionally she glanced over at Susie, but mostly she looked out the window.

Susie, behind her sunglasses, was beginning to wish for a cloudy day, even for rain. You can get tired of anything, she thought. Even sunshine.

"It won't do, Mr. Decker," said Eddie. "You've got to talk about it, whatever the hell it is. You're putting your child at risk."

"No," said Blair. His voice was even deeper, huskier, than when she had first talked to him. "She won't hurt her. I'm sure of it."

"But she isn't *alone* in this, is she?" said Eddie, unable to disguise her anger. "What about the other one? What about the man who wants fifty thousand bucks?"

"I'll pay it," he said quickly. "And I'll get her back."

"Mr. Decker," Eddie began. She looked directly into his eyes. Trying to figure out how to reach him. "Mr. Decker," she said again.

The trouble is, she thought, I've got no damn sympathy for the man. I can see that he's suffering. I can see that. But I don't damn care. I only care about his kid.

She was seriously calculating whether she had

grounds to arrest him. For obstructing justice, maybe. Or public mischief.

And then the telephone rang.

The kid's father answered on the third ring.

"Do you have the money?" Arthur growled, once again disguising his voice.

"I've got it. Right here."

"I want you to drive down to Port Mellon. There's a —"

"Port Mellon?"

"Port Mellon. That's what I said, isn't it? Port Mellon."

"The pulp and paper mill?"

"I don't know what the hell they do there," Arthur hollered. "They made stuff out of wood, I don't know what they make. Just listen, will you? And write this down, so you don't get lost."

He'd been driving around in the Jeep these last couple of days, taking it into four-wheel-drive territory, and on one of his trips he'd found a clearing up there above the mill. Scared the hell out of him, it did. He'd damn near driven off the edge of what turned out to be a cliff. The drop-off was covered in blackberry bushes, so he'd missed it, nearly plummeted right off it. He had sat there with his heart going like a snare drum, looking out over a forest that was *way* down there, and beyond the forest, the sea, with the coastal mountains rising in the background.

And as he looked, and as his heart quieted, he realized that it was the perfect place.

"Okay, I've got it," said the kid's father. He repeated the directions back to Arthur.

"Right. Be there in exactly forty-five minutes."

"Forty-five minutes. Yes. And you'll have her with you? Samantha?"

But Arthur had hung up.

He'd made the call from Gibsons. It took him less than fifteen minutes to make his way to the clearing. He parked the Jeep in the woods, made sure it was invisible from both the clearing and the road, and settled down to watch and to wait.

Susie turned the station wagon onto Harriet Murchison's street. At the curb in front of the house sat an RCMP patrol car. Calmly, Susie pulled over.

"Okay. Here you are," she said.

Samantha opened the door of the station wagon and slid out onto the sidewalk. Instantly, she began to run, the book held tightly to her chest.

Susie watched until the child was safely through the gate, and then drove away, back to the rented house with the long poplar-lined driveway.

Blair Decker turned to Eddie in a panic. "I don't know where this damn place is. I've never been to Port bloody Mellon. How long is it going to take me to get there? Oh, jesus, what if I can't get there in forty-five minutes? Will he kill her? Do you think he'll kill her?"

He was plunging around the kitchen, waving his arms, completely distraught. His sister, who had run inside when she heard the phone, was trying to pat him on the shoulder, but he kept skittering away from her, reminding Eddie of a gigantic dragonfly.

"We'll find it, Mr. Decker. Don't worry." Eddie took the phone from him. "I'm calling Corporal Turner. When he gets here I want you to tell him everything the man said to you."

But Blair Decker didn't hear her. He had moved into the living room and was staring out the window. Then he rushed to the front door and threw it open.

Eddie followed him. Samantha was sprinting through the gate, clutching a book under her arm.

When the unmarked cars pulled up in front of the house five minutes later, Blair Decker was still holding his daughter, and the shoulder of her T-shirt was wet with his tears.

FORTY-ONE

Susie was sitting under the willow tree again, drinking iced tea and wearing her sunglasses, watching the road.

I could have gotten away, she thought at one point.

But not for long.

I could have gotten home.

But no farther.

She thought again of Buddy. And it was true. She wasn't any better than Buddy after all.

Samantha sat on the sofa next to her father, cuddled close, one hand curled next to her face, her plump legs straight out in front of her. Blair Decker's arm encircled the child, whose head was pressed against the side of his chest.

Eddie wanted to touch her, to pat her chubby thigh, smooth her ruffled hair, stroke her rosy cheek.

The child squirmed, and rested a protective hand on top of the book in her lap.

The clothes she had been wearing had been removed and placed in evidence bags, and her aunt had dressed her in a pink dress and white socks and white patent leather shoes.

"Where's Eleanor?" said Samantha to her father.

"She's at school," said Harriet, who was sitting in the rocking chair where she had waited for Blair Decker's call the evening of Samantha's disappearance. "She'll be home soon."

"Now, do you think you can help the sergeant?" said Samantha's father.

Samantha's eyes skittered to Eddie, in the wingback chair near the big fern. "How?"

"Tell me what happened to you," said Eddie.

"They *stole* me," said Samantha. "They just picked me up and *stole* me." She rubbed her fingers across the cover of the book. "She said she was looking for her dog. But her dog died. She didn't even have a dog." She snuggled closer to her father. "I don't want to talk to her any more," she whispered.

Eddie decided to ignore this. "Stealing children is very bad," she said. "We want to find the people who stole you. And we need your help, Samantha."

"What'll happen to them?" said Samantha, peering at her over Blair Decker's arm.

Eddie hesitated. "That depends," she said carefully. "Were they mean to you?"

Samantha nodded her head vigorously. "The man yelled at me. He made me cry. I don't like that man, not one bit."

"How about the woman?"

Samantha lifted *Lassie Come Home* with one hand and tugged at her skirt with the other. "She was mean at first. Then she was nice." She looked at Eddie through half-closed eyes. "She was sad. Her mother died. Like mine did."

"Did she tell you her name?"

The child shook her head. "But I heard it. The man called her Susie. And she called him . . . I can't remember."

"This is a big help to me, Samantha," said Eddie. "I'm writing it down in here, in my notebook, so I won't forget."

Samantha said, "Okay."

"Can you tell me about the house you were in? And what it looked like outside?"

"Well," said Samantha. She slipped from her father's embrace and climbed off the sofa. "First I have to have a ginger ale."

"I don't get all that many rentals," said Joanna Leery, "so this shouldn't take long. Hold on while I get my records, okay?"

"I appreciate this, Ms. Leery," said Cornie Friesen, pulling an interview form up onto his computer screen.

"Here we are. Right. Now, tell me again, who are you looking for?"

"A couple. Late fifties, early sixties. Would have moved in three, four weeks ago."

"Do you know what they look like?"

"Nope. Well, wait," he said, rifling through his notebook, "yeah, here . . . I don't have anything on the guy, but the woman has medium-long hair, mostly gray, she's thin, she wears mostly long dresses. Ring a bell?"

Joanna Leery laughed happily. "Do you know, it does? And it's funny, but I was out there just yesterday, a rental property on a huge lot, two stories, three bedrooms — it was my intention to arrange to take away the junk that's cluttering up the driveway but oh no, she'd have none of it."

Cornie Friesen, phone clutched between ear and shoulder, began typing. "Hold it, hold it. Let's start from the beginning here. What's the address of this place?"

In the Jeep Wagoneer, in the woods, Arthur sat, and waited. When forty-five minutes had passed with no sign of Blair Decker he continued to wait. He had arrived early. This was partly strategy and partly eagerness.

He was very nervous at first, sitting there with the car window open so he'd be able to hear the first faint sound of an engine laboring up the hill toward the clearing. But time passed and he heard no engine — only birds, and the wind that occasionally gusted through the forest, rattling the branches that were concealing his vehicle.

He had backed deep into the woods, bumping over fallen branches and blown-over trees, crunching over ferns and weeds. It was a good thing he wasn't allergic, he thought, batting at the debris that kept flying through the open window: pollen, and bits of foliage, even the occasional insect. He finally closed the window, glancing at his watch. And jesus christ, another fifteen minutes had passed. He had now been waiting a full hour. The guy was late. Fifteen minutes late.

Fifteen minutes later he was still there, waiting, and Blair Decker still hadn't shown up.

All of a sudden Arthur was paralyzed by panic. He couldn't breathe for a minute, he was so terrified. He had seen in his mind a convoy of RCMP patrol cars making its way up the hillside — christ, no, this was no hill, this was a bloody mountain — up the mountainside, heading for the clearing.

He wrenched himself free of this nightmare, fired up the Jeep, and got the hell out of there, hurtling down the mountain, expecting to see the goddamn Mounties around every turn. Even if they didn't know his vehicle, even if they didn't know what he looked like, it wouldn't matter: they'd follow anybody they saw coming down from this mountain on this day.

When he finally reached the bottom he was shaking with relief. He drove another half a mile and pulled over, draping his arms on the steering wheel and collapsing upon them.

After a while he felt calmer. His mind began working again. So the guy was half an hour late. That was nothing. He was probably driving around, frantic, trying to find the way. Arthur scrutinized the road, which wasn't a road at all but a track, rutted and dusty, like the driveway at the rented house. There was only one way up there. He decided to park here and wait a little longer.

Again, he backed into the brush, until he was sure his green Jeep was invisible. Here he would wait for Blair Decker, and when the guy showed up he'd make sure there were no cops on his trail and then he'd follow him up to the clearing and collect the money. The more he thought about it the more certain he became that Decker, who had sounded frantic and disorganized on the phone, had gotten lost but would eventually find his way.

Arthur, resigned to wait as long as necessary, turned the car radio on, real low, for company.

Forty minutes later he was shooting along the road that led to the rented house, his strangled mutterings becoming an occasional bleat of fury. He yanked the Jeep onto the driveway and bumped rapidly toward the house, toward Susie, who was still sitting in that goddamn lawn chair wearing her goddamn sunglasses drinking her goddamn iced tea. He drove all the way around behind the house, parked next to the back door, and rushed inside. He was going to pack up his belongings, something he hadn't thought to do earlier and which Susie must have wondered about. But he hadn't cared about his belongings then, oh no, he'd been going to start a whole new life with the fifty Gs, but now — now — *shit*. He raced up the stairs, turned around in the hallway and raced back down and out the front door. He stood in front of Susie, panting.

Suddenly he sank to the grass, gripping his head with both hands. "Jesus, Susie," he said, his voice trembling. "You should've done what we said. You should've waited until one o'clock." He lifted his face to her. "It's all over the goddamn news," he said. "How the kid's been safely returned." He felt her stare raking his face and turned his head away.

"And how does that matter to you?" Susie said. "What have you been up to, Arthur?"

He got on his hands and knees, pushed himself to his feet. "I could've had a brand-new life," he said bleakly.

She looked at him for a long moment, resisting the impulse to stand up and gather him into her arms, or at least to reach out and take his hand. "Was the old life such a bad one, Arthur?" she said softly.

He didn't answer. "I'm gonna get my stuff," he said. "How long do you figure I've got?"

"I don't know," said Susie. "Not long."

He walked toward the house, slowly at first, then his pace quickened. Susie heard the front door open and bang closed. She would watch him drive away, and if by then the police hadn't come, she would call them.

Again, as she waited, she thought of Buddy. Of the last time she had seen him. They had lived in Kamloops then. Leigh-Anne was asleep in her room, just as Susie had told her, eight months ago, across the remnants of the rose garden.

Leigh-Anne had only just fallen asleep. Susie tiptoed from the kitchen to the living room with a mug of tea in her hand. She glanced through the window and saw that it was raining, a desultory rain, almost silent, almost invisible, falling from a somber gray sky. She put her mug on a small end table and sat down. She considered turning on the television but didn't want to wake Leigh-Anne, and so she was just sitting there, resting, with her eyes closed, when she heard a car pull up in front of the house. A moment later Buddy walked through the door. She was surprised to see him in the middle of the day.

She knew as soon as she looked at him that something was wrong. She thought that someone must have died.

"I've got something to tell you," he said flatly.

Susie stood up, but didn't move toward him: he didn't look approachable.

"Before you find out from somebody else."

"Find out what, Buddy?" She had clasped her hands in front of her. Part of her was listening for Leigh-Anne, hoping she wouldn't wake up. She wanted to tell Buddy to lower his

voice. And close the door, through which a cold breeze was blow-ing, carrying occasional raindrops.

He put out his hands, as if to touch her, but she was too far away and neither of them moved closer. "I love you, Susie."

"You're scaring me."

"I love you. I'm so sorry." He seemed unaware that he had begun to cry.

"Buddy, what's happening?"

"I'm going to be arrested."

She didn't believe him. She thought it was a joke. But she knew it wasn't a joke, because of his tears. She felt herself gap-ing at him. She thought about overdue parking tickets, speeding tickets too expensive to pay. She fumbled for comprehension. "For what?" she said finally. She could move now, and she did, she went swiftly to him and put her hands on his waist, look-ing imploringly into his face.

He removed her hands and stepped away from her, back-wards, and at first Susie thought he would leave the house, through the open door. He put his hands over his face. "I — I — I messed with Katherine."

She felt it in her chest, like a physical assault: she thought she knew now what it would be like to be shot.

And so her body had believed him, instantly. It took her mind longer.

The set of his chin, the glint in his eye, the ripple of his young muscles beneath the smooth sheath of his skin — none of this had consequence any longer, once he told her what he had done, that he had abused their fourteen-year-old babysitter. She wondered if he would ever have told her if the police hadn't been at his heels.

Susie was grieving him now. There had been no room for grief at the time. Then there had been room only for shame and anger, and for obligation to Leigh-Anne. But now she felt it. Grief. For the other parts of Buddy. For the things about him that she had loved. And she won-dered if he might not be dying, somewhere, now, at this very moment, so bitter was her grief and so severe the pain that accompanied it.

I'm pretty sure I did the right thing, though, Leigh-Anne, she said silently, watching the patrol car turn in to the driveway.

She set the empty glass down on the weedy lawn and removed her sunglasses, placing them on the grass, too. The police car stopped several yards away. The doors opened and three people got out, a man and a woman in uniform from the front seat and Blair Decker from the back. They stood there staring at her. She wondered if Arthur was watching from an upstairs window. She found that she hadn't much interest in any of it, in the police officers, or Blair Decker, or Arthur, or the last three months of her life.

The police officers were approaching, the woman in front. She was tall and strong, with a firm chin and an even gaze. "Go back to the car, please, Mr. Decker," she said. She watched until Blair had returned to the backseat of the patrol car and closed the door. Then she turned to Susie. "Mrs. Wilson," she said.

"It's Ms., actually," said Susie.

"Ms. Wilson. You had an accomplice."

Susie thought about this. "Not really," she said. "No. I wouldn't call him an accomplice."

"Where is he, ma'am?" said the other police officer, a redhead with freckles and a nasty-looking scar on his face. She wanted to ask him how he'd gotten it.

"He's in the house," said Susie. "Packing."

"Is he armed?" asked the female officer.

"Armed? Oh, no."

"I'll go around back, Sarge," said the male officer.

"Right," said the sergeant, and she headed for the front door, looking up at the second-floor windows. A thick blonde braid hung to her shoulder, and the sight of this braid caught at Susie's heart. She saw the sergeant's hand move to her holster.

Before she could reach the steps that led to the small porch, Arthur cried out from inside the house.

"Don't shoot!"

The sergeant mounted the stairs and pulled open the door.

"Don't shoot me!"

The sergeant stepped back, holding the door open, and gestured to Arthur to come out. He did so, his hands in the air, and she handcuffed him and took him to the patrol car.

Blair Decker had gotten out of the vehicle. He began walking toward Susie, slowly, and she remembered the light from Leigh-Anne's candles on his face, the etchings of pain and stealth she'd thought she had seen there.

"Mrs. Wilson."

She remembered that he had been ashen when, dripping with rain, he had come to tell her that her daughter was dead.

He came to her slowly, over the patchy grass, and Susie wouldn't allow herself to look away from his face, his eyes. He lowered himself first in an awkward crouch, then onto his knees, and she thought of Arthur, who had assumed a similar position only minutes earlier. Blair Decker took hold of her hands, which remained limp.

"I'm so sorry," he said. "I'm so terribly sorry."

Susie sat there, patiently, while he apologized again and again, and thanked her for not harming his daughter.

Susie could think of nothing she wanted to say.

A second police car turned in to the driveway.

Susie let her head rest against the back of the lawn chair. Behind her closed eyes tears arrived, as if summoned, but finding no welcome there, they retreated.

FORTY-TWO

"It's not up to you, Mr. Decker," said Eddie, who was fast losing patience. "It's the police who lay charges, not you. And the Crown's already on its way."

"But it wasn't your daughter she took. I ought to have something to say about it." He strode from the window to the door and back again, running his hands through his hair, agitated and increasingly truculent.

"For god's sake, Mr. Decker, this is a kidnapping we've got here. And will you please stop racing around my office."

Blair Decker put his hands flat on Eddie's desk and leaned close to her. "Please, Sergeant Henderson. I'm begging you. Don't do this."

"I don't have a choice," she said obstinately.

He looked at her for several seconds. Then, "You wanted to know what the connection is. Between Susie Wilson and me. You wanted to know about Leigh-Anne."

Eddie sighed.

"Okay. I'll tell you," he said.

"You'd better sit down, then," said Eddie and pointed to the black leather chair.

He sat down. "It was a Friday morning," he said, gripping his knees. "After breakfast. Donna — my wife — had taken Samantha to kindergarten. She'd just come back. I was going to take my coffee upstairs and start to work."

"We have to talk, Blair," she said, and she sounded more tired than anything else. "It's been going on for so long — it must be serious. And so we have to talk about it."

"How long have you known?" said Blair. He was profoundly embarrassed and, absurdly, angry with Donna for catching him off guard.

"What's her name?" said Donna, lifting her coffee cup and immediately putting it back on its saucer. "Not that it matters."

"I didn't know you knew," said Blair, but he realized as he said it that he did know, and that he had taken her silence for acceptance. "Donna . . ." He had expected her to interrupt him, but she didn't. She waited.

She was wearing an old sweatshirt and jeans. He thought she looked exhausted, but beautiful. He loved her very much.

And then he thought about Leigh-Anne. He didn't know what to do, where his loyalties ought to lie. Did he have enough loyalty for the two of them? And how, precisely, was he to manage that, even if he found that he did have enough?

He sat down opposite his wife. "I do have strong feelings for her, I guess," he said soberly. He had had other affairs. Shorter ones. But nothing serious. He felt, now, that they hadn't counted in the grand scheme of things.

"Do you want a divorce?" She wasn't looking at him but past him, maybe into a future without him.

"Donna, I don't know. Do you?"

"I've been giving that a lot of thought," she said. "All I know for sure is that I can't live like this any longer. We either get counseling. Or we get a divorce."

Donna was four years older than Blair. At this moment he thought she looked much older than that. And this was his fault. He had caused the suffering that had created new crinklings in her smooth fair skin. He believed that she had known about his other affairs and had tolerated them. This one, it was clear, she would not tolerate.

She lifted her hand and smoothed her hair back from her forehead. "Do you know when we had sex last? With one another, I mean," she added dryly. She still wasn't looking at him.

Blair didn't answer.

Donna got up from the table and went into the back hall. When she returned she was putting on her bright yellow rain jacket. "Think about it, Blair." She picked up her purse. "I'm going out for a while."

He didn't try to stop her — why should he?

He was thinking, Does this mean we have to make a decision today? Will we have to talk it through today? Will I have to choose between them today?

And he was a little bit thrilled. A little bit flattered. He preened, just a little, listening to his wife driving away, listening to the rain.

"It was about an hour later," he said to Eddie, "that the police arrived. To tell me that she'd been killed."

He sat back in the chair and dug at his damp eyes with his knuckles.

Eddie looked him over curiously. He was an attractive man. Intelligent. Well-spoken. A loving father. But she didn't like him much.

"I don't get it," she said bluntly. "Okay, so you were having an affair with Susie Wilson's daughter. And maybe this contributed to your wife's death. Although you don't know that. What's it got to do with Susie? I still don't understand why she kidnapped your child."

"Ask her," said Blair. "She'll tell you."

It was very late when Eddie got home.

She walked slowly up to her front porch. There was a faint fragrance in the air, from somebody's flower garden. It lessened her weariness, lifted her spirits. Aromatherapy, she thought. It was time she got those lilacs planted, time that her own garden produced sweet scents to welcome her home.

Inside, she closed the blinds and drew the curtains. She needed to get out of her clothes and shower, and wash her hair, but she didn't have the energy. She took a beer from the fridge and turned on the TV.

The child hadn't been harmed. No money had changed hands. The victim's father wanted to be a character witness for the kidnapper, for god's sake. The Crown hadn't been impressed. Susie Wilson and Arthur Bentley would get off with conditional sentences, and Eddie wasn't sure that she approved.

Eddie stretched luxuriously and groaned and drank her beer straight from the can.

Susie Wilson would get community work, or a curfew, or probation, or all of the above. Arthur might pull some jail time but it probably wouldn't be much. She wondered if the two of them would have anything to say to each other once this was all over.

She adjusted the volume on the TV, turning it down, not really wanting to watch anything but needing the comforting murmur of the sound, the companionship of the sleek, brightly shifting images. Then she curled up on the sofa with her work diary and for a few moments gazed unseeing at the ceiling, reliving the events of the day.

Susie Wilson been sitting on the edge of the cot in her prison cell when Eddie came to collect her, as calm and prim as if she were paying a call, waiting patiently for her hostess to show up. Eddie, ignoring Arthur's indignant wails from a cell around the corner, escorted her to the interview room.

Eddie stopped to drink some more of her beer. Then she bent again to her work diary, recording Leigh-Anne's love affair, Leigh-Anne's abortion, Leigh-Anne's death. And Susie's revenge.

"I was wrong," Susie had told Eddie. "Oh, I was so wrong." She sat in the uncomfortable metal chair with her back straight, her hands in her lap, and her knees together. She had reminded Eddie a little bit of her mother. "I should never have taken it out on the child." Her eyes were so full of pain that Eddie could barely look at her.

Eddie questioned her about when she had begun to plan the kidnapping and exactly what she had done to carry it out. Susie Wilson answered promptly and fully — she obviously had no intention of withholding anything.

When asked about the ransom her lips thinned and her eyes became slits.

"We were never going to ask for money," she said furiously — as if this made the act less nefarious. "Never."

Then a strange little smile grew upon her face — an affectionate smile. It was so small she might not have realized that it was there. "Poor Arthur," she said. "He just wanted to — take advantage of the situation."

She insisted that she had planned the whole thing, and Eddie believed her. She didn't think Arthur had either the smarts or the patience. After all, he'd got his own directions wrong. If Samantha hadn't shown up when she did, and Blair Decker, instead of informing the police, had tried to deliver the ransom money, he would have wound up waiting in a clearing miles from the one Arthur had had in mind.

Eddie put down her pen and flexed her fingers.

She wondered, had Leigh-Anne gotten pregnant on purpose? Had she hoped that might persuade Blair to marry her?

Eddie rested her chin on her hand, staring at the murmuring television, feeling distinctly melancholy . . . but gladdened, too. Because Samantha had been delivered safely home.

FORTY-THREE

In her office the next morning Eddie stood up, clutching the phone to her ear. "I beg your pardon, sir?"

"You probably won't even have to move. It's only, what — twenty miles from Sechelt?"

"That's right, but —"

"Staff Sergeant Cooper will be taking over from you on the first of September. And I've got someone from Langley in mind to fill your spot. He might have a bit of a problem getting there that soon, he's —"

"Do I get to think about it, sir?" Eddie broke in. "Excuse me. Can you give me some time to think about it?"

There was silence for a moment. "Sure. Oh, sure. Think about it by all means. But I've got to know by the end of the week."

"Fine, sir. I'll get back to you. And — and thank you."

She hung up and immediately sat down. He had offered her the RCMP detachment in Gibsons.

He's right, she thought. I could keep my house. Commute.

Her own detachment.

She rubbed her palms against her pant legs. But what would happen when she got promoted? The Gibsons detachment had fewer Members than the one in Sechelt, which was why it was headed by a sergeant. When she got her staff sergeant's stripe, she'd have to be transferred again.

Eddie stood up and walked around her office. She had always known she would be replaced. But I don't want to leave here, she thought. She went to the window and squinted up at the sky, bright but cloud-covered. I could say no, she thought. And stay right where I am. I liked being Alberg's 2IC. Maybe I'd like this new guy, too. I could stay here until I get my promotion, and *then* move on.

My own detachment. Smaller, yes, but that was okay. Closer to Vancouver. But still on the Sunshine Coast.

My own detachment. Now.

She felt a jolt of pride so stunning it took her breath away.

Also by L. R. Wright

STRANGERS AMONG US

Fourteen-year-old Eliot Gardener hates British Columbia and harbours an anger that he doesn't understand. But he believes himself to be perfectly calm when he raises a machete and attacks his father, his mother, and his sister....

Karl Alberg knew the Gardeners, knew there was trouble, but he could neither anticipate nor avert the tragedy. Alberg attempts in vain to get through to Eliot — who will talk to no one about what he has done.

Meanwhile, Karl and Cassandra are being tailed by a vengeful and bereft man from one of Alberg's earlier cases. Is there any chance that they'll be able to carry out their plan to buy a house, get married and settle down?

Seal Books/ ISBN: 0-7704-2758-8

Also by L. R. Wright

ACTS OF MURDER

RCMP Staff Sergeant Karl Alberg is on a collision course with change. Hard on the heels of his marriage to Cassandra Mitchell comes news of her considerable — and quite unexpected — inheritance. And Alberg is in for another surprise, when Sergeant Eddie Henderson arrives for her new post....

Alberg is also on a collision course with a quiet killer stalking Sechelt. Someone who watches, judges, and deals punishments for the sins of this sleepy British Columbia town's inhabitants. So subtle are the murders, so obscure the motive, no one in Sechelt suspects the deaths are connected. But the killer has made a pact — one that carries a deadline. With time running out, Sechelt's avenging angel must find more suitable victims — and quickly. And Alberg and Henderson must uncover the pattern in these seemingly random murders — before the next "sinner" dies.

Seal Books/ ISBN: 0-7704-2782-0